OPERATION: SKIRMISH

a sweet military romance

Rules of Engagement Military Romance Series

Operation: Camouflage Christmas
Operation: Allegiance
Operation: Reconnaissance
Operation: Skirmish

OPERATION: SKIRMISH

a sweet military romance

DEEDEE LAKE
SUSAN M. BAGANZ

OPERATION: SKIRMISH

Paper back ISBN: 978-1-936501-89-2

 Published by CrossRiver Media Group, 4810 Gene Field Rd. #2, St. Joseph, Missouri 64506. www.crossrivermedia.com

For more information on DeeDee Lake, visit DeeDeeLake.com

For more information on Susan M. Baganz, visit SusanBaganz.com

For more information on the Rules of Engagement series,
visit RulesofEngagementMilitaryRomance.com

Editor: Debra L. Butterfield
Cover Design: Carrie Dennis Design

Dog tag illustration 49930528 © Alancotton | Dreamstime

Printed in the United States of America

To the warriors who have been wounded in the line of duty,
whether those are visible or not,
we thank you for your service and sacrifice.

"Fight the good fight of faith; take hold of the eternal life to which you were called, and for which you made the good confession in the presence of many witnesses." (1Timothy 6:12 NASB)

Definitions

EMDR - Eye Movement Desensitization and Reprocessing
TMI – too much information

MILITARY

ACU – Army Combat Uniform, daily work uniform
ARCP – Army Recovery Care Program
AWOL – Absent without leave
Black Op – black operations, covert military or political operations that may employ measures not generally authorized.
IED – Improvised explosive device
JROTC – Junior Reserve Officer Training Corps
On quarters – temporarily assigned to stay home and recover until released
SAT – Satellite phone
Spec – Specialist, military enlisted rank

FOREIGN LANGUAGE

Greek

Agapiménos – sweetheart
Engonia – grandchildren
Giagiás – Grandma
Mamá – Mom
Papá – Dad

Spanish

¿A cuánto dinero llevarnos – how much money to take us to…
Adios – goodbye
Baño – bathroom/toilet
Bienvenido – welcome
Bueno – well
Compadre – buddy
De nada – you are welcome
¿Dónde? – where
¿Dónde está el baño? – where is the bathroom?
Eres – are you
Gracias – thank you
¿Hay algun pueblo cerca? – is there a town nearby?
Hermosa – gorgeous
Hola – Hello
Mi amigo va conmigo – my friend comes with me
Muchacha – girl
Muchacha hermosa – pretty girl
Muchas gracias – thank you so much
Muy – very
Muy bueno – very good
No más – no more
Nosotras estamos perdidas – we are lost
Nosotras no tenemos nada – we have nothing
Ocurrido - happened
Pierna – leg
Pierna no más – leg no more
Policia – police
¿qué? – what
¿Qué le ha ocurrido a tu pierna? – what happened to your leg?
¿Qué te debo? – what do I owe you?
Señior – senior, mister
Señiorita – young unmarried woman
Señora – lady

si – yes
siesta – an afternoon nap or rest
silencio – silence
un poco – a bit or a little bit
via con Dios – go with God

1

Kristos sang the last note of the song and finished strumming his guitar while grinning at his buddies. After a brief pause the electric guitar player started the next song and Kristos jumped in on his acoustic. Playing at the outdoor patio of the Hernandez Hacienda Mexican restaurant was one of his favorite things to do. The crowd clapped as the band started their next song. The small dance floor was packed. For a Friday night in the middle of July in Colorado Springs, it was about as good as it could get.

A woman dancing erratically caught his eye. Her blonde hair swayed, and there was a slight hitch in her movement to the music, but he doubted anyone else noticed it. She had moved close to the stage when a man came and grabbed her arm. She tossed her drink at him but missed. The liquid hit Kristos in the face, chest, and guitar. He stopped playing as the band continued on. The woman struggled against the taller man's advances.

"Leave me alone!" she yelled.

Kristos set his guitar down, hopped off the stage, and pushed his way between the woman and the man. "Hey, break it up!" he shouted above the noise.

The woman's fierce expression, pursed lips, and narrowed eyes didn't focus on him but the man to his left. Before he realized it, a fist came out of nowhere and connected with his face, propelling him to the stage platform. Kristos rebounded quickly and with a swipe the man was flat on his back on the floor as people moved out of the way.

Kristos motioned to the bouncer at the door who pushed through the crowd as the music ended. This was now a spectacle and not one he wanted to be involved in.

"Paul, can you remove this man for assaulting this woman and myself?"

"Do you want to press charges? Should I hold him for the authorities?" Paul asked, his ginormous biceps flexing as he restrained the attacker who was for the moment not fighting.

"She started it," the man said.

"I didn't start anything. I was dancing and enjoying myself when you decided to accost me and couldn't understand the word *no* coming from my lips," the young woman said as she swayed. Kristos reached out to steady her with a gentle hand on her shoulder. She shrugged it off. "I want to press charges."

Kristos eyed the woman. She was petite, possibly not even five feet tall. Her thick blonde hair came to her collarbone. Her eyebrows indicated her hair was originally brown. Not unusual. She was a pretty little package. Those pale green eyes flashed warning.

"The band will be taking a fifteen-minute break," the lead vocalist said.

"Why don't we go toward the entrance?" Kristos suggested. The crowd thinned as many returned to their seats to watch the tableau playing out before them.

"Come on," Paul said as he led the man and woman toward the front door. Kristos followed behind. He could easily admire the view as the little spitfire walked ahead of him.

Out of the way of the crowd, Paul called the police. Kristos grabbed some napkins to wipe away the beer from his face and hair. Ugh. He'd splash some water on it when he got a chance.

The young woman turned his way. "I'm sorry my drink ended up all over you."

"I'll survive," Kristos said. The manger strode toward him with an ice pack. Kristos grabbed it with a "Thanks, Andy." He placed it up to his left cheek and winced. He'd be boasting a black eye tomorrow. No way to hide that from his family. He wiggled his jaw around. It hurt but Kristos didn't think anything was broken.

Eliza admired the guitar player. His dark wavy hair and short beard and mustache gave him the appearance of a cowboy. He wore boots and jeans, and that smile was something wonderful. She hadn't realized she'd danced her way up to the front of the stage.

"Tornado, what kind of trouble did you get into now?" Gabby asked as her friend stepped closer. Gabby was her roommate on post.

"Tornado?" the intriguing guitar player asked.

"It's a nickname, but I earned it the hard way. Specialist Elizabeth Torres. And you are?" She leaned forward, staring up at his face.

"I'm Kristos Sava. I wish we'd met under better circumstances."

"Were you aware your eyes have grey stars in them?" Eliza asked.

Kristos nodded. "I am aware but appreciate your noticing." He gave a half-smile.

"This is my roommate Gabby Madison." Eliza motioned her arm to the woman next to her.

"Hi, Kristos. Did she do this to you?" Gabby pointed at Kristos' face.

"Sort of. The beer bath was courtesy of Tornado here and the fist to the face was thanks to this, um, guy." He directed his thumb at the now sullen man.

Eliza giggled. "You wanted to call him a gentleman, didn't you?"

Kristos shrugged and turned to the bouncer. "Paul, can you give the police my info? I need to be ready to get back on stage for our next set." He turned to Eliza and Gabby. "It's been fun, ladies, but I need to return to the stage."

Tornado grabbed his arm as he turned to leave. "Kristos. How can I find you again?" She dropped her hand when he stopped.

"I'm not sure why you would want to," Kristos said.

"Perhaps to tender a proper apology?" Eliza offered.

Kristos reached into his back pocket and pulled out a business card. "This is where I work and that's my number."

Eliza grinned. "Thanks. You're cute. I like you."

He bit his lip before replying. "I'm guessing you're drunk. Gabby, I hope you are her ride home?"

"I am. It was nice meeting you." Gabby tugged on Eliza's arm.

"Oh." Kristos put the ice pack on the bar counter. "And thank you both for your service." He turned and strode to the back of the restaurant.

"What did you do?" Gabby hissed.

"I was enjoying the music," Tornado defended.

Soon the police were there and she gave her statement and Gabby escorted her back to their table. The meal she'd ordered had arrived so they silently sat to eat. Tornado was grateful she had a view to the stage. She caught the eye of the cute guitarist and gave him a wink. If she wasn't mistaken, he blushed.

The next morning Kristos walked into the barn to talk to his horses. This was his favorite place to be. He came to his oldest mare, Zena. He'd taken her in because she was no longer useful for breeding, and a bit long in the tooth for a Percheron. "Good morning, Zena. How's my favorite girl?"

The horse snorted and touched her nose to his cheek in the gentlest movement.

"Yeah, some tiny soldier decided to dump beer on me and attract the attention of some creep who thought she was easy prey. And I, like an idiot, stepped in to help her. I should have stayed on the stage."

Zena shook her head.

"You're right as usual ol' girl. She may be a capable woman, but I was raised to treat women with respect and to defend them should the need arise. Just grateful I avoided getting into more of a fight."

The horse started chewing her hay as Kristos patted her neck. "Horses are so much easier to understand than women," he whispered to himself.

"They are, huh?" Kobbe, Kristos' sister-in-law had snuck up on him. He turned to face her.

"Kristos! What happened to you?" Kobbe asked.

"Tried to help a damsel in distress and got punched by the guy inconveniencing her."

"You didn't fight back?"

"I did and called the bouncer. Charges were filed and he's banned from the restaurant," Kristos said.

"And the girl? Was she worth defending?" Kobbe gave a sly grin.

Kristos shrugged. "She was grateful. I doubt I'll ever meet her again. She was drunk. Not my type."

"Sorry."

"She was military though. A specialist, I believe she said."

"From Fort Carson?" Kobbe asked.

"That'd be my guess."

"She must have been cute for a man to bother her and you to step in."

"Doesn't matter, Kobbe. I don't drink, I don't chew, and I won't date girls who do." Kristos grinned at the rhyme.

"Cute, and a good standard to set. I'm sure you'll get lots of questions from *Mamá*."

"I'm sure I will. Now, what can I do for you?"

Kobbe went on to describe a new client coming in for equine therapy and discuss what horse might be best suited for the need.

When she was finished, Kristos grabbed his laundry and headed to the house. If he left it in his apartment above the barn, the entire room would be overwhelmed with the odor of beer. He'd left his clothes out on the landing last night to keep that from happening, and he washed his face twice to make sure the scent wouldn't be bothering him as he slept. Good thing he didn't run into any law enforcement on the way home. He'd only drunk soda but still, the way he reeked he'd be walking a line and taking a breathalyzer test for sure.

He got his laundry started and headed back to his apartment above the stables to make his breakfast. As he fried some eggs he wondered about the spunky young soldier and why she'd been drinking. Women sometimes approached him at these events, but no one ever mentioned his eyes at least until a third or fourth date—if they ever got that far. His last girlfriend, Gloria, had dumped him after realizing he was only ever interested in raising horses. She didn't like the idea that he might expect her to muck out stalls. He chuckled to himself. Even his younger sisters Zoe and Sophia had done that chore over the years. It was part of living on a ranch.

The image of Miss Tornado flashed through his mind. She'd probably tell him she could do it better and proceed to show him. Oh well. She was cute but drinking and tossing beer on him were not clever ways to win his heart.

He wondered what a little pixie like her did in the military to earn the name Tornado. His brother Alexandros and his brother Rusty's wife, Jane, were both Army, so he respected those who served. Didn't mean he was interested in a military wife. Even if he saw her again, she'd likely be deployed somewhere else before long. The Army was fond of that practice.

Let it go, man. She's not your type.

So why couldn't he stop thinking about her?

2

Eliza Torres had been dubbed Tornado by her Army buddies because she was a force to be reckoned with in that team even though she was petite. Today, however, was not going well and she was not living up to her nickname. Her head pounded. She groaned as she rolled over. She dragged herself to a seated position and proceeded to strap on her prosthetic leg. She still had much to get used to with this contraption. One thing on an extensive list to deal with before she'd be thrust from the Army nest and forced to fly on her own into the big cruel world.

Squawk!

"Fine, Ramsey. I'm coming." She hobbled over to the large cage where her blue-and-gold macaw flapped his wings in protest. She grabbed the water dish, dumped it in the sink, and refilled it. She opened the cage so the bird could perch on top. His wings were clipped enough to keep him from flying too far, but not so much that if he flew to the floor he'd land flat on his beak. She handed him a peanut and put some more food in his dish. She pulled out the bottom of the cage and cleaned it out and put fresh paper in there to be cleaned out again tomorrow. Why had she agreed to take this bird?

"Pretty bird, pretty bird, pretty bird," she said in hopes that the bird would talk. The previous owner who'd been deployed told her the bird possessed a good vocabulary. She'd yet to discover evidence of that. The bird did allow her to pet him and would sit on her arm or lap without complaint. She'd never owned a pet before. This was a new experience.

Her phone rang and Eliza clicked to accept a call from her longest and closest friend, at least before she joined the Army. “Hey, Rachel. How are you this morning?”

“I’m good. How are you? You mentioned you were going to go out with Gabby last night? Did you?”

Eliza sat on the chair near the birdcage. “Yes, and I made a royal fool of myself.”

“Oh, tell me more. Spill girl,” Rachel insisted.

“I drank too much beer on an empty stomach. There was a band playing and this one guitar player was really cute, so I wandered over to the dance floor, enjoying the music. I got close to the stage when some jerk decided I needed to give him attention. I tossed my beer in his face but missed and covered the guitar player with it instead. The man came off the stage to help me with the bully and ended up getting punched for his efforts. He has the loveliest eyes.” She sighed.

“The guitar player or the bully?”

“The guitar player.”

“Did you get his name?” Rachel asked.

“Wait, let me see if I can find it. He gave me a business card.” She dug around in her jeans pocket. “Here it is, Kristos Sava. Yummy.”

“You were drunk, tossed your drink at him, he got punched, and you think he’s going to be interested in you?”

Eliza pouted. “Why not? I’m cute.”

“Of course, you are, sweetie, but I doubt a man like that is going to be interested in a woman with your issues.”

“Are talking about my leg?”

“No. I’m talking about how you still haven’t worked through your trauma, much less figured out what you’re going to do with your life once you’re out of the Army.”

“Great way to bring down my morning.” Eliza frowned and sat back down, flipping the business card between her fingers. “Maybe I’ll give him a call.”

“Oh, honey. Don’t,” Rachel begged.

“I will if I want to.” Eliza snickered.

"Of course, you will. You always do what you want." A cry came from the background. "The boys are fighting. I need to intervene. We'll talk soon, OK?"

"OK. Thanks for calling, Rach."

They ended their call and Eliza tossed her cell phone on the sofa. She didn't have a clue what she'd do today. Not quite in the Army and not quite out. She had therapy during the week, but the weekends were her own, and so far she hadn't gained any wisdom on how to move forward in a way that set her on a path for the future. It was beyond frustrating. She went to the bathroom and combed her hair. She paused to stare at herself in the mirror. Dark circles under her eyes weren't attractive. She grabbed some makeup to try to minimize her lack of sleep. Maybe she'd take a nap later. Right. Because that's what highly functioning women did on a Saturday.

Those words didn't quite describe her. She walked into the kitchenette to get breakfast. Their quarters were small but workable. Gabby had already headed out for the day, but she left a note asking Eliza to pick up milk. Why couldn't Gabby do it? Eliza opened the fridge and discovered there was no milk at all. Hmmm. No cereal this morning unless she wanted it dry. They were shy on eggs as well. Great. Well, at least there was something with purpose to do today. Not that it would take very long. The shoppette was only a few blocks away as she still hadn't managed to get a vehicle adapted for her use. In a way she wondered if she really needed any adaptation. With her prosthetic she could still do most things a normal biped could do.

She made some coffee and sat by the window. Ramsey was tossing his nut shells on the floor. She should sweep that up. Why in the world did she even bother getting a bird that in some ways almost seemed as tall as she was if one took his length from tip to tail. Well, she was stuck with him now. But that stupid soldier lied to her about him talking. Would be nice to own a pet that actually liked her and wanted to interact beyond getting treats.

Maybe next time she'd get a dog. She sighed.

She finished her coffee and set the cup in the sink. "Come on, Ramsey. Back in your cage. She tapped the bottom of the door and the bird made his way down, entered, and settled on his favorite perch. Squawk! Squawk!

She locked the cage. "Shhhh, you'll get me in trouble." She wasn't supposed to have pets, especially a huge bird.

Ramsey ignored her and began to groom his feathers.

Maybe he needed a friend? No. She could barely take care of one bird but to deal with two of these huge mess-makers? Not a good option for now. Was she drunk when she agreed to take the animal? At least it hadn't cost her anything other than time to clean up and care for it. Well, and feed it and buy it toys. She'd always wanted a parrot that could talk. The man said this one did. It'd been weeks and so far, not a word.

She put on her walking shoes and grabbed her purse and jacket before heading out to get the few items on the list. It wasn't unusual for the weather to turn chilly in July at the bottom of Pikes Peak.

Once she made it to the sidewalk she grimaced. Sometimes she forgot she needed to be more careful with every step she took. She hadn't fully adjusted to her fake leg. At least she hadn't lost it on the dance floor last night. That would have been embarrassing. She still struggled to believe the real one was gone. Her squad was gone as well. She'd not been able to make their funerals as she'd been hanging on for dear life.

The tell-tale pounding of shoes on the sidewalk caused her to step aside to let a jogger pass her. "Hey." She gave a little wave as he passed but he didn't reciprocate. Sometimes it was as if she were invisible. Maybe that's why the rest of her didn't blow up like her compadres. The IED couldn't see her. The thought at least made her chuckle.

She entered the shoppette and located her items. She did the self-check and was soon on her way back home. She missed the closeness of her squad in Afghanistan. Life on post went on for the units, families, and activities. It was like a large town. It could be easy to feel lost. And alone.

She entered her tiny barracks room and put away the groceries. Her phone rang from the sofa where she'd tossed it earlier. She grabbed it and dropped onto the cushions. "Mom?"

"Good morning, Eliza. How are you doing?" Mrs. Torres asked.

"As well as can be expected. A little tired."

"Were you out late?"

"Too many questions, Mom. What's up?"

"I wanted to share some news. Are you sitting down?"

"More like stretched out on the sofa. Sounds like something big. Did you get a promotion?"

"No, sweetheart, remember I mentioned Nigel to you?"

"Yeah, old high school sweetheart, right? His wife died of cancer a few years ago?"

"Right, well, since we reconnected, we discovered that old spark was—"

"Mom, TMI. Too much information. I don't want to hear about your sparks."

"Eliza. You are a grown woman and while your father died a long time ago, I'm still a woman with needs."

"Mom! Stop it." Eliza groaned and closed her eyes. Her mom, barely able to give her the birds and the bees talk, now was talking about sparks? What was going on?

"Fine. Nigel proposed to me last night." Mrs. Torres paused. "I said yes."

"You're getting married? Wow. Um. I guess congratulations are in order." She tried to sound chipper.

"Thank you. I wanted you to be the first to know."

"When's the wedding?"

"We'd like to do it soon. Nigel got a promotion and his work will take him to Arizona. I'm already searching for work out there. I'll be putting the house up for sale next week."

"Wait. What? You're selling the house?"

"Yes, dear. I'll box up your stuff but I'll need a place to send it pretty soon. I understand this is an inconvenient time for that, but I can put it in a storage place until you figure out where you're going and what you're doing next."

Eliza shook her head. Her mom was marrying someone and moving. The only home Eliza ever knew would be gone. There was no more "home base" for her to return to. She'd thought of returning to Nashville to hang out there with her mom while she figured things out, and now that door was closing before she could even get her prosthetic toe in to stop it.

"Eliza?"

"I'm sorry, Mom. You threw a few curve balls at me so rapidly I couldn't catch them. Sounds like this is happening fast."

"Perhaps for you, but Nigel and I have known each other for years. We both understand what we want. I hope you can be happy for me. Maybe you'll be able to come to the wedding? We're keeping it quite simple and low key. Mostly family. Not a big gathering. No dancing."

"Is that because you're afraid I can't dance?"

"Nothing of the sort. I believe you are more worried about what others think of your injury than is reasonable. We want a simple service, that's all."

"And then you're moving."

"Yes. I'll be sad to leave our home, but it's never been the same since your father passed and you left for the Army."

"You're lonely? You have friends."

"It's not the same. Someday you'll understand how the love of a good man can be more powerful than anything. I hope you can be happy for me."

"I am happy for you, Mom. I look forward to meeting him. Do I need to call him Dad?"

"Nothing of the sort. You can call him Nigel. We're all adults and his grown children will call me Joy."

"How many kids does he have?"

"Three, but they are all married now. One is expecting a baby this fall."

"So I get to meet all of them at this wedding?"

"That would be the plan."

"When you figure out the date, let me know and I'll do my best to be there."

"I love you, Eliza."

"Love you too, Mom."

Eliza ended the call and dropped the phone to the floor. Ramsey squawked again.

Home was going to disappear. Mom would no longer be in Nashville but moving to where? Arizona? Isn't that where people retired to?

What was she going to do now? She closed her eyes and draped an arm over her head as if blocking out the light would keep hard truths away. Loneliness ate away at her and soon the tears trickled down her cheeks.

3

Kristos walked into his parents' kitchen to find his mom, Roda, bustling about. He strode over to her and gave her a kiss on the cheek.

"Oh, you startled me." She turned toward him. "*Agapiménos.* What happened to you?"

"I tried to rescue a damsel who apparently wasn't in as much distress as I thought and the guy who was bothering her punched me."

"It looks horrible. Are you on the worship team tomorrow morning?"

"No, thank goodness for that. I'm tempted to watch the feed live from the comfort of my laptop."

"You will do no such thing, young man. If you acted with honor, and I have no doubt you did, then there is no shame in showing your face at church."

"Fine. I'll be there." He surveyed the dining room table. "Feeding everyone tonight?"

Roda smiled. "Yes. All my children should be here for dinner."

"That makes this a special occasion. Why is everyone coming?"

She shrugged. "Alexandros said they had news and so did Russell. Zoey and Sophia said they had plans with friends later but would be here."

"Anything I can help with?"

"Yes, agapiménos. Stir this pot, will you?" She bustled off as he grabbed the spoon she'd been using.

Soon the dining room was full and the chatter that was common here filled the space. Eventually *Papá* cleared his throat as Mamá put the last platter on the table.

"Let's join together in prayer for our meal." Everyone joined hands, including Jane and Rusty's son, little Mark. "Heavenly Father, You have richly blessed us throughout the years, even with the trials and heartaches. Thank You for Your faithfulness and for the loving hands that prepared this meal. Amen."

"Amens," chorused around the table and soon plates were passed.

Rusty, Kristos' second oldest brother, frowned at Kristos who sat across from him. "I'm guessing there's a story that goes with that black eye?"

Roda shook her head. "We won't discuss that now. Maybe later. He was honorable. Now, both Alexandros and Russell have news they wanted to share tonight. I for one am eager to learn what it is."

Alexos glanced at Rusty. "You have news too?"

Rusty nodded. "You can go first. You are technically the oldest." The smirk on Rusty's face indicated this was a bit of an insult although a friendly teasing one.

"I will go first then." He reached to grab his wife Kobbe's hand. "We wanted to share the good news that we are expecting a baby."

Kobbe's face grew pink.

"Congratulations." Roda was up out of her seat giving Alexos and Kobbe hugs. Tears were streaming down her face. "You don't know how happy this makes me." She glanced to her husband. "We will have more *engonia*." Their parents always threw in Greek words when they got excited.

She sat back down, and Rusty grabbed his wife Jane's hand. "Well, before you get too comfortable, Mamá, we are also happy to announce a similar event."

"*Ayeye!*" Roda jumped up to kiss both Rusty and Jane on the cheeks. "I am the happiest of mothers to be so blessed."

Alexos jumped up and Rusty rose as well as they gave each other a hug murmuring their congratulations to each other.

Kristos shook his head, grateful he was a long way from the responsibility of a wife and children. He had his horses, and he was fine with that for now. Someday he wanted more. Soon the conversation was in full swing with baby name suggestions and questions to Mark about how he felt about being a big brother.

Zoe spoke up during a quieter moment. "I'm still going into the Army so don't expect me to be babysitting."

Sophia shrugged. "Sure, leave it all to me."

"I'm the grandma. I get first dibs on babysitting," Roda protested.

"Best not to ask me," Kristos offered. "I'll probably put them on Zena far too early."

Excited chatter filled the dining room. Soon the meal ended with Zoe and Sophia tasked with clearing the table.

Kristos excused himself to return to his apartment. He locked the door and settled down in his comfortable recliner. He grabbed his guitar, which still held the faint scent of beer, and began strumming a worship song. He adored his family and was sincerely happy for his brothers and their wives. At the core he was an introvert and appreciated the quiet moments alone here, or on horseback.

How would a wife ever fit into that? It didn't matter. He was fine on his own.

"Eliza. Wake up, already."

Eliza moaned and rolled over.

"What is it, Gabby?" she grunted. Peeking through a partially opened eye she glimpsed her roommate looming over her.

"It's Sunday and you promised you'd go to church with me, remember? Now get up and get ready."

Eliza found that mornings since the *event* didn't come as easily as it had before the big boom. That's about all she could remember of it. She sat upright and dropped her leg to the floor and grabbed for her prosthetic to put it on.

Wait. When had she ever promised Gabby she'd go to church? Church? God didn't want anything to do with her. If He couldn't save all of her when the event occurred, what was left wasn't worth saving either. Maybe it was faulty logic but she clung to it. She went to get ready. When she finished, she stepped out into the main living area and Gabby groaned.

"What?" Eliza asked.

"That's what you choose to wear to church?"

Squawk! Squawk! Ramsey scolded her as well.

"What's wrong with this?" She wore a clean Army t-shirt and her blue jeans and tennis shoes. She debated wearing an Army baseball cap as well but opted to leave that off.

"Don't you own anything nicer? You dressed better going out to dinner Friday night than you do to worship God."

"Who said I was going to worship God? When did I make this promise anyway?"

"On the way home from dinner." Gabby folded her arms across her chest. She was wearing a nice top, dress pants, and sandals. Her prosthetic arm wasn't covered as usual.

"You're not wearing a jacket?" Eliza asked.

"Why should I? I don't need to hide my arm. I'm functional and if anyone has a problem with that, it's on them."

Eliza shrugged. "Do you expect me to wear shorts and show off my leg? I haven't shaved the other one in over a month I think."

"TMI. No. It's just, well, you could put on nicer clothes."

"This is who I am. I'm comfortable. It's probably the only comfortable thing I'll deal with this morning." Eliza put her hands on her hips and tilted her head in a whatcha-going-to-do-about-it attitude.

Gabby dropped her arms. "Fine. But maybe that cute guy will be there."

"And if he is? He's not going to want to have anything to do with me after his beer bath the other night. Remember?" Eliza grimaced.

"You're right."

Ramsey flew over to land on Eliza's arm. "Fine. I'll get you some fresh water."

Soon they were in Gabby's car headed off post to the Good Shepherd Community Church.

Eliza closed her eyes during the drive. Why? Why had she ever agreed to this outing? She prayed she wouldn't embarrass her friend while there and that she wouldn't snore during the sermon. She didn't need anyone preaching to her about how to live her life. She'd been through the fires of hell already.

4

Kristos strode through the doors of the church. He'd grown up in the faith and couldn't remember a time when he didn't believe in Jesus. His father went from rancher to preacher. When Kristos was old enough to step in and keep the ranch going, he did. He loved his life on the ranch.

He found a spot toward the front and sat down. Occasionally, he would serve on the worship team here but not this weekend. He could sit and relax and focus on the most important thing in his life: Jesus Christ.

Worship began and he stood, glanced around, and spied someone familiar. No. It couldn't be that little Tornado from Friday night. Here?

Come on, Kristos. All are welcome at the foot of the cross.

I'm sorry, Lord. I was being judgy. I don't have a clue what hurt lies in her past or what brought her to the stage. If You brought her here, do a work in her heart and draw her to Yourself.

There was no answer as he poured himself into singing the songs that were familiar and meaningful to him. Lord, forgive me for not looking at the log in my own eye and being too quick to look down on Tornado. It was easy enough to do as she was petite.

And cute.

And a drunkard.

Lord, Your Word tells me to stay away from people like that.

All through the message Kristos wrestled with his own critical heart toward the young woman and how that conflicted with his—OK he admitted it—attraction to her.

What was he to do after the service let out? Avoid her? Approach her? It wasn't as though he could act like she wasn't there, and if they chanced to meet, pretend he hadn't noticed her. He wasn't an actor.

Horses were easier. They didn't lie and could sense the undercurrents going on in him or any rider. Maybe that's why he seemed to be the one kid in the family to reach adulthood without much drama. Working the ranch and caring for God's magnificent creatures, the horses, kept him grounded and sane.

That was until a Tornado grinned at him on the dance floor.

The final song ended, and he still had no clue what he was going to do about Tornado. Did he need to do anything?

The sanctuary for Good Shepherd Community Church was unlike anything she'd ever seen before. Eliza had not stepped foot into a church since her father's funeral.

Great. Her mother was going to have a church wedding. Might as well get comfortable.

When the music started, she craned her neck to check the guitar player. It wasn't the guy from the bar. Not that it mattered. Of all the churches in the Colorado Springs area, why would she even imagine that she'd run into him here?

He was too good for her. He was honorable and never tried to come on to her—only protect her. She repaid him by flirting shamelessly. Her own face grew warm at the memory. Thankfully everyone stared at the words on the screens to sing along. The music was pleasing but the melody and words were strange. She listened with interest and reluctantly sat down when the worship leader asked them to.

As if the skies parted to let the sun shine, she spied him. Kristos. The man from the bar. He was here after all. Oh, why had she insisted on dressing so shabbily? She'd refused to take Gabby's cautions to heart.

What did it matter? If he was a church-going man there's no way he'd ever be interested in a heathen like her. Inside she was like a tornado, causing collateral damage as she spun out of control. The thought sobered her. She'd never considered herself that way. Emotions and memories swirled around inside her, colliding with fears, uncertainty, and what if's.

Was her moniker from the military an apt description or a prediction of her future? Or both? Leaving a path of death and destruction behind her? Pain at the back of her neck indicated intense stress. She rolled her head around on her shoulders not caring what people around her thought. At least she wasn't falling asleep.

The pastor stepped up on stage. His last name was Sava. Was Kristos his son? Great. She was crushing on a pastor's kid? Granted the man was an adult and had been playing at a restaurant with a dance floor. Didn't Christians have a ton of rules? Don't drink. Don't smoke. Don't dance. Don't go to movies.

She glanced around at the congregation. Some were here in blue jeans and others were more business casual and still others were dressed in what down South they'd call their "Sunday best."

Not that she understood much of that. She wasn't raised in the church. One of her squad-mates, Hal Zarenski, mentioned God a few times and asked her once if she was going to heaven. She'd blown him off. She was aware he attended chapel and he possessed a peace that wasn't from over-confidence. It went deeper than that. Maybe if he'd lived longer and she hadn't lost a limb, she'd have been able to learn more. Why had she been so stubborn and opposed to him talking about it all? What few things he said indicated he had assurance he'd be in heaven. His grieving family were kind enough to send a get-well card and tell her they were praying for her. It didn't make sense. She'd been driving the truck.

Right. Like an IED would wave a red flag of warning. If they'd been the lead truck they might have escaped serious harm but their truck had been second. From what she understood the first truck ran over the IED and there was a delay causing her truck to explode. She touched above her eyebrow where a scar remained from the incident but she hid it under her bangs.

Pastor Sava was sharing from some book called Romans. What was Romans?

His voice boomed. "Romans chapter 1, verses 18–20 clearly state: 'For the wrath of God is revealed from heaven against all ungodliness and unrighteousness of people who suppress the truth in unrighteousness, because that which is known about God is evident within them; for God made it evident to them. For since the creation of the world His invisible attributes, that is, His eternal power and divine nature, have been clearly perceived, being understood by what has been made, so that they are without excuse.' Think about this. We live in a beautiful area with breathtaking mountains. Did you ever wonder how they got there? How did the trees get planted? How did the grass grow? Some of you struggle to keep a green lawn in the drought of summer, yet the grass on the mountains grows unaided.

"The sun rises and sets. The moon controls the ocean waves. Eyes that see and ears that hear cannot be manufactured by human ingenuity. Our bodies and our brains are incredibly complex. Where does a thought come from? How do emotions exist? Science can't find them with a microscope. Where does the wind come from and where does it go? All these things and infinitely more testify to the truth that there is a Creator. His name is Jesus.

"If you haven't recognized the God of creation, the Lord of the universe, in all you've seen, heard, and experienced in this world, take note. Paul writes in Romans that you have no excuse. When God is quiet, His creation cries out in worship and testimony to Him."

Pastor Sava paused, and his eyes scanned the crowd; when they came to her, they paused for a moment.

Eliza gulped. The moment passed and she let out a deep breath she hadn't realized she'd held.

What if God's creation was calling out to worship Him? It didn't mean she needed to. The mountains? A big pile of rocks and dirt. What was so amazing or spectacular about that? Wasn't like she'd be going rock-climbing anytime soon. What about poisonous snakes? If God's creation was so good, what about His supposed people? People created bombs, wars, and all kinds of horrible things. Humans did unspeakably cruel things to other people.

"Now, maybe you don't own a carved image as an idol like they did in the Old Testament, but what about your phone and social media? Do you spend more time on that than you do with our Lord? How about television? We can worship many things without even realizing we are doing it. We can even worship ourselves. Our image, the way we present ourselves to the world. Our finances can be an idol as well.

"None of these things are inherently evil on their own. The use of a cell phone allowed my son Alexos to rescue his brother Rusty a couple of years ago during a fire. Being entertained isn't a terrible thing, but if that's all you do, you are missing out on time with God. We were created to worship God, serve Him, and submit to Him. We live near Fort Carson so some of you are military and understand the chain-of-command. We have a Supreme Commander in Jesus and He asks us to obey and follow Him. There is a battle waging in this world between our enemy, Satan, and those of us who follow Christ. We have everything we need for the battle when we are submitted to Him and walking in step with the Holy Spirit."

Pastor Sava continued. "All of creation is without excuse. That's what Paul writes. That means the human traffickers are without excuse. Child abusers are without excuse. Thieves are without excuse. Paul writes later in 2 Timothy chapter 3, starting in verse 1: 'But know this: Difficult times will come in the last days. For people will be lovers of self, lovers of money, boastful, proud, blasphemers, disobedient to parents, ungrateful, unholy, unloving, irreconcilable, slanderers, without self-control, brutal, without love for what is good, traitors, reckless, conceited, lovers of pleasure rather than lovers of God, holding to the form of godliness but denying its power. Avoid these people!'"

The pastor paused. "Sounds harsh, doesn't it? If we are to avoid people who exhibit these traits, we might need to avoid our own selves. Who among us hasn't been ungrateful? Unloving? Boastful? Lacking self-control? I believe Paul here doesn't necessarily mean for us to avoid these people at all costs because these things could apply to many of us on a given day. However, his stating that those who indulge in these sins, persist in them, refusing to repent and turn toward God—those people we are to avoid. Don't hang around with people like that.

"But you might say, Pastor, how are we to reach the lost if we need to avoid them? It's a great question. Scripture commands us, as we go about our lives, to witness to the power of God. That doesn't mean we want a close relationship with them, or join them in their willful, sinful state. Remember Romans. They are without excuse.

"Satan, however, wants to keep us blind to the truth of God. Paul has said we, the epitome of His created work, are without excuse. We can blame others. We can run from the truth. If you are choosing to ignore the call He has for You to follow Him, willfully put your head in the sand or turning a blind eye, then you are without excuse and the Bible makes it clear that your future is determined by that one choice.

"And make no mistake. It is a choice. A willful choice. God made Himself clear. You can choose to ignore the truth, but God's redemptive plan to rescue a sinful human race is still in play. If you choose to ignore Jesus, you've made a dangerous decision.

"It is a decision. Either way. I beg of you to follow Christ. Heed His calling on Your heart and follow Him. After the final song there will be people up front to pray with you about anything, especially your decision to accept Jesus Christ."

Soon the people around her were standing and singing.

I have decided to follow Jesus.
I have decided to follow Jesus.
I have decided to follow Jesus,
No turning back, no turning back.
The world behind me the cross before me.
The world behind me the cross before me.
The world behind me the cross before me,
No turning back, no turning back.
Though none go with me, I still will follow.
Though none go with me, I still will follow.
Though none go with me ,I still will follow,
No turning back, no turning back.
Will you decide now to follow Jesus.

Will you decide now to follow Jesus.
Will you decide now to follow Jesus,
No turning back, no turning back.

Someone else stood up front and prayed. Eliza couldn't wrap her heart or mind around it all. Part of her wanted to go up and ask for prayer, but something held her back. There was an internal skirmish going on between herself and God. Why would God want her anyway? If He were that interested in her, why did her truck blow up killing her friends?

You're making excuses.

Huh? Where did that thought come from? Just her brain focusing on the pastor's words: You are without excuse.

She straightened her shoulders and followed the people out of the row and down the aisle and toward the back of the sanctuary, hoping all the while no one would talk to her, lest she break under the strain of the battle going on inside.

5

Kristos stepped to the front to be available to pray with anyone. He spied Eliza leaving. Her face set with determination, lips pursed, and eyes narrowed. It was as if she wanted to run away instead of walk to the exit. The little hitch in her step was more pronounced. He wondered what caused it. Lord, get ahold of her heart and help her to see you as the Great Physician…and Counselor. You are aware of her deepest need—especially for You.

Soon a few other people came forward for prayer. The younger crowd tended to gravitate toward him. When he was finished, he strode to the back of church, hoping Eliza would still be there, but she was nowhere to be found. Perhaps that was for the best.

He spied his father finishing up a conversation with someone.

"Hey, Papá. Great preaching this morning."

"Thanks, son. Now we trust Him to bring the fruit."

"Amen."

"See you at lunch?"

"No. I'm meeting Michael, Jeremiah, and Peter for lunch. Dinner?"

"Sounds good. See you later."

Kristos strode out of the church to his 1968 Pontiac GTO that he referred to as GOAT, meaning, greatest of all time. The black convertible with the white interior and white cloth retractable roof was one of his prizes and perfect for a drive on this beautiful sunny day. He arrived at the restaurant where he'd be meeting the guys. He went inside and snagged a table on the patio where he could keep an eye on the vehicle and wave his friends over. He was grateful for the shady overhang to protect them from the sun.

Jeremiah arrived first, followed quickly by Peter and Michael. Kristos greeted them each with a handshake, a half-hug, and pat on the back.

"It's been a while, guys," Kristos said after they'd ordered their food.

"Well, Holly and I tend to hang out more now," Peter said.

Jeremiah nodded. "Genna's been kind of my date on the weekends. I enjoy spending time with her. No offense, bro."

Michael cleared his throat. "Remember Bridget?"

The men all nodded. "Well, I proposed to her last night—and she said yes!"

"Wow. Congratulations, Michael," Kristos offered. "Any idea of when the big day will come?"

"This fall. I'm hoping to talk her into hiring your horses and carriage for the event."

"Get me a date so I don't double book," Kristos said. Mentally he was trying to remember what he already had scheduled but couldn't.

"I'm not that close to tying the knot," Jeremiah offered. "But maybe someday." His goofy grin indicated he was smitten.

Peter cleared his throat. "Yeah, Holly and I are doing well, but it hasn't been long enough to be sure."

Kristos shook his head. "But you said the same thing about Sarah, and you dated her, what? Three years? How long do you need?"

"Maybe I have commitment issues. But what about you? You haven't had a girlfriend for over two years now," Jeremiah said.

"True. I haven't met anyone that piques my interest. My father encouraged me to keep my standards high and I'm in no rush. I'm keeping busy enough."

"I heard from Jake over at the restaurant where you play, that some cute chick dumped beer all over you Friday night. Maybe she's the one?" Michael joked.

Kristos shook his head. "I doubt it. Some guy harassed her. The beer was meant for him. I tried to help her out and got sucker punched by the guy. Charges were filed and she walked away unharmed."

"Oh, playing the knight in shining armor routine, huh? Just wait till she sees you on the back of Delphine...or is Zena your favorite?"

Kristos' face grew warm. "I was trying to be a gentleman. She was nice enough I suppose. I didn't get to hang out long enough to find out as I needed to be back on the stage. I'm not interested in a girl that drinks. I'm not a teetotaler, but I don't like social drinking. Not after Carlos."

The men all frowned and nodded their heads. Carlos had been in their high school graduating class and snuck some beer on graduation night and never made it home, ending a promising future with a car wrapped around a tree.

Kristos cleared his throat. "In better news, that gal showed up at church today. I didn't get to talk to her, but the fact that she showed up was a positive sign."

"Are you interested in her? Does she have a name?" Michael asked.

"She's cute but I doubt she's my type. Tornado or Eliza or something like that? It was a crazy night."

"Isn't your mother anxious for grandchildren? I hear about that quite often from my mom." Michael sipped his water while raising an eyebrow.

"Since Rusty and Jane already have a son and are expecting another child and Alexos and Kobbe recently announced they are expecting, the pressure is off. I can hang out with my horses. They are sometimes better company. Far less drama than a woman." Kristos sat back as the server put their food in front of each of them. "Should I pray?" Kristos asked.

"Sure," they all chimed in.

"Heavenly Father, You are the source of all love and friendship and I'm grateful You've allowed us to be friends all these years. Bless our time together and even though events happen to change the quantity of time with these three men, I ask that You would help the quality. Bless this food. Amen."

Everyone chimed in with their amens and began to eat. Conversation veered to jobs and the latest movies. Kristos ate and listened. He loved his friends and time with them. It saddened him that life changes—OK—women—were creating more separation between these men. They'd been there to fill a gap when Rusty was injured, and again when

Alexos left. They'd commiserated when his girlfriend dumped him.

Would he ever be good enough for anyone? Did it matter? He was content with his life as it was, wasn't he? No. He wanted what his parents had—a home of his own and wife to love and children of his own to someday set on top of one of his giant horses and teach them about the power of strength controlled by discipline.

Maybe his dream was too idealistic.

"So, Kristos, you going to continue playing with the Dry Gulch Band?" Michael asked.

Kristos shrugged. "I'm content to fill in when they need me but don't see myself doing more. Sometimes showing the horses conflicts so this gives me the freedom to say no if I want."

"Sounds reasonable. You're good though. If you wanted, you could become the lead for the band permanently or start your own. According to the ladies you're easy on the eyes," Jeremiah said.

"Um, I appreciate the compliment, I think? My mom gets on me about my man bun and keeps offering to cut my hair. She doesn't mind the beard though. She says it gives me an air of distinction. Whatever." Kristos grinned and took a sip of his water. "I want a woman who wants me for who I am inside and isn't trying to change me into someone else or some imaginary perfect man."

"Here! Here!" Michael cheered. All four men raised their water glasses to cheer.

"Didn't your previous girlfriend believe it was her job to make a man out of you?" Peter asked.

Kristos groaned. "Don't remind me. She wanted that in more ways than I was willing to agree to before marriage. I wasn't about to propose and have a wedding for that alone."

"Abstinence is not fun. Partly why I'm pushing for a wedding sooner than later." Michael's face grew pink.

The rest nodded in agreement but stayed silent. Some things were not comfortable to talk about at lunch in a public place.

As they prepared to pay the bill, the men each tossed some cash onto the table for the tip. Kristos rose. "It was great. Let's not wait too long to do this again."

Kristos headed to the register to pay and then with a wave to his friends got back in his car and headed for home.

He parked the car in the pole barn built primarily to house some of the farming equipment but also contained several classic vehicles. He put the top up and draped a cover over it to protect the vehicle from dust. He strode across the yard to the horse barn. The horses were in the meadow, enjoying the lovely day. Kristos sat on the top of the wooden railing and watched them. His Percherons were like giants next to the few smaller breeds that Kobbe used for her therapy business.

One horse gamboled toward him, her head lifted high as she shook out her mane.

"Good afternoon, Zena. How's my best girl doing?" Kristos patted the side of her neck as he leaned into her. What was it about this old lady, past her breeding, that brought him comfort? He'd been offered the horse for free if he paid to transport it. He'd agreed. She'd lived a good life and birthed many wonderful foals, but here she got to exist and be the grand matriarch of the herd.

And sometimes she was his closest confidant—after God.

"Why do the guys think I need a girlfriend right now when I have you?"

Zena whinnied.

Kristos grinned. What did he have to complain about? He possessed a comfortable apartment above the barn. He was self-employed and doing well with the stable. He had good friends and a family that was growing. He already loved being an uncle to Mark, Jane's son who Rusty adopted. Now two more were coming? He grinned. At least he wasn't the one changing diapers. Although mucking out stalls was worse.

Soon Zena went to graze, and Kristos jumped down and headed to his home. He needed to practice his guitar to keep his skills sharp.

Why did the thought of playing to a certain petite blonde Tornado flash through his mind. Forget it. She's not your type.

Really, then who is?

There was no answer.

6

On Monday, Eliza dressed in her camo and headed to the Soldier Recovery Unit to meet with the therapist Captain Alli.

"Good morning, Specialist Torres. Come in," the psychotherapist said. "Have a seat."

"'Morning, Captain." Torres gave a salute and found her seat. She hated these checkups. She'd rather be doing her physical therapy than sitting here. The captain had been wanting to try some new therapy with her to help heal her trauma, but Eliza resisted.

"Did you have a good weekend?" the captain asked.

"It was OK."

"What did you do?"

"Tried to get my parrot to talk. Went to dinner with Gabby and ended up dumping my beer on some poor guitar player. I was aiming for a guy who was pestering me."

"Why don't you tell me about it?"

Eliza told the story but withheld the fact that she drank one too many beers or flirted with Kristos.

"How did you feel on the dance floor?"

"Hmmm?" She had been enjoying remembering Kristos. He was dreamy but would never be interested in her. "Oh, the dance floor? Awkward. I can't manage to glide as I walk so it feels weird. They might need to adjust the prosthetic. It was sweet for the guitarist to try to protect me. I'm sure I could have handled it myself though."

"By throwing your beer at a man pestering you and can't respect a no?"

"Well, when you put it that way...Maybe I could have removed my leg and hit him with it? Kind of a roundhouse kick to the head but using my arm instead to propel it?" Eliza chuckled.

The captain smiled. "How is your balance on one leg?"

"I could have leaned against the stage." Eliza twisted her lips to the right and left before shrugging her shoulders.

"How would you feel exposing your leg like that?"

Eliza slumped back in the chair. "Embarrassed." She sat straighter. "I understand up here," she pointed to her head, "that I'm not to blame and that I should be proud of my Army service. And I am." Her voice became more strident as she fought tears. She placed her right hand over her heart. "It's here that I have the problem. Here I'm to blame and I failed my squad."

"You still blame yourself for a buried bomb blowing your truck up?"

"You do have a way of getting straight to the point."

"Changing the subject. How is physical therapy coming?"

"It's going. I work hard. I sweat. I'm getting better with my walking. I walked a few blocks to the store the other day to get a some groceries and brought them back."

"Still no vehicle?"

"I'm not sure I'm ready for that. A car costs money and adapting one costs even more. I'm not even sure where I'm going to be living or working when I'm done here."

"I thought you were going to Tennessee?"

"I considered it. Mom announced she's getting married and moving west. She's selling the only home I've ever known."

"If it means that much to you, why don't you purchase it?"

"I can't afford that yet, and I have no idea where I want to live. I can't invest in a property if I might be working somewhere else."

"Have you considered what it is you want to do?"

"Ah, the crux of it all. No clue. Still no clue. Do I want to go back to school? If so, for what? My dad was a long-haul truck driver but even though I can drive big trucks, I don't believe that's the career for me."

"We have time to sort this all out."

"Yeah, so you keep saying and I'm still stuck."

"Have you talked to your friends about it?"

"Friend? I've talked to Rachel some, but not too much. She's busy with her husband and children. We still talk, but there are too many distractions. I'm a problem no one can solve and don't want to burden her with that."

"How about Gabby?"

"My roomie? Our disabilities are different. She's more positive, further ahead in the program, and keeps busy. She's been on my case to get up in the morning and scolded me for drinking too much Friday night."

"Did you?"

"What?"

"Drink too much?"

"Define, too much."

The captain sighed and waited.

"Fine. I drank too much. I'm the size of a middle school kid. I can't handle a lot of alcohol."

"What does drinking help?"

"It numbs me. I can experience some things more…like the rhythm of the guitar and the soft crooning of a cowboy. The vibration of the bass through my foot creating a tingle throughout my body. Desire…" Eliza closed her eyes and sighed.

"Desire for what?"

Eliza opened her eyes and brushed an errant hair off her face. "Desire to be loved. To be seen as whole and worthy of attention."

"One guy paid you attention."

"Sure, but I wasn't interested in him. He was a bully trying to take advantage of my small stature."

"And this," the captain glanced at her notes, "Kristos?"

"He's out of my reach, but with the buzz I had, I didn't possess any fear of rejection at the moment. I guess the alcohol made me bolder."

"How did you feel about it the next morning?"

"Embarrassed. I did toss a full glass of beer on the poor guy. He never yelled or made a fuss about it, just kept on playing and singing as if it never happened. Then he tried to protect me. I can't remember if I said thank you..." Eliza stared at her fingernails.

"You could write him a note."

"I caught a glimpse of him again on Sunday morning. Gabby dragged me to church. He was there but I was too chicken to talk to him. I think his father is the pastor. Kristos is out of my reach."

"Did he treat you as if you were?"

"No. He was courteous but not flirtatious. He was working so maybe that had something to do with it."

"Considering he could have been angry with you, that's a positive."

"I believe he could see I was aiming for the bully and not him."

"But you didn't apologize?"

"I don't remember. I can't even remember what I ate for dinner. I think I enjoyed it."

"Alcohol makes you feel...but erases your memory and manners?"

"Maybe so."

Later as Eliza headed to physical therapy, she took a few moments to sit outside in the shade and do nothing.

She was stuck. Like a 4x4 sucked in deep mud, she was in first gear and trying to rock herself out but dug in deeper. She wasn't sleeping well but had refused the sleep aid the doctor recommended. She didn't want to rely on medication in the future.

But you'll abuse alcohol?

I don't—

Eliza paused and closed her eyes.

A soft male voice disturbed her peace. "Do you mind if I join you?"

She sat up straighter and surveyed the man who was only a few inches taller than her. He had crutches.

"Please. Take a load off. Relax," she offered. She tried not to stare, and curiosity was rampant within her.

"You're wondering why I have crutches," he said.

"Of course, I'm wondering. But that's none of my business."

"I thought sharing our stories helped us heal."

"Hasn't worked for me yet."

"You're injured?"

She lifted her pant leg to reveal her prosthesis.

"Wow. I'm sorry. I lost my foot but they can't guarantee I won't lose my leg below the knee yet. Healing isn't what it should be."

"So why are you out here? They aren't keeping you in a hospital bed?"

"Nah. I'd rather the bed go to someone who can really use it. I need to learn to make it in the real world sooner or later. I decided not to wait."

"Well, good luck with that."

"How did you, um, you know—?"

"Lose my leg? I drove a truck over an IED that had been detonated by the lead vehicle. I was the only survivor." Her voice was strangely detached from the retelling.

"Whoa. I'm so sorry. I hear there's a support group that has meetings. Have you gone?"

Eliza shook her head. "No. At least not yet."

"I'm Cooper. You are..."

"Torres."

"Oh, you're Tornado?"

Eliza frowned. "That was my nickname. How'd you know?"

"My brother was in your platoon. He spoke of how brave you were and how you worked harder than anyone else to prove your worth."

"Cooper...Cooper...I'm sorry I don't recall."

"Oh, he was Specialist Marshall. We have the same mom, but different fathers, and Greg is two years older than me. Lucky duck is still overseas having all the fun."

"Yeah, funny how you can miss being over there, isn't it? I'm sure your family is happy you survived whatever did that to you."

"Not as noble as your injury. I was repairing a truck when the jack let loose. Guess I didn't set it well."

"Ouch. Here or over there?"

"Here. I was about to be deployed to South Korea. Guess that isn't going to happen."

"I'm sorry."

"Hey, it's not your fault. It was either my mistake or faulty equipment. We were on an exercise so it could have been a little of both. It doesn't matter. Playing the blame game doesn't help me move on in life."

"Sometimes it's hard to shift gears," Eliza whispered.

The young soldier next to her nodded. "Isn't it though?"

Private First Class Cooper glanced at his watch. "Guess I better get in there, time for physical torture. No pain, no gain, right?" He released a wry chuckle. "God bless you, Tornado."

"Thanks. You too." Eliza wondered what he meant about God blessing her. He hadn't so far. Granted she could be in far worse condition but was it a blessing to be alive at all? She should have been in a box cloaked with a flag like the rest of the men in that truck. It didn't make sense. Everywhere she turned she was tripping over someone's faith in God. Fine. If it made them happy, good for them.

Eliza's mother would have been heartbroken if Eliza had passed away. She remembered her mother's visit while Eliza was at Walter Reed. The gray pallor on her mother's face as she sat by Eliza's bedside, head bowed. It only now dawned on her that her mother might have been praying. Apparently, her mother hadn't asked for the right thing. Not that her leg was ever recoverable to be reattached. Maybe it was a blessing that she still had her knee?

The throbbing, pulsing soreness defied her to defend that position. Way to go, God. You'll need to do better than that to prove You're real.

She rose and made her way into the building. She failed to notice the beauty of the sunshine on the mountains. Eliza faced her biggest obstacle once again—herself.

7

Kristos couldn't shake Eliza from his thoughts. What was up with her anyway? She flirted with him and avoided him. Maybe she needed to be somewhere? And why did God keep impressing her on his heart? He sat down on a bale of hay as the cool breeze flowed through the barn. The horses were out, and the stalls were cleaned. Murial, one of the Percherons, hung around closer to the barn. She was due to give birth soon. This would be the second foal for his stable.

Lord, I don't understand why Eliza is heavy on my mind, but You do. Draw her to Yourself. Heal the wounds of her past and free her from whatever is haunting her. She's cute, but You are aware I don't want someone who drinks to excess. Anyway. She's Your child, please help her.

Jane stepped into the barn. "Oh, Kristos. I was wondering if you'd seen Kobbe?"

"Not this morning, why? Anything I can help you with?"

"Probably not, just not sure when Mark is scheduled next."

Kristos rose and walked toward Jane. "We can check her schedule." He unlocked the office door off the side of the indoor corral Kobbe used for therapy. He stopped and Jane almost bumped into him. "Whoa. I'm not even sure where to look." The desk was piled high with papers and a wicker rectangular basket was stacked high with receipts and bills.

Jane stepped in and gasped. "I suppose bookkeeping isn't her forte?"

"It isn't, but I didn't realize she'd gotten this far behind."

Jane stepped over to the desk to find a calendar. "I think this is it.

Hmmm. Tomorrow at four. OK, that's all I needed. Thanks, Kristos."

"You're welcome." Kristos backed out of the room and locked the door. He didn't enjoy the bookkeeping for the barn and his horse breeding, but bills needed to be paid, feed ordered, and veterinarian appointments scheduled. He didn't necessarily enjoy all that, but at least he didn't have insurance papers to file and all the stuff Kobbe needed to do on top of writing progress notes for the clients. Or were they patients? It might be helpful if she hired someone to take care of the billing, and insurance, and appointments. Only Kobbe could do the notes. Speaking of which, he had some office work to do himself. He headed to the stairs to his apartment. His office was in a small room where he could close the door at the end of the day and try to forget about business. Someday he'd have his own barn and office. Land was expensive and each horse he owned was pricey too. It would take some time before he was able to break away from the family ranch to have his own.

But did he really want to?

He sat at his desk and started sorting through the bills. He went online to place some orders and he double checked his documentation on each horse in his stable, including the smaller ones Kobbe used. Those horses belonged to his parents. Kobbe currently didn't pay for food or housing for the animals since they'd already been here. She was family. Still, the animals all needed to be cared for. There were also horses they boarded for a fee. Income and expenses. His goal was to make sure there was more of the income so he could be paid.

His phone chimed, alerting him to a message. It was one of the bandmates.

Langer snapped this photo Friday night. She's a cutie. Thought you might like it.

Kristos clicked on the image and enlarged it. He was by the front door when Eliza briefly flirted with him. He hadn't recalled her booping his nose as the photo indicated. His expression didn't make sense. He was smiling?

He texted back. *Thanks*. He wouldn't confirm or deny anything. It wasn't any of their business anyway.

He sent the photo to his email so he could pull it up on his laptop. Once he'd done that, he opened it up on the big screen. The woman was petite, and he towered over her. She was smiling and quite pretty. He suspected blonde wasn't her natural color given her dark eyebrows and roots. Did women have the opportunity to dye their hair when deployed? Of course, she wasn't deployed here at Fort Carson.

The fact that she was military should mean he needed to put her behind him, out of his mind and thoughts. She'd be gone before he knew it, to parts unknown for an indeterminate amount of time. Not good wife material and that was what he wanted most. He didn't want to date for the fun of it anymore. He wanted the real deal. An authentic partner, a lover, a friend, a mother to children they might have. In other words, a wife. He envied Michael planning a wedding to Bridget.

Oh, right. He emailed the open dates he had in the fall to Michael along with a suggestion for a possible location. That would be coming up fast.

Eliza slumped in her chair as the doctor checked her stump. She hated that word.

"I think we need to modify your prosthetic. You've worn this for a while and it doesn't fit right as you gain strength and mobility. I hate to ask you to use your crutches more or a wheelchair, but I'm not happy with your leg and the way this is wearing on you. Does it hurt?"

"Throbs, aches, sometimes pain. Always discomfort, even at night. I thought that was normal. Kind of phantom leg syndrome or something like that."

"Do you get the urge to scratch and itch on your foot?"

Eliza nodded. "Imagine my surprise when it isn't there. So the pain is real?"

"On the edge here, yes. Eventually this prosthetic will become more natural for you, and you won't even think much about it as it becomes part of your body, at least mentally. Physically, it shouldn't hurt."

"OK. I guess you adjust my leg and I go without for a few days?"

"Yep. That's correct. Wheelchair or crutches while your stump heals. When this is ready, I want your stump to be well."

"Thank you."

Eliza was given a wheelchair to use. She called a cab. Maybe once her repaired prosthetic was in, she'd be moved out of the complex care platoon and on to the veteran track. Of course, her therapist didn't think Eliza was ready for that yet.

Eliza would need to prove her wrong. Not that she was in any hurry to go anywhere.

There was nowhere to go.

Once back in her quarters, she nudged the coffee table so she could move around more easily. She maneuvered to the sofa and sat staring at the wheelchair she'd used for more time than she liked. She hated that people stared when she used it, even on an Army post. Off post, in public it could be worse. Gabby wanted to return to Hernandez Hacienda restaurant again on Friday.

Would Kristos be there? She pulled his business card out of her pocket. Why had he given it to her? She couldn't recall.

Eliza already said she'd go…but now she'd be in a wheelchair. Three steps forward and two steps back.

This is temporary.

She'd never be normal. What man would want a one-legged woman? At least she didn't need to shave that leg. Humor, even if it was a bit dark, helped her cope.

But Kristos would see her and learn the truth. Not that she could keep that kind of secret forever from any man, but she'd hoped someone would fall in love with her before they learned about her missing leg, and it wouldn't matter.

So far, no one had. There'd been no dates. No interest. No time.

Was she even worthy of that? Who wanted a messed-up Army casualty? She was a bigger mess in her mind and heart than with her leg.

Ramsey squawked.

"Fine, I'll let you out." She opened the cage door and the bird climbed up to the perch on top of his home. He bobbed his head.

"Is that a thank you? Oh, I wish you would talk."

She moved from the wheelchair to sit in the recliner. The crutches were close by. Her phone rang.

"Hey, Rach. What's up? Usually I call you," Eliza said, forcing herself to sound cheerful.

"I have a few moments to rest while the littles take a nap. Thought I'd see how my bestie is doing."

"Fair to middlin'. Gotta go without my prosthetic until it's modified."

"And you went to church? Last Sunday?"

"Yes, ma'am."

"Well, what did you think?"

"It was, um, interesting. Kristos was there. His father preached."

"Ohhh, that sounds good. Did you talk to him?"

"Kristos or his father?" Eliza grinned.

"Either one, silly," Rachel said.

"Neither. I left as quickly as I could."

"Are you going back this weekend?"

"I'd need to go on crutches or in my wheelchair. Then he'll know," Eliza groaned.

"That you are a lovely young woman?"

"Ha! Surely you joke. Gabby hoped to go to the Hernandez Hacienda again on Friday, the food was amazing, but if he's there…"

"He won't be able to dance with you? Or you won't be able to douse him in beer?"

"All of the above." Ramsey settled on the arm of the chair and fluffed his feathers. Eliza reached over to pet him and loosen up some pin feathers. Gabby would hate the mess, but the bird enjoyed the preening.

"Listen, Eliza, you need to get yourself together and get a plan for your future. What are you waiting for? All I hear are excuses. My leg, my mom's getting married, his dad is a pastor, God can't love me so why bother?" Rachel's voice had a sing-song, snarky quality to it that only a longtime friend could use.

"Hush your face. Did you listen to the sermon or something?"

"I don't even know the name of the church, why?" Rachel asked.

"The pastor spoke about how we are without excuse in knowing God and that all of creation cries out in worship."

"Oh, from Romans, right?"

"Yeah, I guess."

"So…?" Rachel asked.

"You mentioned I was making excuses. Am I? Really? My reality is that life is hard and I'm confused and this abrupt change in my life has left me unsettled. Discombobulated. I don't know which way to turn."

"I realize that, honey, but life happens to all of us, and then we have choices to make. Your inability to make any decision concerns me. That and your drinking. You never used to like beer."

"Ugh. Please, don't lecture and nag me."

"Why? You're tired? You're frustrated? Scared? Lonely? Hungry? I bet you didn't eat lunch yet, you always used to get hangry when you skipped lunch." Rachel teased.

"Hangry. Hungry and angry all wrapped up into one Tornado—at least that's what Cliff Barnes used to tease me. Why don't you tell me what's going on in your world?" Eliza asked, fully aware that it was an excuse to get her out of talking more about herself…and her excuses.

When she hung up a short time later, she realized that's all she really was…a bundle of excuses. The only problem was, she had no clue what to do about it.

Kristos picked up the phone on the first ring. "Dad? What's up?"

"Wondering if I can talk to you about an upcoming mission trip we have planned."

"The one to Mexico?"

"Yeah. Mateo was going to lead the team and can't do it now. He doesn't want to leave his wife for a moment."

"Right. Fighting cancer is brutal. Totally understand. He should be with her."

"Exactly. That means there's a leadership gap. You've gone a few times. I realize you didn't plan on it this year but could you pray about not only going, but leading the trip?"

"I don't view myself as much of a leader, Dad."

"I think you have hidden depths you've not reached yet, and this would be a valuable experience for you. I believe you possess the ability to do it. I've been praying and your name is the only one that I keep coming back to."

"Wow. Thanks. It's a big responsibility. How many people are going?"

"We don't have our full team together yet. I was going to announce on Sunday the final cutoff dates. I wanted to make sure there was a point person before we forged ahead with the plans."

"It's a little short notice, but I'm sure my assistant, Caden, would be willing to work full time for a week or so while I'm gone."

"First pray about it, then talk to Caden, and let me know. If I don't have solid leadership, I can't risk sending a team even with the organization we'll partner with on site."

"I get it, Dad. You take the spiritual, emotional, and physical safety of our team seriously. You sure you don't want to go? It's been a few years."

"Not this time. Let me know, son."

"I will."

They disconnected their call, and Kristos rose and walked to the kitchen to refill his coffee mug. Mexico. He'd experienced some tremendous moments in Mexico when he went as a younger man. Funny. Like he was so old now. He strode to the living room and settled into his favorite chair. He'd never led a team on a trip like this. He was more of a behind the scenes support person. Why had his father chosen him? Alexos or Rusty would have been better choices for leading a team. His Spanish wasn't particularly good either.

God, what are You up to with all this? His life was good. There was a rhythm to his days and weeks, and he found joy and comfort in working with the horses. Was God asking him to step out in faith?

He wondered about Eliza. She continued to pop up in his thoughts. He wondered if she'd be back at the restaurant on Friday night. He wasn't playing this time, but planned to go with Peter since Peter's girlfriend was out of town for work. Would he see the pint-sized Tornado again?

He hoped so.

OK, Lord, whatever You want, just make it clear to me…soon.

He rose and instead of returning to his office, went downstairs to check on Muriel.

The horse was already on her side in full labor with the hooves sticking out. Kristos grabbed a chair to sit in the corner of the stall. This was Murial's first time, and he wanted to be there in case she had any difficulties. After a few hours there was a foal on the hay, struggling out of the sac surrounding its hind legs. Was the little one fully gray like the mother? He couldn't tell yet. Before long, the foal struggled to his feet and upon closer inspection Kristos determined it to be a colt. "Hmmm. Welcome, little guy. Murial, you did a beautiful job. How about we name your son Malachi? Does that sound good?"

Murial gave a soft whinny and shoved him away with her head.

"I get it." Kristos put his hands up and backed away, marveling at the wonder of God's creation and how a horse understood exactly what to do. "You want to bond with Malachi, and I'll leave you two alone for now. Congratulations, Murial."

She nodded her head and focused on the new colt finally locating his first meal. Kristos stood and watched from the other side of the pen as the mother and son got acquainted. It was beautiful. The rest of the horses were in the pasture until Kobbe needed one of them for her therapy clients.

He'd never imagined that some of his Percherons would be used for equine therapy. Even Zena sometimes helped. Despite her old age, she was as steady as they came, as well as Adonis and Ajax who were geldings and often used to pull wagons for events. The few Gypsy horses and Morgans, as well as one Shetland pony named Shelby, rounded out the horses who were sometimes used. Thankfully, most of those had been owned by the Savas for a few years and were also great for slow trail rides. He was grateful they weren't raising performance horses although he admired barrel riding and other events like that. Personally, he preferred the draft horses, which was why he'd been networking and building up his own stable of Percherons. There weren't a large number yet, but if he kept working hard, he'd have a great stable. Who knew? Maybe someday Malachi would be a stud for future horses and he'd make money with him.

He strode back up the stairs to his apartment and office and went back to record the new birth and document the lineage of this colt. He grinned. A boy.

As awestruck as he was at the birth of this foal, how much more would he be at the birth of one of his own children? His two older brothers' wives were expecting babies. As happy as he was for them, he was envious as well of their happiness in marriage and the starting, or continuing, of their families.

Kristos only had horses, which as wonderful as they were, weren't quite the same as a woman. He sighed as Eliza popped into his thoughts again. *Really? Come on, Lord. If these thoughts are not of You, please take them away. I don't want to be taunted by someone I can't or shouldn't have.* Of course, he was making a snap judgement based on a glass of beer. And her flirtatiousness. The glass had been full. What if it was her only drink that night? He stunk so much of beer by the time he was face to face with her, he wouldn't have been able to tell if it was on him or from her when she came closer.

Argh! Stop it. Stop thinking about her.

Eliza.

He liked that name. He had no doubt she lived up to her Tornado nickname as well.

Why did that make him grin?

Eliza sat down with the vocational counselor on Friday. She hated needing to go anywhere with her wheelchair. It made transportation more difficult. Even though it was collapsible, she depended on someone else to help her, and she did not like being dependent on anyone.

Except her team, but she pulled her weight with them all.

Except for when she failed—and three men died.

Losing a leg was minor to that, although their death was instantaneous and her recovery was long—painful at first, and torturously slow.

"Eliza, let's go over your evaluations. You earned an associates in business, right?"

"Yep. I ended up a truck driver and I was good at it."

"You want to drive trucks when you leave the Army?" The captain frowned at the wheelchair.

"I thought I could do anything I wanted. There are adaptations, right?"

"Sure there are, to a certain degree. It would be difficult and you're on the petite side. Are you thinking long-haul trucking or delivery work? You'd need to be able to lift and carry a heavy weight."

"I have no clue what I want."

"You don't want to work at a desk? Paperwork bores you?"

"I don't know. I never tried it."

"You got a degree in business. Why not go back to school for a bachelor's degree. Business or anything else?"

Eliza shrugged. "But—" She stopped. She was making excuses again, wasn't she?

"Yes?" the captain asked.

"What do your evaluations indicate I'd be good at?"

"You scored high in business. Human resources might be an option? Or accounting if you wanted to go on for a certified public accountant degree or become a certified tax specialist? You could even work for the Internal Revenue Service."

"I guess that at least would be government work, right? Good benefits?"

"You're worried about benefits? How about something that will give you a paycheck to start? While you will get retirement pay as an E4, you'll likely want to be doing something to bring in extra income and give you purpose."

"I'll think about it."

"You could start taking some classes, begin working toward something?"

"Maybe."

"Listen, Specialist, you suffered a loss of more than your leg and your friends. I'm here to help you figure out your next steps. We want you to succeed and thrive in life after the Army. I'm going to make a suggestion—a challenge as it were."

"OK?"

"I want you to consider doing something outside of your comfort zone. I don't care if it's a sport you try, we have many adaptive sports, even for those in wheelchairs. Or a class. Or something to serve someone else. Just do something, anything, outside your bubble to prove to yourself you can. You might find you unlock something deep inside you that will help steer you on the path you should take."

"You sound almost like you're preaching to me."

"I am a person of faith, and that might help you as well, but you're stuck. So take a step to get unstuck by trying something new."

Eliza let out a long breath. No excuses. "OK."

"Before your next appointment at least have a plan. I don't particularly care what it is. Do something new."

Nodding, Eliza unlocked her wheelchair and spun it to the door after the captain graciously opened it for her. She got a ride home and back to her quarters. Gabby wasn't home.

Something new? Whatever would she do?

9

That Friday night the August heat was slowing Eliza down. She struggled with the crowds to get through the entrance door to the Hernandez Hacienda Mexican restaurant she and Gabby decided to revisit. There was a band playing but with a quick glance she realized Kristos wasn't there. She sighed in relief. She slowly made her way to the table with Gabby pushing the wheelchair. It was such an obvious handicap, and the stares were like pointed daggers igniting the spots where she'd experienced burns from the explosion. Would she ever get over this sense of being a spectacle?

"Chill. It's a morbid curiosity. People want to know your story, that's all."

"And you get to be invisible."

"My story isn't as dramatic…and given how well I'm doing, I hope to be rejoining my unit in Georgia at Fort Gordon."

"You'll be moving out."

Gabby sat and turned to Eliza. "I'm sorry to say it, but yes. You'll get a new roomie, I'm sure. Maybe someone new to the program who you'll be able to encourage and help along."

The conversation stalled and dinner was uneventful. Eliza couldn't eat much and continued to worry that someone would trip over her wheelchair. The music tonight failed to cheer her or get her thinking about dancing. She drank—too much. By the time Gabby wheeled her to the door with a to-go box on her lap, Eliza was comfortably numb.

A man bumped her. Instinctively, she reached out with her good leg to kick him as he passed.

"Not nice," Gabby whispered in her ear.

Eliza shrugged. "Some people are rude."

"Doesn't mean you need to be as well."

The man came back her way with his fists clenched. "Did you kick me?"

Frowning, Eliza leaned her head back to see him. "Must have been my phantom leg. It has a mind of its own."

Before anything more could be said, Gabby pushed her out the door. Once back in the car with the wheelchair tucked away in back, Gabby settled into the driver seat. "I'm worried about you. The drinking. The attitude. What's going on?"

Eliza shrugged. Gabby started the car and headed back to Fort Carson.

"Not going to answer me?"

"Not sure what to say." She wasn't about to confess her confusion and fears to her roomie who would soon be returning to duty. Jealousy welled up within. Great, one more irritating emotion to deal with.

Once back in their barracks, Eliza checked on Ramsey. "How ya doin', Rams?"

The large parrot squawked and turned his back to her. Seemed like she was making a mess of it with everyone tonight.

"Eliza, I'm serious when I said I'm concerned. I'm your friend, on your side, but you've got to realize your whole life is ahead of you. You've the opportunity to start it fresh with the help of the Army. Grab on to that and go for it. You can do this. Only losers give up." Gabby went to her own room and the door shut without a sound.

Eliza grabbed the crutches and hopped to her room, shutting the door with less decorum. She brushed her teeth and readied for bed. Sitting on the edge of the mattress, she checked her knee. The doctor informed her she was fortunate to have kept the knee. She should be grateful. It's not like she had gorgeous legs forcing her to abandon dreams of being a model. She was average in looks, although deceptively strong from the Army training and the physical therapy after surgery.

She dyed her normally black-brown hair blonde, but she wasn't sure she liked it. She certainly wasn't having more fun. So why had she done it?

To wipe away the gal who had been fearless and cocky. That girl had guts. She earned her place in the platoon. A woman who had been respected and considered an equal. The woman they depended on.

The woman who let them all down.

Yet the same face stared back at her in the mirror. What was the point? Blonde or dark brown, she was the same failure. She turned off the bedside lamp and crawled under the covers. Hitting the pillow a few times didn't help. She cried herself to sleep.

Kristos arrived at church on Sunday and was about to find his seat when he spied the blonde spitfire wheeling up the walkway, her wheelchair pushed by her friend. Kristos went to hold open the door for them.

"Thank you," the pusher said.

"Good morning. I'm Kristos. We met last week."

Gabby grinned and reached out a hand to shake it. "That's right, I'm Gabby. You're the guy who got a beer bath courtesy of this klutz."

"Hey!" Eliza protested.

Kristos recognized the dig as a friendly one. "I guess that would be me. I believe the drink was meant for another man who conveniently avoided it."

"We're holding up traffic," Eliza whispered loudly.

Gabby shook her head. "Guess that's my cue to find us a place to sit."

"I can show you where most people park their chairs so they can be out of the way of the aisles. There are a few spots up front or some here in the back."

"The back is fine with me," Eliza said.

"Thanks, Kristos," Gabby said as she pushed the wheelchair away.

Kristos frowned. What made Eliza so prickly? The wheelchair? He hadn't realized she'd been injured but that explained the slight hitch in her step when he'd seen her the first time. Only one shoe showing today. Probably getting a new leg or something like that. After pointing them to a spot, he walked out of the sanctuary to join the worship team in back. He was singing one song this morning as part of the plea for people to join them in Mexico. Funny how he'd be leading a team to be missionaries in another country to reach the lost, when a stubborn gal, who probably lost more than her leg, sat in the back of the sanctuary, equally lost.

Soon the service began, and it wasn't long before Pastor Theodore Sava called Kristos to the stage.

"Kristos has agreed to lead our mission team to Mexico, but we have plenty of room for others to sign up to join us. Kristos has been on this trip before. Son, why don't you tell us why you're heading up the trip this year?"

"You asked me to."

The crowd chuckled.

Pastor Sava grinned and stepped aside.

"On a more serious note, my father did ask me to head up the trip when the original leader was unable to go. I prayed about it and began to recognize that all my objections were lame excuses." Kristos almost choked, realizing how awful that word could sound to Eliza sitting in the back row. "Excuse: I've never led a team like this before. True, but having gone several times I am aware of the environment. Growing up in our large and ever-increasing Greek family, I understand a little about chaos and relational dynamics. And how will I learn to lead if I never try? My dad saw something in me that he believed could be a good fit. One excuse eliminated. Another excuse: I don't have the time. Who does? But I have a helper who is more than capable of taking the reins as it were..."

His father chuckled.

"Excuse three: I don't speak Spanish. Silly since I've been there before and took the language in high school, but the most important words are, *Hola. Gracias.* And '*¿dónde está el baño? Via con Dios.*

"My father once told me: 'No fear. No limits. No excuses.' That quote hangs on the wall at the stable. I'm here to challenge you to examine your reasons for not going on this trip. Of course, some will have valid ones that you can't get around, but ask God to show you what reasons are valid and which ones are excuses. This trip can be challenging work, but also filled with joy and can be life transformational. I challenge you to join me and the rest of the team as we go. You can find me in the lobby after the service to talk more about it if you wish."

Kristos picked up his guitar and began to sing a song he'd written yesterday.

Lord, You're calling me to go
But all I want to do is say no
You said all things are possible with You
Help me do what You want me to do.

Trusting You is a start
Since the day You came to live in my heart
Still I struggle to go when You tell me to
Help me do what You want me to do.

I've never been alone
Since my heart became Your home
You tell me to witness as I go
Help me to do what You want me to do

By Your Spirit within me
I can rely on Your strength
To do what You want me to do
Help me do what You want me to do.

He finished and walked off the stage. Once in the back hallway as the worship team started their set, he leaned against the wall. He'd toyed with writing music before. Had it fallen flat? Or had the ballad reached the hearts of the people God was calling to join him in Mexico?

Guess he'd find out after the service.

He came through the hallway toward the back of the sanctuary and slid into a rear row. He could view Eliza and Gabby out of the corner of his eye. What was she thinking? He frowned. Of course, she was missing a leg. If anyone had a good reason not to go—it would be her.

Why did that make him sad?

Eliza could barely breathe. If she had her leg she'd have risen and left. Gone. But she stayed and when Kristos sang it was as if someone pierced her heart. Why would God want her to begin with—much less on a mission trip to Mexico? She wasn't even sure she believed in God.

She recalled the words of her counselor challenging her to do something outside her comfort zone. And Kristos' words from his father: No fear. No limits. No excuses.

It came back to excuses. According to Pastor Sava, she was without excuse from knowing God existed. Sure, she'd heard about Jesus and His death and somewhat magical return to life, but that didn't mean she needed to commit herself to the man. Was He God? There was so much she didn't understand but her heart ached to learn more.

Why would God even want her? And live in her heart? What did that even mean? Even if He wanted to save her, why would He want her to go to Mexico? Didn't missionaries talk about Jesus? She couldn't do that.

It was out of her comfort zone.

She would need her prosthetic leg.

She'd never traveled with that before.

She didn't know Jesus.

God wouldn't call her to go to Mexico, would He? Surely her counselor would be suggesting something else: skydiving perhaps, bungee-jumping, whitewater rafting, hunting grizzly bears even. All of those sounded saner than Eliza Torres traveling to Mexico.

Those weren't excuses.

Or were they?

Kristos exited the sanctuary as the closing song started. He waited by a small table that had information and a sign-up for the trip. Would anyone stop to sign up? If no one did, there wouldn't be enough people to go, and he'd be off the hook. Somehow, he didn't think God would let him off that easy. He chuckled to himself. Maybe he'd meet some sweet Christian senorita down there, fall in love, and bring her back to the United States.

So why did Eliza's image flash into his mind. She wasn't the woman for him, of that he was certain.

The woman he'd been thinking of emerged from the sanctuary being pushed by her friend. They headed straight to him.

"Kristos, your song was lovely," Eliza said.

She didn't possess that hard edge, that mask of bravado he'd observed before.

"Thank you."

Gabby grabbed an information brochure and scanned it. "Oh, pooh. I don't have any leave to use for this. Otherwise, I think it would be a fun trip."

"We'll be working, fixing up some buildings, specifically a church and school. We'll have worship services for the village and share about Christ. No air conditioning. Fairly primitive conditions."

"Like we haven't dealt with that, right, Eliza? Military life is no cakewalk to be sure. Eliza, you have some leave saved up. This is something you should do."

Eliza paled; her eyes grew wide. "Me?" She pointed to the wheelchair.

"You'll get your leg back this week. Don't be so wimpy. A girl who can drive an Army truck can surely handle a hammer or a paintbrush." Gabby grabbed the packet of information and shoved it in the pocket on the side of the wheelchair. "We'll talk later. I agree with Tornado here, your song was moving. Thank you for sharing it."

Gabby turned to wheel Eliza out as Kristos stared after them. Someone else was challenging the petite soldier to go to Mexico? Why did that make him smile?

Kobbe, married to Kristos' brother Alexos, strode up to him. "You know her?" She motioned to the departing women.

"Yeah, met them a week ago. The one in the wheelchair is Army. She wasn't in a wheelchair then. I'm assuming her friend is Army as well."

"You should tell her about our therapy program. Why didn't you realize she had a wheelchair?"

"She was standing unaided with what appeared to be two feet."

"Likely a prosthetic."

"I have very little acquaintance with either woman."

"She's the one who dumped beer on you?"

Kristos rolled his eyes. "Yeah."

Kobbe nudged him with her elbow. "That will be a fun story to share with your kids someday."

"Excuse me? Why would I share that story?"

"An obtuse Sava. Because it's how you first met. Duh. See you later. Don't forget to tell her."

"Wait, Kobbe. What's going on in your office? I needed to get in there the other day and it was a disaster area."

Alexos came to stand by his wife and chimed in. "Paperwork is not Kobbe's forte, is it, agapiménos."

"I have other strengths," she defended.

Kristos grinned. "I'll keep an eye out for someone who could help you. You could use it. Other than progress notes for your clients, almost anyone else could do the insurance billing and manage the books, right?"

"Almost anyone except me," Kobbe admitted, twirling a long red strand of curly hair around one finger.

Alexos chimed in. "That's a great idea, Kristos. It's a job that a wounded military vet could do. I'll contact the Army Recovery Care Program. They're often looking for ways to help wounded military establish a new life after the Army and given that you already work with wounded veterans, this might be a way to expand your care, by giving employment to someone who needs it with an employer equipped to deal with any kind of residual trauma."

"I'm not sure I have enough work for a full-time employee. I'm not making that much yet."

"Kobbe, it's someone we could both use. I could use some help. I manage well enough, but I believe that between the two of us and given that we share the use of some of the horses, we could put together a decent package for employment," Kristos offered.

"Why don't we sit down later and hash out some job objectives, duties, and possible pay and benefits?" Alexos offered.

Kobbe nodded. "I think that sounds like a promising idea. Especially with us having a baby on the way, it's possible someone could also help with the therapy when I'm further along."

"Great. I'll see you later. Where should we meet?" Kristos asked.

"Come to our place. We'll serve you a nice lunch," Alexos offered.

"It's the least we can do since you helped Alexos with all the finishing touches of our home." Kobbe smiled at both men.

"Sounds good. See you later. I need to be here through the second service."

Alexos and Kobbe mingled some more before leaving. Kristos admired his brother and had missed him when Alexos was overseas. With Alexos gone and Rusty having surgeries after his accident and needing so much help, much of running the ranch fell to Kristos. He'd made it profitable by boarding horses and helping riders learn to care for and train for dressage or other things. Those horses helped pay the bills and funded his purchasing his dream horses, the Percherons. Over the years he'd managed to accumulate more horses and now had a few horses of his own. Hugo would be a great stud soon and now Malachi. With the breeding program and two colts, he'd be sitting pretty down the line. Living frugally helped, but he'd learned some of that from Rusty who used to live the van life on their parent's property while building a successful adventure business.

A few other people came to chat and get information. Kristos went into the next service believing God was going to assemble an awesome team for this trip.

And who knows, maybe Tornado would be there. Was he up for that challenge?

Kristos grinned. *Yes, God. I am.*

10

Eliza sat on the sofa. Gabby was in her room packing some of her belongings. She'd gotten notification that she'd be moving by the end of the week to join her unit in Georgia. Lucky duck. Not that Eliza believed in luck, but not believing would assume someone had a choice.

She'd had no choice about losing her leg. An explosion decided that for her.

She'd had no choice about losing her childhood home. Her mother was selling that to move to another state with the man she would marry.

She'd had no choice when her father died.

She'd had no choice about leaving the Army. It wasn't only the leg, although that was a big part of it. It was the emotional stuff that her therapist kept telling her she wasn't dealing with.

What stuff?

She didn't remember the explosion…or at least she didn't think so. There were dreams. More like nightmares. At times she woke up in a cold sweat afraid she'd screamed out loud.

Eyes sweat too, right? She wasn't one for crying. Crying wasn't the Army way.

Ramsey flew to sit on the arm of the furniture next to her.

"Do you want to be petted?"

Squawk!

"Fine. I wish you'd talk to me, Ramsey. You're a handsome man but I guess if you don't bite me, I should be grateful. I have no doubt that ginormous beak of yours could do some serious damage should you choose. Wonder why your previous owner lied about your vocabulary? He obviously wanted to get rid of you quickly before his deployment. Why he even bought a bird when he knew he was about to be deployed makes no sense to me. But many enlisted and officers have children as well while in the Army. You're not allowed to give those away. You came dirt cheap and at least I'm not alone."

She began rubbing the pin feathers on and behind Ramsey's head. She'd need to vacuum up the waxy residue later. If he didn't poop or pee anywhere other than his cage, she'd be content with this kind of clean-up.

The packet for Mexico sat on the sofa next to her. She pulled off the paper clip holding things together and began to sift through it. She had enough savings for such a trip. Could she handle it with her leg? What about her sleep issues? It wasn't like there'd be a therapist on call to talk to. Well, maybe there would be if they at least had electricity and a cell signal. Living in primitive conditions didn't bother her, nor did hard work. Physical therapy had made her strong so she could handle living without the bottom part of her right leg. She needed to get a vehicle.

What a rabbit trail her brain had traveled down. The car would be necessary once Gabby moved out. She should have bought one sooner. She set aside the Mexico paperwork. What was she thinking anyway? She couldn't do it. She shouldn't do it.

Excuses, excuses.

She grabbed her laptop from the coffee table and put it on her lap. Ramsey was content to hunker down for a nap by her side. She clicked open the page with information on vehicles for sale on post by soldiers who were deploying and wouldn't be needing them. She found a car and saved the information. Tomorrow she might get an opportunity to check it out in person. The thought of doing at least one thing to propel her toward independence caused her to smile.

Maybe she wasn't doing too bad after all.

Kristos sat with Alexos and Kobbe at their kitchen table.

"Thanks for the meal, Kobbe."

"You're welcome. We appreciate your help with the house and moving."

Kobbe rose and took the dirty dishes to the sink. "There are still a lot of things to be done with the house, but we're pacing ourselves. Next up is a crib I think?" Her cheeks turned pink as she glanced at Kristos' brother.

"Ahem, well, thanks again. I'm sure you'll have many years to personalize this place and make your mark here. You'll be able to do some more decorating other than Alexos' I-Love-Me wall." He was referring to a display of mementos from Alexos' Army career as a helicopter pilot. Kristos shot Alexos a wry look to take any sting from the comment. "Anyway, home is more about people than it is about property. You're getting a good start on that."

"Thanks.," Alexos said. "Let's get some paper out and start figuring out what kind of person we would search for to handle the office for Kobbe. It'd be nice if she had more time to serve people instead of on the phone with insurance companies, doctors, and sending out invoices."

Kristos grabbed his laptop. "I figured we could start typing it out on the computer. Easier to make changes."

The next hour was spent hashing out the role and tasks the office manager would deal with for the therapy business and Kristos' stable. Weighing out the cost of everything and the increased income they could both manage to bring in to pay for this person.

"I'm not sure we can realistically do a full-time position unless I found others willing to do this kind of therapy alongside me," Kobbe said.

"That's a great idea. They could build their own clientele. Kind of like building a therapy practice, except here we have horses to help," Alexos cheered. "How many people do you think we could find to help?"

Kobbe shrugged. "I can check with my brother-in-law, Bernard, to see if he is aware of anyone leaving the military who might want to do this. Even if several were part time while starting up another office practice, it could be a terrific opportunity."

"We have a few other spaces that could be made into offices so they could do both from one location," Kristos offered.

"Wow, this is getting bigger than I anticipated when we started. Why don't we start with the office personnel first so I can get organized and pray about the rest. Perhaps it will be organic and God will bring the right person our way," Kobbe said.

Kristos frowned. "You think God would do that?"

"Yes," Alexos and Kobbe said in unison.

"OK. This together thing is adorable but also a little strange. Please don't start finishing each other's sentences."

Alexos chuckled and pulled Kobbe into his lap when she returned to the table. "Togetherness is a big part of marriage, little brother. Someday God will bring a gal your way so you can experience it as well."

Kobbe wrapped an arm around Alexos' back. "It's not all roses, Kristos. We've had our challenges too."

"Right, like who wants anything other than white paint on the walls?" Alexos asked.

Kristos cleared his throat and rose to his feet. "I'll let you hash that out, but I'd say paint colors is not a hill you want to die on, big brother." He closed his laptop and tucked it under his arm. "I'll head out for now. I'll clean this up and email it to you both, and we can keep praying about how we want this to look. Wouldn't hurt to come up with more of a name for your services. I should do that as well. Sava Ranch is nice enough, but I'm thinking it lacks some pizazz."

"Do you want to stay and brainstorm that?" Kobbe asked.

"Nah, I need to spend some time praying. It's hard because while I want to specialize in Percherons, we have Morgans, a Shetland, and the Gypsy horses as well as the ones we board. How busy do we want this place to be?" Kristos asked.

Kobbe grinned. "Shelby, the Shetland, was a lovely gift for my practice, Kristos."

"Shelby is a sweet little filly. She seems especially tiny next to the Morgans and Percherons. Let's leave how busy we will be in God's hands."

"Thankfully I'm tall enough to handle using those for therapy as well. Still the smaller people who come benefit from starting out on her. She's perfect."

Kristos ducked his head at the compliment. "My pleasure, Kobbe. I'll see you at the stables."

"Bye!" The couple waved Kristos off. He went outside and got in his truck and headed to his apartment. Once parked, he set his laptop aside and stepped in to check on Muriel and her little colt, Malachi.

"We'll have you both out in the pasture soon."

Malachi scampered around the pen, finally stable on his long legs. Muriel whinnied and shook her head.

Kristos reclaimed his laptop and headed up to his apartment and office. He plugged it in and grabbed a tablet of lined paper and a pen. He had a small porch off the back where he could see the mountains. He sat down and started to think.

Mountain View Stables? That had a nice ring to it. He checked his phone search engine. Nope. There was already a stable in Fort Collins with that name. He did a search for ranch names in Colorado but thankfully none of the others appealed to him. He finally had the list narrowed down to three: Mountain Shadow Stables, Mountain Meadows Stables, or for the fun of it because he had some of the world's largest horses and those were his passion: Tall Tail Stables.

The more he looked at the names the more he was drawn to Mountain Shadow Stables. He'd need to find out what Kobbe would call her company. If either of them wanted to be on the map as a force in Colorado, they needed good branding.

He set aside the papers and squinted. It had been a full day. The sun was shining and the weather was nice. Time to go for a ride. He changed into his work jeans and some boots and headed downstairs. He strode to the gate to the pasture and gave a low whistle. Zena trotted his way.

"Hey, girl. Wanna go for a ride?" he asked.

Zena whinnied and nodded her head. He walked toward the half door and unlatched it, letting her back into the barn. She stopped by the tack room, and he brought out a rug and placed it on the horse. He tossed the saddle over and cinched it. He put on her bridle and after making sure Zena had a good drink, they headed out to one of the shaded mountain trails.

The air was cooler under the tall aspens that grew on this part of the property. Occasionally, he could glimpse the soaring tops of the Rocky Mountain Range. Zena didn't need much urging to keep moving forward. He let her pick her path when the trail divided. She was acquainted with them all. Sitting atop the large horse and experiencing the flexing and power of the muscled beast beneath him infused him with confidence and courage. Like he could tackle anything. But could he really?

Eliza. Why did she continue to weigh heavy on his heart and mind? He'd seen her, what? Three times?

Lord, I'm trusting You to bring me the right woman at the right time. Please remove thoughts of Eliza if they are not of You. I want my pursuit of a woman to be honorable, but why am I confused about this particular soldier? The lack of a leg doesn't worry me, but there's a hardness there I can't explain, and it causes me to hesitate. I'm taking this need to be cautions as a nudging from You.

Sure, women flirted with him in the past. He'd always been clear that was not how he was going to select a potential life mate.

How else would he find one? Sitting on Zena wasn't going to bring women into his life to be noticed, that's for sure.

Was he being too picky? Of course, he wanted to be attracted to her.

Eliza was loveliness in a pint-sized package.

He wanted a woman who loved God.

Eliza was attending church but that didn't mean she was a follower of Christ.

He wanted a woman who would love horses since his life and livelihood were surround by them.

Could Eliza even ride a horse? With a prosthetic she could. He wondered if she'd tried hippotherapy?

There were no other women on the horizon in his life. Not at church or in any of the other places he went. He discounted women who approached him when he played guitar and sang. He didn't want a groupie, but a partner.

He wanted a family full of life and love like his parents had…and now Alexos and Kobbe as well as Rusty and Jane.

Zena shook her head and pawed at the ground with her hoof.

"What is it, girl?" he whispered.

A bobcat blocked the path up ahead of them at the curve.

"Shhhh."

Kristos reached for his semi-automatic pistol, released the safety, and aimed with his finger off the trigger.

Moments passed and neither the horse nor the bobcat moved.

With a flick of its short tail, the cat turned and strode off into the trees. Kristos released a breath he hadn't realized he'd been holding before engaging the safety and put the gun back in the holster. Zena could have killed the bobcat without his interference, but he didn't want to risk any harm coming to her.

"Time to head back home." He turned the horse around and they returned to the barn at a trot. Zena apparently had enough of wildlife and wanted the safety of the barn. Kristos couldn't blame her. At least it wasn't a grizzly. He'd forgotten to take his rifle.

Note to self: go into the woods fully armed next time.

11

Eliza was meeting with a new treatment team member today. Hopefully she'd get her leg later in the afternoon. She hated this wheelchair, but it was easier than doing crutches all the time.

She wheeled into the office. "Specialist Torres, I'm here for my appointment."

Without looking up the nurse said, "Go have a seat. I'll tell the doctor you're here." The nurse raised her head and gaped. "Oh, um. I apologize."

"It's fine. I'll keep the seat I have for now." Eliza wheeled herself to a spot and backed in to have a view of the room. There were a few other people there.

A nurse appeared at the door. "Specialist Torres?"

"Here." Eliza wheeled forward.

"Follow me." She led Eliza down one hallway and then to another. She opened the door to a room and motioned her in, placing a file on the desk. "Make yourself comfortable. Captain Travis will be with you soon."

The door closed softly, leaving Eliza all alone in the room. This wasn't a normal doctor's office. She'd been fighting this referral for quite some time before agreeing to see a psychiatrist. She wasn't crazy so why did her therapist want her here? It didn't make any sense.

A rap on the door preceded the entrance of a tall man with dark hair. He closed the door and strode in with confidence. He came around to the side of the desk and pulled up a chair. He sat down facing her and picked up the folder.

"Specialist Eliza Torres. It says here you've been in the Army Recovery Care Program for a few months. Why don't you tell me a little about yourself and why you're here?"

"Yes, sir. I'm Torres but my squad called me Tornado. I'm a—I mean, I was a truck driver until an IED blew up my truck killing everyone except me. That's how I lost part of my leg. I don't remember the event. Once I finish my program here, I will be medically retired from the Army." She said all of this in a matter-of-fact voice, keeping any emotions locked up tight. She hated telling her story.

"Where are you from originally?" the captain asked.

"Tennessee."

"Family?"

"Just my mom." Eliza sighed.

"Will you be returning home?"

Eliza shook her head. "Mom is getting married and selling the house."

"How do you feel about that?"

Eliza closed her eyes and took a steadying breath. "It doesn't matter. It is what it is."

"I would think it would matter. How long had you and your mother lived in that house?" The captain continued his inquisition.

"All my life, she worked hard as a nurse to keep it after my dad died."

"How old where you when that happened?" His gaze was steady, and his tone of voice was comforting.

"Thirteen."

"Where you close to him?"

"Yes. He was an over-the-road truck driver but when he was home, he was fun to be around." She blinked to keep tears at bay at the memory of time with her father.

"Are you an only child?"

Eliza nodded.

"How did he die?" the captain asked.

"Complications from diabetes."

"How long has your mother been a widow?"

"About ten years?" Eliza said. Had it been that long?

"Are you happy she's found someone to love?"

Eliza shrugged. "I guess. I've not met the man and now he's taking her away."

"Where?"

"Arizona."

"No place for you in the new family?" the captain asked.

"I don't want to impose. It would be weird, like a third wheel."

"I'm sorry about that. Have you made any decisions about where you'll go or what you'll do next?"

"No." Eliza frowned and gritted her teeth.

"Why not?"

"I don't know."

Captain Travis nodded. "Any nightmares?"

"Some. Who doesn't have nightmares?"

"Have the frequency or subject of the nightmares changed since the, what did you call it, event?"

"Maybe." She avoided his gaze now.

"Headaches?"

"Sometimes."

"Do you believe you have a problem?"

Eliza paused before answering in a whisper. "I have lots of problems. Who doesn't?"

"OK, what kind of problems do you have? Can you be specific?"

"Sure." Her voice grew in volume. "I have a parrot who won't talk. I don't have a vehicle and when I get one, I need to adapt it for this." She motioned to her leg. "My mom is abandoning me. I have no clue what I want to do with my life because I originally planned on the Army being my career. I have no idea where to live, or what job to apply for. I'm tired of being alone. I miss my squad."

"How have you been coping with these issues?"

"Avoiding them. Sometimes drinking," Eliza confessed.

"Are you someone who likes spontaneity or structure."

"Structure."

"You had no trouble with the structure of the Army?" the captain asked.

"No."

"But now your life is unsettled with no plan and a lot of unknowns."

"Exactly." Eliza wanted to add a *duh* to that response.

"Do you feel stuck?"

Eliza nodded. "So stuck it sucks. My life is aimless except for various appointments for therapy, or physical therapy, occupational therapy, career counseling, oh, and getting my prosthetic back today so I can walk again."

"Any relationships?"

"My roomie, Gabby, but she'll be moving at the end of this week."

"No one else?"

"My friend Rachel from high school. She's married with kids and living in Tennessee."

"Do you communicate with her often?"

"Whenever we can manage it. A couple of times a week now that I'm back in the States," Eliza said.

"How do you like the group therapy sessions?"

"I haven't gone to those." Eliza folded her arms across her chest.

"Why did you do that?"

"Do what?"

"Fold your arms. It's a defensive posture," the captain said.

Eliza glanced down at her arms but didn't move them. "Just felt like it."

"Are you anxious?"

"Well, these are a lot of questions. Why wouldn't I be anxious? I didn't want to come and see you, but my therapist insisted, so here I am. I'm a broken toy soldier. Can you fix me?"

Captain Travis grinned. "Is that how you perceive yourself? A little bit of glue and a fresh coat of paint and you're fine?"

"I wish."

"Listen, Specialist Torres, I can't fix you. I can help you get there but the majority of the work needs to be done by you. This is your one life and only you can live it. You have choices, but maybe there's too many choices so you're paralyzed from making any decision. We can help you narrow that down. May I make some suggestions?"

"Sure."

"I don't think you're a candidate for medication, but if you need help sleeping, we can offer you something for that."

"Nah, I'm good."

He nodded. "These are not mandated but merely suggestions. There is a newer therapy out there called EMDR which stands for Eye Movement Desensitization and Reprocessing. While you described the event as if it were nothing, I suspect you're struggling with some trauma from it and this could help you process that and move past it."

"Sounds weird. Anything else?"

"My sister-in-law runs a horse therapy clinic at the Sava Ranch. She's a trained and licensed counselor in equine therapy can help in surprising ways, and you get to be around horses, which is fun."

"I've never ridden a horse. With my leg…"

Captain Travis shook his head. "You get your prosthetic and check her out. You'd be surprised. Kobbe Sava is a good listener as well. You might be amazed what gains you can make if you try this."

"But I need to find a career. Figure out where I'm going to live and all that jazz."

"Yes, you do. My suspicion is you can't make those decisions until you get past the event and these are ways that might help."

"I don't know." Eliza fidgeted.

"I won't force you. I'd like to see you back in four weeks. Whether you do any of that or not is your choice, but I want to talk about your progress next time."

"No medication?"

"Not at this point. I'm not sure you need it and hate to prescribe if there are other options available."

Eliza frowned. "OK."

"Here are pamphlets with information on both therapies. Give it a shot. There's nothing to lose and everything to gain."

"No excuses," Eliza whispered.

"What was that?" Captain Travis asked.

"Nothing. I'll take your counsel under advisement."

"Good." Captain Travis rose and opened the door. "Check in at the desk to make your next appointment. I'll be praying for you, Specialist Torres."

"Oh, um, thanks." Eliza rolled herself out and down the hallway. A psychiatrist who prayed?

She made the appointment and stopped outside, parking under a tree to read the pamphlets since she had time before her next appointment.

Sava. Sava. Kobbe Sava. Was she related to Kristos? She glanced at the photos. What could it hurt?

She flipped to the other one. It seemed like a lot of hocus pocus but if a military psychiatrist thought it could help would she be foolish not to try it? She closed her eyes and took a deep breath.

Had she been too comfortable being broken? Had she assumed the identity of a victim? She was a victim, but a survivor as well. Who was victimizing her?

She was. The brutal truth took her breath away. If anyone else said that to her she'd have ripped their heads off with choice words.

A tear escaped and traveled down her cheek. She'd been so lost but only because she kept herself going in the same maze, like a pig content to roll around in the mud, not caring how filthy she was getting. That was her. A flat tire going nowhere fast.

But how could she change?

I'll be praying for you.

Why would he say that? Why would God be interested in her? Or was that something else she'd been avoiding, assuming she'd be rejected and abandoned once again? If the God of the universe ditched her, she'd be irredeemable. By avoiding Him she was saving herself from that reality.

But was she? Irredeemable?

Apparently, Captain Travis didn't think so.

She could only save herself. God couldn't be relied on for that. If He'd cared, her dad wouldn't have died, her mom wouldn't be selling their home, marrying a stranger, and moving away. She wouldn't have lost her team—or her lower leg.

She glanced at her phone. She'd better head over to get her leg so she wouldn't be needing this wheelchair anymore.

Then she needed to call a soldier about a car.

12

ristos sat down for lunch with his buddies Michael, Jeremiah, and Peter, to catch up on life at a little sandwich shop in Colorado Springs.

"So, Michael, you set the date?" Kristos asked.

Michael nodded. "Yeah. We're opting for sooner rather than later. Just getting more challenging to, um, not…well, you know."

"Be intimate?" Jeremiah asked.

"Yeah."

"I believe you're blushing," Peter stated with a grin on his face.

"Come on, men. We've all had this challenge," Kristos said. "It's not easy and yet you have a lifetime ahead of you. We can keep praying for you both as you strive to wait."

"We have the date and the venue selected. I'll text you the info, Kristos. She really wants that fancy carriage and the gray Percherons pulling it."

"Adonis and Ajax are the perfect gentlemen for the job. How remote is the site?"

"It's a bit of a ride. We'll need a large wagon pulled by horses to help the guests get there as well as the wedding party. It will take several trips."

"Any contingency plan in case of bad weather?"

"We'll host the reception in the barn, but Bridget is set on us doing the ceremony out in the meadow, although she agreed to her mother's request that we at least put up a canopy to protect us from the sun if not any unexpected weather."

"Got it. We'll do our best. I'll get Caden to help with the event. He's great with the horses and proven himself skilled with a team and the wagon. I'll handle delivering your bride myself."

"Thanks, Kristos. I never understood how stressful planning a wedding could be. So many tiny decisions."

"You're doing some counseling too, aren't you?" Jeremiah asked.

"Yeah. Pastor Sava is working with us through that. I admit to having some cold feet with the responsibility of all of this."

"Adulting isn't easy, but at least you'll have a helpmate. Bridget seems like a great gal," Peter said.

"Speaking of gals, how is that spunky young woman you met the other week, Kristos?"

Kristos frowned. "Who? Oh, Eliza? She's been to church twice and might be coming to Mexico. Oh, and she's missing part of her right leg."

"And you just found this out?" Jeremiah asked. "Seems like that would be hard to hide."

"She must have had a prosthetic hidden by her jeans at the restaurant," Kristos defended.

"Does that put you off?" Michael asked. "I'd find it kind of weird."

Kristos shrugged. "No. Why should it? She's Army and obviously lost her leg. With Kobbe having her equine therapy at the barn, we've seen soldiers with a variety of disabilities. They're human beings just like us. Many of us have issues, just not always as visible."

"So, you going to ask her out?" Peter inquired.

"Hadn't crossed my mind. I don't have her contact information for starters."

"You have her name. I bet you could figure it out," Michael suggested.

"Listen guys, I'm happy for you and your relationships, but I'm not going to rush anything. We're barely acquainted." He wasn't going to admit she'd been on his mind and he'd been praying for her several times a day. "Changing the subject, are any of you joining me on the trip to Mexico?"

"I wanted Bridget and myself to go but she said it's too much with planning the wedding."

"Genna wants to come. I'm still trying to see if I can get vacation to go. Summer is a busy time in the construction industry. Everybody and their brother wants an addition, a pool, a sunroom, or garage. We've got too many jobs lined up." Jeremiah sighed and took a drink of his iced tea.

"We could use your skills. Even if you can't come it would be a great experience for Genna," Kristos offered.

"Holly and I are too new in our relationship. She hasn't come to church with me yet, preferring her own. I mentioned it to her but she's not on board. I might be coming though." Peter grinned.

"Hey, Kristos, you playing with that band anymore?" Michael asked.

"Not lately. I'm working on some stuff for church and the mission trip." Kristos took a bite of his sandwich.

"You're taking your guitar? That makes me happy," Jeremiah said. "Extra incentive to get off work."

"Hey, I'm sorry we aren't asking you to sing or play at the wedding. I really wanted you as part of the wedding party and with the transporting of the bride, I thought it might be too much to ask."

"It would be too much. I appreciate the thought but if you asked, I would have said no. Are you having a live band at the reception? I could do a song for you then if you like."

"That'd be awesome."

"Anything in particular?" Kristos asked.

"I'll let you choose. I'm tired of making decisions!" Michael snagged a french fry off Kristos' plate.

"I'll figure out something. No worries," Kristos said.

"Invite Eliza as your plus one," Jeremiah whispered to him. "I dare you."

Kristos shook his head but didn't give any other response. Bring Eliza? What was his friend thinking? They weren't even an item. Had barely spoken. Was he that desperate that a petite woman gives him a beer bath and he's thinking he'd ask her out? Utter foolishness.

They guys chatted some more and went their separate ways. Kristos headed back to the ranch, where he stopped to check in on Murial and Malachi. The colt was growing stronger by the day. Murial was a natural and great mother and watching the two of them together made him grin.

Someday, maybe someday he'd have a wife and child of his own. To watch a woman he loved holding their child and being able to be part of that kind of love in a family. He wasn't in a hurry but after his last girlfriend broke it off, he wondered where and when God would bring the right woman his way.

He wondered who he would even invite to be his plus one for Michael's wedding. Eliza popped into his mind. Was it because of Jeremiah's taunt or because he was interested in her? Anyway, he'd be too busy to be any kind of companion for a guest. There was still time to figure it out.

Even with her right foot prosthetic, Eliza needed an adaptation to her new-to-her sport utility vehicle. Having something between a sedan and a minivan gave her easier access to getting in and out of the vehicle. If she remained in this area, it would be useful in winter. She was pleased with her purchase, and it was now with a mechanic on post who specialized in adapting vehicles. One step closer to independence. She arrived home and opened Ramsey's cage.

"How's my sweet boy today?" she asked the bird.

Ramsey squawked and climbed to the top of the cage where he fluffed his feathers and flapped his wings as if to say "It's about time you got here." She grinned and went to get a glass of water and sat down in a chair, grateful for her prosthetic and the ease of moving around without crutches or a wheelchair. Her phone rang.

"Hey, Rachel, what's up?" Eliza asked.

"I had a few spare moments and was thinking of you, wondering how it's going."

"It's a good day. I purchased a car but have to wait until it's tricked out for my leg, which I got back today. It feels much better than before."

"That's progress. Any more Kristos sightings?"

Eliza shook her head even though her friend couldn't see it. "At church on Sunday. First time he'd seen me in my wheelchair but didn't appear to care. He's heading up a mission trip to Mexico and Gabby dared me to go."

"Will you? That sounds like it would be awesome."

"Rougher conditions could make it more challenging," Eliza excused.

"You're Army tough, you've been in poor living conditions and rocked it. Your prosthetic leg will be fine. You should do it. Might be a good way to get better acquainted with this Kristos fellow."

"I'm not sure. Maybe I've been around Army guys too much, he wears his hair pulled back in a man bun, has some facial hair…"

"You're saying he's not your type, but you were trying to flirt with him at a bar where he was playing guitar."

"Yes, his hair wasn't pulled back that night. He has dark wavy curls and I normally don't like longer hair on men, but on him…"

"You liked him then, but not now because he wears a man bun?"

"We don't have anything in common."

"Hmmm, a love of music, church…I'm sure you'll discover other things the better acquainted you are."

"Maybe so but going there for the sole purpose of stalking the leader seems a poor reason for the expense and challenges a trip like that would entail," Eliza said.

"You texted me that one of your counselors told you to think outside the box. This would qualify. I think you should go. I wish I had had an opportunity like that before I settled down with children. Now I may never go to another country. We don't have the money."

"It would be sweet if you were able to join us. That'd be very cool," Eliza said.

"I'm not volunteering to come be your wingman for this guy, although the thought is tempting. Some days anything sounds better than two toddlers fighting and screaming 'Mommy, Mommy, Mommy,' a zillion times a day. And for all that, I wouldn't trade them for the world. Oh, Eliza, I want that kind of happiness for you."

"I've never had much experience with little kids. I doubt I'd be a good mom. Doesn't matter anyway since I'd need a husband first…or at least would prefer to do it that way."

"A good option and far easier to handle if there's a loving man in your corner. I don't understand how single moms do it."

"So, you think I should throw all caution to the wind and go to Mexico?"

"What real excuse do you have not to go?" Rachel asked.

Excuses again. "I'll think about it."

"Someone's crying, so I'd better go figure out what trouble they've gotten into. We'll talk soon."

"Yeah, thanks, Rach." She ended their call and Eliza sank into her chair.

Mexico. Should she go? Was her disability a good excuse? Not really. They were working to make her as able-bodied as possible for the real world. Maybe Mexico would be a good test of how well she'd do outside the protective fold of post life. She'd talk it over with her counselor tomorrow. Sometimes it felt like all she did was counseling, testing, going to physical therapy, answering questions, and being challenged to confront her trauma.

She wasn't traumatized. The event happened. It was over and done. People died and she had a foot that sometimes itched but she couldn't scratch it. Why did everyone think she had issues to resolve?

Maybe because:

She had no clue what she wanted to do.

She was terrified of life outside the Army.

She had no one of her own to watch her six in civilian life.

She'd been drinking way too much.

All the above.

Multiple choice and *All the above* was the answer. She sighed. Yup, event or no event, she had issues.

She picked up the Mexico Mission package Gabby had grabbed on Sunday and began paging through it. Helping with kids, cooking meals, construction work, evening worship services she'd need to attend, witnessing…Wait. What? Witnessing? Witnessing what? The work? It didn't make sense. The rest she could do. Her cooking skills were adequate. She could handle listening to singing. Working with kids? Well, no experience since her high school babysitting days; she'd met some kids overseas and those interactions had been positive. Those kids were grateful for the American soldiers' presence there.

Would the Mexican people be grateful for Americans coming to help them?

How would everyone react to her leg? She would want to wear shorts at times if it was warm out.

When did she ever worry about how she looked? She gave up much of that in the Army where everyone looked similar. Yeah, so that's why she bleached her hair blonde? She wasn't even sure she liked it that color, but it was her way of not being herself. Separating herself from who she was before the event.

The only way she could figure out who Eliza "Tornado" Torres was, was to try something new. Shake herself out of the inertia she'd been stuck in since recovering from her physical injuries.

No excuses?

She took out the paperwork for the trip and began filling out the information. She was going to Mexico.

13

ristos was at the back of church again on Sunday and Eliza strode up to him. She was breathtaking in her sapphire blue top and black slacks.

"Good morning, Eliza…or do you prefer Tornado?"

She shrugged. "Morning, Kristos. Eliza is fine. My squad called me Tornado but maybe that's a moniker that belongs in the past. I'm not sure."

"I'm sure there was a reason for the name that describes part of you."

"Maybe. I've never seen a tornado. I hear they're destructive, so maybe it's not a term I would want to embrace any longer."

"Were you destructive in the Army?"

She shook her head. "I drove a truck. The only one I destroyed was my last day overseas."

Kristos nodded. Interesting that she didn't say how. Given the missing leg he suspected it might have been an IED. "Sounds like a story for another day."

"Or never." Her curt reply stunned him, but she continued. "I filled out the paperwork for the Mexico trip." She handed him the envelope.

"You're going?"

"Yeah, why? You said no excuses. I couldn't think of any strong enough to keep me from going—other than my own fears, and it's time I acted despite that."

"What are you afraid of?"

"I'd rather not talk about that right now." She said with her hands on her hips, as if daring him to push her.

"Would you like to meet for lunch to discuss the trip further?" Kristos asked, wishing he could take back the words. Why would he do this?

Her arms dropped to her side. "Maybe. When and where?"

Kristos gave a time and location, wondering if she'd show up. His curiosity about her had gone up several notches, and those pouty lips were a temptation of their own. "See you then?" he asked.

"Sure. I'll be there." A soft smile made those lips even more tempting. He broke his gaze away to her eyes. She gave a slight nod and departed.

Alexos came to his side. "Was that her?"

"Who?"

"The girl who dumped beer on you? She's cute. Not as beautiful as Kobbe, but I suspect she has what it takes to land the next Sava man at the altar."

Kristos shoved his brother away. "Leave it be, man. She's going to Mexico. That's it. There's nothing more to it."

"You keep deluding yourself, but I recognize the look of a lovesick puppy." He hurried away to find his wife.

Kristos shook his head and conversed with a few others before he left his post as the second service started. He had enough time to run home, change into more casual clothes and meet Eliza at the restaurant. Why did a tiny thrill of excitement strum through him at the thought of time spent with the petite Army powerhouse?

Once at the restaurant he waited outside and spied her arrival in a sport utility vehicle.

She exited the vehicle with a grace that surprised him. In her denim jeans she had a lithe elegance. She strode toward him without the hitch in her step he'd noted at their first meeting. Was that only a few weeks ago? When had he ever met someone and started praying for them without needing to be reminded? With this woman it had been involuntary. Spirit-led.

He needed to move cautiously. She attended church but that didn't mean she loved Jesus.

Why did you ask her to lunch? Hmmm?

"Hi, Kristos. I've heard this place has good food."

He opened the door and let her pass through before following. "Yep. That's been my experience. You'll have to judge for yourself."

Kristos motioned with his hand that they wanted a seat for two and were shown to a booth. No chance to practice being a gentleman by helping Eliza with her chair. He sat down across from her and the server handed them their menus.

"I like the physical menus. I know a lot of people like doing the online thing but still, I prefer this," Eliza stated.

"You probably didn't use your cell phone for everything overseas."

"Nope. Usually turned it off. Wasn't a lot of use for it there."

"Have you adjusted to being back on American soil?" Kristos asked. "My brother who was Army, struggled, and my sister-in-law returned recently. She's still at Fort Carson for now."

"It can be a culture shock, but coming home this time was harder since I left part of myself over there."

"You didn't say specifically what happened."

"There was an event. People died. I lost my leg below the knee and was sent home. Once I'm done with ARCP, Army Recovery Care Program, I'll be medically retired."

Not surprising she wouldn't or couldn't talk about what happened. "I'm sorry for your losses. Will getting out be a good thing?"

"Not what I planned for when I signed up. The Army was my plan A and there was no plan B."

The server came and took their orders and left.

"I'm sorry that it's another loss for you. It was hard for Alexos to give up that dream but eventually he found a new path, fell in love, and is content with his life. You'll get there in time."

"Was he wounded in combat?" she asked.

"If combat frisbee counts, yes. Any other type, no."

She giggled. "He was sidelined playing combat frisbee? Ouch."

Kristos grinned. He liked the sound of her voice and that little bit of unexpected happiness that leaked out of her. "Yeah. He's adapted. He came home to heal and eat plenty of our Mamá's Greek cooking.

Thankfully my family doesn't live too far away, which made it possible for him to get to and from therapy on post for his left ankle."

"You said you have a sister-in-law still in?"

"Yeah, Captain Jane McIntire Sava, serves in intelligence, she has some time left to serve and just announced her and my brother are expecting a child. Not sure how that will all work out. They don't live on post. She had a child from her first marriage, and he's a sweetheart."

"Wow, two Army connections in one family. Why didn't you ever join?" she asked.

"I fell in love with Percheron horses and always worked on the ranch. Early on I wanted my life to be that, working with and taking care of those magnificent animals."

"How do they compare to Clydesdales?"

"A little bigger, both are draft horses. Kobbe, my sister-in-law, does therapy using horses and sometimes she uses the Percherons." Kristos took a sip of water.

"Horse therapy?"

"Yeah, why?"

"I got some information about that. It was suggested that it might be helpful for me," Eliza said.

"I find riding a horse is the best therapy."

"And what do you need therapy for?"

Kristos shrugged. "Probably nothing. I'm not perfect. I've had a decent upbringing and my family is kind of awesome. I've no complaints."

"Didn't go on to college?" Eliza asked.

"I have dyslexia, made studying hard so I dropped out. I still do some studying on my own when I can. Audiobooks help."

"I hadn't considered that. Good adaptation."

"You could call it that, I suppose. I never thought of it that way. So where do you hail from? I detect a Southern accent," Kristos asked.

She grinned. "Nashville."

"Are you going to stay in Colorado when you get out?"

"I'm not sure where I'll go or what I'll do. That's been my challenge," Eliza said.

The server brought their meal.

"Do you mind if I pray for our food?" Kristos asked.

"Does it need it?" Eliza asked.

"Not necessarily, but I always do."

"Fine."

Kristos bowed his head. "Heavenly Father, thank You for this food and this time with Eliza. Bless our conversation and be glorified today. Amen."

She didn't say a word but began to dig into her meal.

"Other than driving a truck, what other skills do you possess?" Kristos asked. He had to admit the idea of a woman driving a truck was hot. He'd have had a difficult time being in her squad with her as the driver, even if she were wearing camouflage. She was too attractive not to notice and want to pursue.

"I have an associate's in business. I could go back to school, but I'm not sure what I'd want to study."

"Business doesn't do it for you?"

"Not sure. Numbers come easy to me."

"That's a gift. Now why did you decide you want to come to Mexico?"

Eliza set down her fork and sighed. "That's complicated. Matter of fact, everything in my life is complicated." She picked her fork up and took a bite of her food.

Kristos frowned. She failed to answer the question. "I'm sorry. You realize this isn't a vacation getaway. It's a work trip that will emotionally and spiritually challenge you, maybe physically as well."

"I'm in shape physically. I may be small but I'm mighty and can do more than you might think. Emotionally and spiritually? Now you're scaring me."

"I'd love to have you on the trip, but I wanted to make sure you weren't viewing this as an escape from your problems."

"My problems would be an excuse not to go, but I've recently been encouraged to try something. Do something. Anything—outside my comfort zone. No excuses. You said no excuses. I'm trying to push past all the excuses I can think of."

"I don't mean to discourage you but wanted to be honest about how challenging the trip can be. I've come back a little different every time I've gone. My heart grows bigger, and I leave a little bit of me there on every trip."

"Sounds like you enjoy it."

"It's challenging work and a pain to make arrangements to be gone, and to organize, but yeah, at some level I enjoy the challenge it presents. The understanding that I'm making an eternal impact by doing temporal work helps."

"Explain that."

"Sure. I may work on a church building—that won't last forever. The lives I get to speak into, those interactions, sharing Jesus with lost people, that has an eternal impact."

"Do you preach too?"

"Not so much me, but sometimes it's the one-on-one conversations that have the biggest impact on a person's heart."

"Would I—need—to—pr-each?" she stuttered.

"No, but you would be interacting with people and those conversations can be life-changing for those individuals."

"Is this a requirement to go? That wasn't in the paperwork."

"No. Be yourself. We're all at various stages of our journey. There's not a specific benchmark to meet to be able to go."

She nodded and continued eating. Kristos focused on his food. What was her issue? Was she shy? Or unsure of how to share her faith? Either way she'd grow in those areas on this trip and the thought of getting to spend more time with her made his heart do a little jig inside his chest. Odd. That had never happened before with any woman he'd ever met.

When the meal was completed, Eliza laid her napkin down. "That was delicious. I'm definitely coming back here. Thank you for the invitation. I haven't had much of a chance to get out since arriving at Fort Carson."

"I noticed your roommate drove you to church."

"Yeah, she did. I'm happy to say I just bought an SUV this week and they made the adaptations for me faster than I expected. I'm grateful to be behind the wheel again. It's been a while."

"How long since you've driven?"

"Since, um, January when the event occurred." Sorrow washed over her at the thought of her guys no longer being around. One minute they were vibrant, strong men, and the next they'd vanished.

"Hey, are you OK?" Kristos asked, his eyes were kind.

She nodded. "I'll be fine eventually. Sometimes grief hits out of the blue. I lost friends and while I miss my leg, I grieve for them more."

He nodded. "I get it. Grief can be messy from what I've been told. I've not experienced much yet. I'm sorry you had to go through that. I didn't mean to bring up a bad memory."

"It's OK. There really isn't a memory there to bring up. One day my friends were alive and a day later I wake up and they're gone. Poof. Almost like some evil magic. I can't understand why God would let that happen."

"Now you're getting into deep waters. God is good but He does allow the consequence of sin and the free will of others to run their course. He promises to be with us in the midst of all that ugliness. It's the price we pay for sin entering the world. Somehow God allowed you to survive."

"I wish I could understand the rhyme or reason for it."

"Some things are above our human reasoning."

Eliza frowned. "Are you content with that?"

"I wouldn't say content. Human pride wants to assert that we're capable of anything and superior enough to understand it all—but God is infinite and perfect. Sometimes I need to rest on truths I can't fully grasp and live in gratitude for the gift God gave in His Son Jesus and the Holy Spirit that can enable and empower me to live my life right here and now."

"Whoa. That's a lot to chew on. Not much of that made sense to me."

"What part?"

The server stopped by and left the bill. Kristos put down his credit card and the server departed.

Eliza was done talking about God. There was too much to unpack. "Thank you for a lovely meal. I've enjoyed getting better acquainted."

Kristos frowned and opened his mouth as if to speak but the server returned. "One moment." He added the tip, signed the slip, and put his card back in his wallet. "I've enjoyed our time together as well, Eliza. I think Mexico will be an interesting trip for all of us."

Eliza wasn't sure if she should be happy about that. *Interesting* sounded ominous to her. "Yea, I think so too."

They rose from the table and Kristos followed her through the restaurant to the front door. "Can I walk you to your car?" he asked.

"Sure."

"I'm curious about how they adapted it for you."

Eliza shrugged. "Come, take a look." She unlocked the car and stepped back so Kristos could peek inside.

"Interesting. Even with the adaptations I could still drive this too?"

"If you needed to, yes."

"Cool." He stood and turned to her, allowing her access to her car interior. "Thanks again for meeting me." He held out a hand.

Eliza shook his hand and the current of electricity was so strong she thought she experienced it all the way through her prosthetic foot. She released his hand. "Thanks for the invite." She sat down and he closed the door for her. Once she started the engine, he gave a little wave and strode away.

Coming or going, he was a delight to watch.

Heat rushed to her cheeks. She was grateful no one could witness that. She drove back to post but it was more like riding on a magic carpet.

14

Kristos was at the Mexican restaurant again on Friday night, playing with the band. He scanned the crowd as he played, wondering if Eliza would show up. He thought he'd spied her walking in with someone, another woman who might have been missing an…arm? He couldn't be certain through the crowds and almost missed his guitar solo on that song. When the set was over, he set the guitar aside and stepped off the stage. Eliza was there waiting for him.

"I thought I'd caught a glimpse of you entering," he said.

"Yeah, my new roomie, Livie, wanted to get away from post, so I suggested this place and she agreed. Livie, meet Kristos, Kristos, Livie."

The woman next to Eliza was tall and dark with sleek black hair and a brilliant smile.

"Good evening, Livie, welcome to Colorado Springs."

"Thank you. It's a pleasure to meet you, Kristos. Eliza mentioned you. Said she's going to Mexico with you in a few weeks."

"That's the plan." He glanced at Eliza. "Should be an interesting trip for the whole team."

"I would be interested in going but there's still a lot of healing to do before I can be exploring the world again." Livie bent her left arm, and a bandage covered the part of her forearm where a hand would originally have been.

"I'm sorry you both were injured in the line of duty. Thank you for your service."

"I appreciate that. Thanks." Livie turned to Eliza. "I'm headed back to the table. It was a pleasure meeting you, Kristos."

"Same here." He barely noticed the statuesque woman retreating.

"She's a beautiful woman and could have been a model," Eliza said.

"Really? Why would you say that? You possess your own brand of beauty, was that ever a dream?"

"What? To be a petite model? Never crossed my mind. Not a ton of Hispanic models. Jamaican ancestry like Livie? Now she would be stunning in anything."

"Appearances aren't everything, Tornado. Character and personality are more important."

"So, what exactly do you look for in a woman if it isn't her appearance?"

"Well..."

"Deep subject," she said.

Kristos chuckled. "Right, and far too complicated for the few moments I have left here. Wanna do lunch again on Sunday after church? We could talk more about it then."

He could kick himself for extending the invitation. She wasn't his type, was she? Well, at least tonight she wasn't dousing him with beer or flirting shamelessly.

She nodded. "I'm game if you are. Any opportunity to gaze into those remarkable eyes should never be passed up." She winked and walked away. If he had never seen her in a wheelchair, he'd have no clue she was...what? Disabled? That title didn't fit the pint-sized powerhouse who strode away from him. He wasn't even partial to blondes. What had gotten into him lately when it came to Eliza? He shook his head, took a sip of his bottled water, and went to the stage for the band's next set.

He'd been wrong about the flirting. Why did her mention of his unusual eyes make him want to grin? Because most people didn't notice the star shape in them, and it meant something to him that she did. He glanced toward where they sat but couldn't see past the crowds and wall supports. Didn't matter. He'd see her Sunday.

The next day as Kristos worked cleaning the stalls in the barn, he wondered what possessed Eliza to go on this upcoming trip. The challenge? His little talk? Was God leading her through His Holy Spirit? Was she even a believer? What limited studies, messages, and teachings he'd paid attention to, he understood there was a concept of prevenient grace. *Prevenient* wasn't found in Scripture, but it did sum up the idea that God used the Holy Spirit to draw people to Himself while convicting the world of sin and unrighteousness. Part of accepting Jesus was understanding how desperately one needed a Savior.

Being raised in a Christian home it was all he understood until the summer before his junior year of high school when Rusty was injured at camp and there was no guarantee he'd survive. That day hit Kristos hard. What if it happened to him? That day, Kristos knelt by his bed and pleaded with God to save him. It wasn't until later that he was baptized. His parents had been so busy worrying and caring for Rusty that Kristos hadn't told them till later.

Sometimes it took a serious event to wake a person up to the desperate need of a soul for a Savior. Had Eliza's event, as she called it, done that for her? Or was she still searching? He needed an answer on that before their relationship went any further. Rusty may have married an unbeliever and Jane came to Christ, but Kristos had no such compulsion toward Eliza. He liked her. Maybe she'd be a friend if nothing else.

Could men and women be friends?

He wasn't going to even try to answer that. He'd lunch with Eliza on Sunday and work up the nerve to ask her about her faith.

A car pulling into the parking area not too far from the barn caught his attention. He strode to the barn door to investigate who was coming.

Eliza? What was she doing here?

Kobbe strode out the door to the pen. But of course. Eliza was military and injured. She would be getting help from Kobbe. Why did the thought of seeing her here make him so happy? *Foolish heart. Settle down.*

"Good morning, Kristos," Kobbe said as she came to stand by his side.

He gave his sister-in-law a nod. "Hi."

Eliza drew close.

"Morning, Eliza. I didn't expect to see you out here," Kristo said, certain he was grinning in a goofy way.

Her face brightened as her smile spread, showing her teeth. "I wondered about you when I read the last name. I have an appointment with Kobbe Sava."

Kobbe extended her hand. "I didn't realize you two were acquainted. I'm Kobbe, married to Kristos' older brother Alexos. I'm glad you could come out here today so I could show you around. Mountain Shadow Stables is Kristos' business, but he rents part of the barn and allows me use of many of the horses for therapy, although one is mine specifically. Come and I'll show you around and we can talk about how I might be able to help you."

"Sounds good. Nice to see you, Kristos," Eliza said as she walked off with Kobbe.

Kristos stared after the women until they went into the pen where Kobbe did the majority of her therapy. He returned to the stable to finish doing his cleaning work, wondering if he could hang around in case Kobbe wanted to introduce Eliza to the horses.

His phone rang. Waiting was out of the question. He hit the button and strode up the stairs. "Hello, this is Kristos Sava with Mountain Shadow Stables."

Eliza had the distinct impression that Kristos was happy to see her.

"This corral is where most of the therapy happens. We can close it in the winter months so it's warmer and open it up on nicer days to let the breeze through. I have the ability for more than one therapist working here, but as of yet I'm the only one. What exactly is the issue your therapist wishes you to work on?"

"Trauma from an event overseas where I lost part of my leg." Eliza lifted her jeans to show the prosthetic. "It's from the knee down."

Kobbe nodded. "I'm sorry for your injury. Thank you for your service. My dad was Army so I'm an Army brat, and I'm married to a retired Army helicopter pilot. Let's go to my office, and I can get some releases of information signed so I can get your medical records and be in communication with your team."

"OK." Eliza followed the red head to the office. When the door opened Eliza was shocked. "Wow, looks like a disaster area in here."

"Yeah, bookkeeping and insurance are not my fortes. I'm not administratively gifted, I guess. Kristos suggested we hire someone to help us get this organized."

"I would think that would be a good thing. If I were available to work in the civilian arena I'd apply. This seems doable."

"What do you think would need to be done?" Kobbe was logging into the computer and printed out some documents.

"I'd organize into some piles and establish a filing system. Do you do your books on the computer?"

Kobbe shook her head. "I have no clue how to do that."

"There are some simple enough programs that will help you track income and expenses, as well as payroll so you're withholding the right amount of taxes."

Kobbe frowned. "I'm not even sure how much I'm making yet."

"That's not good."

"It is what it is. Here are the releases of information and it allows communication both ways. Fill in the various professionals on post you've been working with and I'll send in the requests for records."

"OK." Eliza set a pile of papers aside to make room at a desk to write.

"I'm sorry. I should have handed you a clipboard."

"It's fine." Eliza finished filling out and signing the forms and handed them back to Kobbe.

"If you wanted, I could do a little bit of organizing right now—sorting through this all so you can make better sense of it."

Kobbe shook her head. "That's sweet of you but I think that might be a conflict of interest. I can't have you doing work for me for free, and not at all until you complete therapy with me. Most of what is here is highly confidential."

"Understood. If you're working with vets, you might want to employ one who might have a good grasp of the billing with veterans benefits. I'm not there yet but it wouldn't take much for me to learn it."

"Is that something you want to do?"

"For something like this, I'd be interested. Working in a big business or an accounting firm? No. I never considered the possibilities of working for a small business like this. It would be something pretty cool to be a part of."

"I'll keep you in mind. Kristos said he might be able to use help as well although he seems to be managing his stuff well."

Something sparked inside Eliza, a thrill of excitement at the possibility of working here when she was out of the Army. And Kristos? He'd make it all the yummier. She resisted the urge to lick her lips.

"Here's a package for you to take home and some paperwork I'd like you to fill out to help me understand you from your perspective, not just the medical experts." Kobbe handed over the manilla envelope and glanced through the releases. "Oh, you see Captain Travis?"

"Yeah. He's the one that recommended this place."

"Wonderful." A smile came across Kobbe's face.

"Why? Do you know him?"

"Yes. He's really good at what he does. I'm glad you get the benefit of his care."

"That's right. He mentioned you're his sister-in-law."

"How about I introduce you to the horses? That's usually everyone's favorite part of the tour. Most are out in the paddock right now but they do come when I call. Kristos has them well-trained."

Eliza nodded her agreement to Kobbe's plan. Maybe she'd see Kristos again.

They walked out of the office and Kobbe locked the door. They walked through a wider hallway to the main stable area.

"Wow, this is bigger than I expected," Eliza said. "And so clean."

"Kristos is meticulous in his care of the horses." Kobbe led them to the closest pasture where the horses grazed.

"Shelby!" Kobbe called out and a Shetland pony headed their way. "This is Shelby, a wedding gift from Kristos. She's great at working with many of the kids we deal with."

Eliza marveled at the sweet horse. "She's adorable."

"Thanks. Go on, Shelby."

Kobbe soon introduced Eliza to Sabrina, a gypsy horse, and her two fillies, Sassy and Sarah. The horses kept getting larger. The three Morgans, Delphine and her fillies Dorothea and Danielle, were gorgeous.

"Now on to the horses Mountain Shadow Stables is most known for, the Percherons."

Soon two geldings, Adonis and Ajax; as well as Rafael, a stud; Hugo, a young colt; and Muriel and her recent colt, Malachi, were presented.

Eliza was stunned. "I cannot imagine how you can get a normal human up on some of these larger horses and use them for therapy."

Kobbe nodded. "We have ways and they are amazingly gentle. Finally, you need to meet Kristos' pride and joy, Zena. She's retired from most things and was given to Kristos when her previous owner didn't feel she was up to pulling carriages anymore. She can be great for horseback riding though and therapy."

Zena ambled toward the rail and whinnied.

"Wow, she's stunning." Eliza patted the side of the horse who towered over her at least as much as the others if not more.

"She's beautiful and a treasure. I'm honored that Kristos will sometimes suggest her for clients."

Eliza frowned. "Does he participate in your work?" Would she be seeing him when she started coming here?

"Not often but if I need help, he's generally available. He's a stand-up guy. You're probably already aware of that," Kobbe said with a soft smile on her lips.

"We're not well acquainted."

"I'm guessing you'd like that to change." Kobbe was leading her back toward the large opening to the barn closest to the parking area.

"Maybe. I've got a lot of stuff to figure out. Adding a relationship to that wouldn't be wise." *Oh, but I'd sure like to.*

"Love often takes us by surprise and it's rarely convenient."

"Who said anything about love?" Eliza protested.

Kobbe raised her eyebrows. "I'll get back to you about possible dates to start once I get the medical records so I understand anything that might be a concern. Have a good weekend, Specialist Torres."

"You too. Thanks for the tour." Eliza slowly walked back to her vehicle, taking in the ranch property with fresh eyes. The place was tidy and neat, except for Kobbe's office. The house farther back was a two-story and had flowerpots on the porch with lovely bright colors. The entire place could have come out of some magazine. It was picturesque and welcoming. As she got to the car, she paused to glance back at the barn where she'd last spotted Kristos. She noted stairs going to the second story and windows with curtains inside. Someone lived up there? Maybe Kristos did. As if summoning him, a body passed the large window, and her suspicion was confirmed. The handsome cowboy lived above the stables.

Love often takes us by surprise and is rarely convenient. Kobbe had said that. Would love ever be part of her life? Everyone she loved or cared for left her. Her father, her mom. Even her friend Rachel left her when she married and settled down with her husband and started having kids. It was like the world continued to move forward while Eliza was stuck in park.

She frowned, got into her vehicle, and drove back to post.

15

liza dragged her new roommate, Livie, to Good Shepherd Community Church on Sunday. Entering the building, she didn't spy Kristos.

"Are you searching for someone? Perhaps that attractive cowboy from Friday night?" Livie asked.

"Maybe." Eliza gave up and they found seats off to the side and midway up so she'd have an unobstructed view of most of the church. She was starting to realize that there were several people from post who attended here. Interesting. She didn't realize the Christian faith was that prevalent.

"I'm glad you brought me here. I was planning to go to chapel on post but it's nice to be with civilians as well, isn't it? Kind of an exposure therapy to prepare for when we need to live among them once again."

"Yeah. I hadn't thought of it that way," Eliza said, keeping her eyes focused on the gathering congregation.

"There he is," Livie said, "over there." She gave her finger a little flick in the direction.

"I appreciate your being discreet," Eliza whispered.

"Anytime."

The service started. Eliza kept watch on Kristos and was amazed at how he immersed himself in the worship. She turned her focus to the stage and the words on the screen. She'd heard them before somewhere.

> Through many dangers, toils and snares
> I have already come;

'tis grace hath brought me safe thus far,
and grace will lead me home.
The Lord has promised good to me,
His word my hope secures;
He will my shield and portion be
as long as life endures.
When we've been there ten thousand years,
bright shining as the sun,
we've no less days to sing God's praise
than when we've first begun.

The worship leader ended and began praying, but Eliza's thoughts careened through her mind. She had been brought home safe. Was that God's doing? All along she'd been blaming Him for not keeping the others alive and for the loss of her leg. Was her survival a gift?

What was grace, really? And what was this good God had promised? The music seemed to move Kristos as she witnessed him wipe away a tear as they all sat down.

A cowboy who cried?

When had she last cried? About anything? Oh, there'd been tears shed over the pain of therapy to be sure, but all her tears for the past few months seemed to have been locked away behind a thick dam in her heart to keep her from being vulnerable.

Drinking numbed the pain somewhat. Her therapist cautioned against it and challenged her to try Alcoholics Anonymous if she needed help to stop.

She didn't need any help. She was a soldier.

So why did the concept of grace—whatever that was—make her want to cry? Or take a drink?

Pastor Sava was once again behind the podium. She'd begun to appreciate his warm voice even when his words challenged her.

"Turn to the book of Luke, chapter fourteen. We'll get started there." He paused and the sound of pages turning filled the room.

Did everyone here own a Bible?

Livie nudged her and pointed to the open book she held in her lap.

How had Eliza not even noticed her roommate brought one with her?

Pastor Sava prayed. "Heavenly Father, we come to You this morning in awe and reverence for the wonderful ways You work to draw us to Yourself. Open our hearts to Your truth as revealed in the Scriptures and change us to become more and more like Your Son, Jesus. Amen."

A few amens murmured around the room. Had this happened the past few times she'd attended or was she only seeing things in a fresh way? The possibility confused her.

"Jesus was speaking to his disciples and others in story form. Scripture calls them parables. We'll start in verse sixteen.

"'But He said to him, "A man was giving a big dinner, and he invited many; and at the dinner hour he sent his slave to tell those who had been invited, 'Come, because everything is ready now.' And yet they all alike began to make excuses. The first one said to him, 'I purchased a field and I need to go out to look at it; please consider me excused.' And another one said, 'I bought five yoke of oxen, and I am going to try them out; please consider me excused.' And another one said, 'I took a woman as my wife, and for that reason I cannot come.'

"Now can you imagine the audacity of these people? If you received an invitation for a free meal, I'm sure many of you would be eager to take up that offer and attend. Especially a feast. A banquet. Now usually one doesn't invite enemies to dinner, do they? Imagine this man who extended this invitation. The guests are aware of the date and time but fail to show so he sends his servants and each one has an excuse."

He went over the excuses in the text. "It is obvious these are not the real reasons the people cannot come to dinner.

"The song we sang talked about being in heaven for ten thousand years. God is planning an exquisite banquet for those He invited to be in His family. Now Jesus first preached to the Israelites. These were God's people. He was the promised Messiah, but many didn't accept that. He was inviting them to His Father's mansion, and they had excuses of their own. Many of their excuses were about as strong as what are given in this story. And those people not only spurned him, rejected him, but also killed him.

"Jesus rose again. And as God's servant, He is the ticket needed to gain entrance to this feast. But listen to what Jesus tells us as the parable continues.

"Now imagine this. Jesus is saying that those who rejected his invitation to the grand hall of feasting with God the Father, will never be able to come. Instead, Jesus' message was also extended to the Gentiles, which I suspect includes most of us in this room. Those not of Jewish descent. He also went further to include the poor. The disabled. The blind. Those who limp…"

Eliza tapped her prosthetic with her good foot. Why would God specifically mention that in the Bible?

I'm inviting you, Eliza.

Startled, she glanced. Was that in her head? No one else seemed to notice anything. Weird. She returned her attention to Pastor Sava.

"It is by God's grace that even though others refused to accept the invitation to Jesus, that we are also given a spot at the dinner table. We need to be careful not to be like those who were first invited and give lame excuses for not coming. 'May I be excused?'" he said the latter in a whiny voice, "Is pathetic. When dinner is served, it is served. It's that way at our home. If Roda, my wife, prepares a meal, we sit down to eat. We don't wait for long if someone's been invited. The food is hot and fresh and tastes best then. Trust me, she's an awesome cook, who would ever want to miss her meals?" He patted his stomach. "Obviously, I haven't missed many myself."

The congregation chuckled.

"When God extends that invitation to follow Him and accept the invitation of salvation in Jesus, why would anyone make an excuse? As Romans one states, 'we are without excuse.'"

He paused before continuing.

Eliza fidgeted in her seat, swallowing hard.

"We skipped two verses of 'Amazing Grace' so let me read them to you now. 'Yea, when this flesh and heart shall fail, and mortal life shall cease, I shall possess, within the veil, a life of joy and peace. The earth shall soon dissolve like snow, the sun forbear to shine, but God, who called me here below, will be forever mine.'

"What more invitation do you need? If the Holy Spirit is tugging at your heart, don't resist. Accept the invitation to the banquet, to an eternal hope of joy and peace with Jesus. Being forever His. His Holy Spirit seals us. He gives us a reserved seat at the dinner table. His grace and mercy are unending.

"We all have our disabilities, don't we? My back isn't as strong as it used to be, and the older I get the more I forget. Just because others might not notice doesn't mean any of us are without a need for our Savior. The richness of life in Him, worshiping at His feet, cannot be overstated.

"No one will twist your arm. Jesus extends the invitation, but He doesn't force you to the table, into a relationship with Himself. You must decide to follow Him.

"We have prayer partners on the side of the sanctuary who would love to pray for you and with you. If you need help deciding and acting on the information you learned today, please stop and let our prayer partners pray for you."

Pastor Sava stepped aside as the worship team took the stage and another song was sung.

Eliza stood with the congregation but didn't sing. Tears stung her eyes. She inhaled deeply. *Settle down, Eliza. You have too much to deal with right now.* The last thing she needed was to try to figure out this God thing.

Love often takes us by surprise and is rarely convenient. That's what Kobbe said yesterday, but she was talking about a love between a man and a woman—wasn't she? So why would those words pop up in her mind?

I'm inviting you, Eliza.

She couldn't escape church fast enough.

On the ride back to post, Livie talked about the service. "I like that pastor. He preaches the truth without watering it down. I'm grateful for the Lord's goodness to me."

"Even though you lost your hand?" Eliza asked.

"I could have lost so much more. I'm alive to continue to bear testimony to His faithfulness and grace. What a glorious assignment to be used by Jesus even in my struggles and pain. Sure, I'm sad about my upcoming medical retirement. I miss my hand and all the things it allowed me to do. I could focus on those issues, but I choose to think about all I *can* do. Every breath is a gift from Him. I love how Jesus used even the disabled who in those days were considered useless, to be His special guests. It doesn't matter if my body is whole; Jesus loves me right where I am and I get to dine at His table, on His Words, every day because of His amazing grace." Livie paused. "I'm sorry if I sound like I'm preaching, but I found this morning uplifting. Thanks for taking me. I can't wait to return next week."

Eliza remained silent. They headed to their barracks. Eliza changed into more casual clothing. "See you later, Livie."

"Enjoy your time with the hot cowboy. I wish I could join you, but I promised my parents I'd call today via video, and I'm thinking you don't need a wing man for lunch." Livie gave a wink and waved Eliza out the door.

16

Eliza drove to a different location this time and in spite of GPS she almost got lost. She arrived at the restaurant a few minutes late and sat in the car to pull herself together. Why did she fear she would shatter if…if…? She couldn't finish the sentence. She wasn't even sure what to talk to Kristos about. Would he talk about his faith? Would he tell her she couldn't go to Mexico? Why was she here?

She'd sure love a beer about now to calm her nerves, or anything alcoholic. She'd promised herself she would never drink if she were driving so that was out of the question. She needed to pull up her big girl panties and go meet the boy.

A knock at her window startled her. Her hand went to her chest as she glanced up.

Kristos. That smile could melt anyone's nerves but right now she needed more than that.

She gave a tentative smile and opened the door. Grabbing her keys and purse, she exited the car.

"Sorry I startled you. I saw you drive in and thought I'd come see if you were OK when you didn't get out of the car right away."

"I'm fine, thank you." She lied. Between the turmoil this morning and the zing from his innocent touch that traversed her arm to jump start her heart again, she was a bundle of nerves.

"Great. Let's go eat. I'm starving." Kristos walked by her side and opened the door to the restaurant for her. He followed her inside to the host.

"How many?" the woman asked.

"Two," Kristos answered, and they traipsed after the server to a booth. "Thanks."

The server walked away leaving menus on the table. Kristos picked up one and Eliza slowly grabbed hers, tempted to hide behind it.

Soon their orders were placed, and she was forced to surrender her menu. As tempting as hiding behind it was, she couldn't stay there forever.

"Did you like the ranch?" Kristos asked.

"Yes, it's beautiful. You maintain the property well."

"Thanks. I have help. There's a young man in high school who gives me a hand with much of it. Now that it's summer I sometimes use him for weekend events, weddings, fairs where they want the big horses, parades. He's loving it and I appreciate the extra set of hands."

"Sounds like you keep busy. I'm surprised you have time to get away to Mexico."

Kristos shrugged. "It happened to fall during a time when I'd not committed to anything and Caden can handle the daily stuff while I'm gone. If he has challenges, my older brothers are often available."

"So not a huge sacrifice."

"I need to pay him as he's working more hours, so I do sacrifice some of my profit margin for that and I paid for the trip just like everyone else. Airfare, meals, lodging…it still comes out of my pocket."

"Fair enough."

The food arrived.

Kristos held out a hand across the table. "I'll pray for the meal."

Eliza reached her hand across to his and once again that tingle traversed her arm. He bowed his head.

"Heavenly Father, thank You for another beautiful day and the generous way You have provided not only for our salvation but for our physical needs as well. Bless our meal and our conversation. Amen." He gave her hand a little squeeze before releasing it.

"When will you start working with Kobbe?" he asked.

"Once she gets all she needs, we'll make appointments. Hopefully, that won't take long." She dug into her side salad.

“Sounds fair. Have you ridden before?”

“No. All those horses are taller than me. I suppose if I managed to climb into massive Army trucks, I should be able to manage climbing onto a horse, assuming I don’t need to drag myself up there.”

Kristos chuckled. “I would have a tough time getting up on a horse like that. Some have been trained to come down on a knee to enable you to get up on them, but we do have steps that can be used. It’s not typical for Kobbe to use the Percherons. The gypsy horses are trained to come down and do an excellent job. They get the most use in those type of situations.”

“Do you have other horses too?”

“Sure do. We board horses. The owners can come any time to be with their horse and ride if they wish. We provide the shelter, a meadow for them to be out in, and food. I also muck out their stalls daily. Not my favorite chore but the horses appreciate it.”

“I guess I didn’t realize how much goes into owning horses.”

“Having a horse is not an easy expense. Thankfully, I get to indulge my passion for the Percherons because of the boarding and the other events we do with the larger horses.”

“Cool.”

Silence hung between them.

Kristos took a drink and set down his fork. His gaze was filled with warmth. “What’s on your mind Eliza? You seem preoccupied.”

“I’m mulling over some of what your father preached on this morning.”

“A startling sermon. Sometimes people think they have all the time in the world to get straight with God, but life is filled with uncertainties as you are aware, and our lives can be gone in an instant. There’s not always an opportunity for a deathbed confession of faith. It sounds harsh but when life is done, you’re either sitting at the banquet table or in a very dark and lonely place filled with torment.”

“Doesn’t sound like the workings of a good God,” Eliza protested.

“Ah, but it is. He is also a holy and just God who cannot tolerate sin. That’s why He sent His Son Jesus to die for us, so we can be free of the penalty of sin, which is death and eternal separation from God. However, God gives us the choice whether to accept or reject that gift. If anyone tosses that gift aside, they've chosen hell. There's no in between."

"But aren't most gifts fun? How is being a Christian good?" Eliza asked.

Kristos resumed eating. He chewed his mouthful before speaking again. "Depends on the gift, doesn't it? Now if I gave a child a pony, say Shelby, the Shetland pony. You met her yesterday. Would they find it fun?"

"I can imagine the excitement over such a gift." Eliza wondered where he was going with this. Didn't every little girl want a pony growing up?

"But the child needs to learn how to care for the horse, how to lead and ride the horse, feed it, shelter it, clean up after it. None of that can take place unless the child says, 'This is my horse,' and chooses to exercise ownership of it."

"I don't think I follow," Eliza said.

"Probably not the best analogy. When we receive the gift of salvation, we take ownership of our faith. We need to learn how to exercise it, keep our lives free from sin which, like cleaning out a stall, is a daily chore because we live in a messy world, and we fail often. We feed our faith by going to church, reading Scripture, worshipping, learning, and being encouraged by other believers. If we, however, reject the gift of salvation, in our example—ignore the horse—it will grow weak and die."

"That sounds horrible." Eliza's heart grew heavy with grief at the image of an emaciated, weak horse dying.

"It is horrible. When we die, or Christ returns, for anyone who failed to accept the gift and nurture it, it's worse than starving a horse to death. The person who has done that has dug their own grave, chosen hell for eternity with all the pain and agony of separation from the Almighty God who created and designed humans to give Him glory. The horse didn't choose to die, did it?"

"No."

"But we do when we turn from God and the loving gift He offers us. Is living a life of faith easy? No. But nothing worth having is easy, is it? Even a seed needs to push through dirt before it can fully sprout and bloom. God is with us every step of the way."

"Wow. This is a much deeper conversation than I anticipated. I didn't grow up going to church. Had never stepped inside one except my dad's funeral, until Gabby brought me a few weeks back and now I'm going to Mexico, and some of what you're saying is as difficult to grasp as the Spanish we'll hear down there."

"And yet one must start somewhere, right? You don't learn to speak Spanish overnight. For fluency to grow, it takes years and practice and good teaching and even exposure to others who speak it. In some ways the Christian faith is like that as well. It takes time. You don't need to be perfect and understand it all to take that simple step in accepting the gift," Kristos explained.

Silence hung between them as they ate.

Kristos spoke again. "Why did you decide to join the Army?"

"Good question. I didn't have a clue what to do with my life and the Army sounded like a safe bet. I already had an associate's degree but wasn't sure that's what I wanted to continue doing. The college fund my father set up couldn't finance anything more so I joined the Army and ended up driving a truck."

"My brother Alexos was in the Army. He said everyone swore an oath to defend the Constitution and obey the orders of the president of the United States. Is that correct?" Kristos asked.

"Yes. What of it?"

"When did you last read the Constitution?"

"It's been a while."

"How do you feel about our president?"

"Let's not go there. I'm not much for politics," Eliza said.

"Yet you swore an oath to obey him. If he told you right now to get on a plane and go to war, you would go."

Eliza nodded. "He wouldn't do that."

"How do you know? Political leaders have sometimes asked their military to do unconscionable things."

"I volunteered for that."

"Meaning you had a choice."

Eliza nodded.

"Same is true of God. He becomes Commander-in-Chief and unlike any president, He is perfect and holy and according to Romans 8, wants to work all things together for good to those who are His. He does that for His glory and for our good as well."

Eliza wasn't sure what to say. She'd barely eaten and her appetite was gone. Something deep inside was unsettled and Kristos' passion was intoxicating to listen to. Those stunning eyes pleaded with her to take that step.

I'm inviting you, Eliza.

That sweet face with such an earnest desire to help her understand. She wouldn't mind waking up to that every morning.

Wait. What?

Love often takes us by surprise and is rarely convenient.

"Has anything I've said made sense?" Kristos asked.

Eliza nodded. "Between you and your father, I have a lot to think about."

"Do you own a Bible?"

"No. I've never had one or read it."

"When we leave, I'll give you one and bookmark where you should begin reading. You currently serve a president you don't personally know who doesn't care about you as an individual. God, however, does. Will you at least read it?"

"Sure. I'm willing to give it a try."

"And call me with any questions—or my father if you prefer."

"OK."

The server gave her a to-go box and Eliza put her food in there. Kristos paid the bill and they headed to the parking lot.

Kristos had been praying for Eliza from the moment after she'd dumped beer on him a few weeks ago. He'd wondered if God placed her on his heart because she was the woman God selected for him. It saddened him to realize he was wrong about that. God only wanted him to share about Jesus and today he'd dumped a truckload on Eliza.

She strode by his side, barely coming to his shoulder. Everything in him wanted to plead with her to accept Jesus. The Holy Spirit held him back. When they got to the car, he reached into the back seat and pulled out a Bible. It was worn and had some notes in it but was a good translation. He pulled the ribbon and placed it in the book of John and handed it to her.

"Start here."

"But this is your Bible," she protested.

"It's one of them. I've read different versions over the years. You'll find some scribblings in the margins from me, just ignore them."

She accepted the Bible and placed the to-go container on top of it. "I'll give it a try. Thank you. And thank you for lunch as well."

"My pleasure, Eliza Torres." He would have liked to add that like a tornado she'd ravaged his heart, but love and romance weren't in the cards, and he didn't want to confuse her with those things. "The greatest love you will ever have is with Jesus. Nothing else can compare. Find your hope in Him and life will seem vastly different."

She nodded and turned to walk to her car. Kristos waited until she was in and the engine started before he got into his own vehicle. As he drove away, he prayed God would draw Eliza to Himself, that God would heal whatever wounds were deep inside. He also prayed he would stay pure and keep Eliza at arm's length. Friends, but no more. That'd be even harder on the mission trip. *God, I am certain You will use Eliza in ways she's not even aware of yet to bring honor and glory to Your name.*

17

Eliza arrived home to find her roommate gone. After putting the food in the fridge, she opened Ramsey's cage. The bird ignored her and continued to devour some of the shelled nuts she'd put there that morning. Eliza sat down in her favorite chair and opened the Bible to where Kristos had marked with a silky red ribbon. She began to read.

Her phone rang. Eliza hit the accept button. "Hey, Rachel, what's up?"

"I was going to ask the same about you. It's been a few days."

"Got my leg, doctor wants me to try something called EMDR and equine therapy. Went to visit the ranch where the horse therapy is and lo and behold, Mr. Kristos Sava is there."

"Did you almost die?"

"No, silly. It was cool to see him in his own happy place I guess you could say. He was friendly but mostly all business and I didn't get to talk to him long."

"I'm sorry. That had to be disappointing," Rachel said.

"Not really. We met for lunch today."

"Two weeks in a row? Are you dating him?"

"I doubt it. He is a Christian with a strong faith. He's leading that mission team."

"Why would that be a problem? You're a good girl with a strong moral code."

"Who also has had a tendency to drink too much since the event."

"I'm sorry. Can you join AA?"

"We'll see. I've not had a drink for about a week now."

"And the temptation?"

"Was fine until this morning."

"What happened this morning?"

Eliza explained the message at church and some of what Kristos talked about.

"Sounds like you got preached to. Guess that dims the glow for that guy."

"Not necessarily. He was so passionate as he spoke and it didn't feel like preaching or a sales pitch. He earnestly sounded as if he cared about me and my soul. He had nothing to gain by that."

"Are you sure? Does he get brownie points in heaven if he brings along so many souls?" Rachel's tone dripped with disdain.

"I don't believe it works like that. He gave me a Bible and I've been reading…in the book of John. Interesting stuff." Eliza put the ribbon in the spot where she'd been disturbed, closed the book and set it on the side table.

"Don't go getting all religious on me now."

"There's something about this Jesus that, umm…I can't explain it well. I need to understand more about it."

"I guess that's OK."

"So how is your honey and the kiddos?" Eliza asked and settled back to listen to stories about a life she'd yet to experience.

When the call ended, Ramsey flew over to stand in her lap.

"I do wish you'd begin to talk, Ramsey. I don't understand why you don't."

Eliza longed to grab the Bible again but the door opening distracted her. Livie walked in.

"Hey roomie, how was your afternoon?" Livie asked.

"It was—interesting. Where were you? I was surprised to find you gone."

"Just met a friend from therapy, we sat at a coffee shop to chat. It's a beautiful day out there."

"Who is this friend?"

Livie shared her interest in a man also in therapy for a similar injury. Eliza listened but longed to continue reading the Bible. Ramsey flew back to his cage to take a nap.

"Enough about my possible beau. How was lunch with Kristos?" Livie asked.

"Interesting. He can be quite passionate when he talks about Christ," Eliza said.

"Like father, like son, huh?" Livie grinned. "I'm happy for you."

Eliza frowned. "I'm not sure why. Gabby got me started with church, but I have no idea how this Christian thing works. I've got too much on my plate to be trying to figure that out as well."

Livie's expression changed. Her lips drooped and the sparkle left her eyes. "First of all, I'm sorry I never asked about where you were spiritually."

"It's OK."

"No. It's not. I love Jesus and yet often I find I'm too quiet about my faith. As if treating you well was going to help you see God better without understanding my motivation."

"You need motivation to be kind?" Eliza asked.

"Some days, yes. Don't you?" Livie asked.

"I never bothered to worry about it."

"Well, I should have tried to discover this truth earlier."

"We're only a few days into being roommates. Not a lot of time to establish a friendship." Eliza reassured Livie.

Livie gave a half wave of her hand. "It's kind of you to be so generous. Listen. I won't push you. I'll be happy to attend church with you and if you have any questions, hopefully I can help give you answers."

"Why won't Ramsey talk to me?"

"Seriously? That's the question? What's that over there?" Livie pointed to the book on the end table.

"A Bible Kristos loaned me."

"Wonderful. And you've been reading it?"

Eliza nodded.

"Good. I'll be praying that the Holy Spirit will draw you to God so you can experience a love like no other. I'll also pray that you'll give up fighting it."

"Why would you say I'm fighting it?" Eliza gulped. Had her skirmish with God been obvious?

Livie shrugged. "Just a feeling I got at church. Like there's a tug of war going on for your heart between your own prideful independence and the God calling you to trust Him."

Eliza wasn't sure how to respond to that. "Even if I wanted to give in, how does one do that? Is this a battle?"

"Yes. For your very soul and your eternal destiny."

"Now you're sounding like Kristos."

"I'm liking your handsome cowboy more and more." Livie grinned.

"And to my other question? How?"

"It's as simple as saying yes to God. Admitting to Him your desperate need for salvation from your sin and agreeing to submit yourself to Him. You committed to the Army, giving yourself to God should be a much easier decision."

"You'd think that, wouldn't you? How did you make that decision?"

"I was raised in a home that loved Jesus. My mother was always singing His praises throughout the day and my father would read to us from Scripture at night. It seemed a natural thing. It's like I grew up in the faith. When I was in high school, I finally chose to be baptized."

"I need to do that too?" Eliza asked. Was there more that would be required of her?

"The thief on the cross wasn't baptized but Jesus promised him he'd be in paradise with Jesus. You might not have gotten to that part yet."

"No...not yet.

"Listen, Eliza, Jesus loves you and wants to be a part of your life. Living for Him will give you more joy than being a soldier in the Army ever could."

I'm inviting you, Eliza.

Kristos strode into his parents' home for dinner. He wasn't especially hungry, but Sunday night was family dinner night and whenever any of the family could, they tried to be there. With Zoe and Sophia still in high school and busy with a variety of activities and work after school, sometimes it was the only time they could all be together.

Mark ran to him. "Uncle Kristos! Up!"

Kristos picked the little boy up. It was amazing he had been mute for so long and now could speak so well. The family all praised God for that. It was one of many miracles God worked due to Rusty's faithfulness in obeying the Lord's call to marry Mark's mother, Jane.

"Mark, you're almost getting too big to be picked up anymore."

"I'm big."

Kristos grinned and tickled the boy who giggled. "Yes, you are."

Rusty strode into the room with his support dog, Lola, a fox-like Shiba Inu.

"Hey, bro. Looks like Mark has your number. How ya doin'?"

"Been keeping myself out of trouble," Kristos offered as he set Mark back down. The little boy went to play with some toys on the floor.

"Everything going well with the Mexico plans?"

"Yes. I'm looking forward to the trip and seeing what God will do."

"I can't wait to hear about it."

"You'll need to wait until we return or are at least on our way back. If I remember correctly, the village we're staying at has limited access to a cell signal."

"Do you need a satphone? Just in case of an emergency they come in handy. I have an extra."

"Might not be a bad thing to have handy."

Rusty patted him on the back. "I'll bring one over the next time I come home and leave it for you by your door."

"I appreciate it. We've never had difficulties before, but there's unrest all over the world and I'd be naïve to think that we'll be exempt from that."

"Well, I pray you won't have need of it."

They headed to the dining room.

"Come on, Mark," Rusty called, "time for dinner."

Mark jumped up and ran ahead of them to the table.

"Where's Zoe?" Kristos asked. He'd been worried about his sister who announced her intention of joining the Army after graduation. She wasn't taking any JROTC classes. She said enlisted was fine for her.

Kristos' mom, Roda, hustled in with a pan of food. He took it from her and placed it on the table.

"Zoe got called in to work."

"I thought you asked her to get off on Sundays?" Alexos asked as he strode in with his wife, Kobbe.

Dad walked in. "She's independent and doesn't like being told what to do. She says she asked and had no choice, but I struggle to believe that's true."

"Is she really at work?" Sophia asked. She was the youngest of the Sava clan and liked to stir things up sometimes.

"We put that app on her phone like you have; she resents us for it. I have threatened to take the phone away."

"I never had a phone when I was in high school," Alexos said. "I think we rely too much on technology."

"Maybe so, but without the GPS locater I gave to Mark we might have never found him when he'd been taken," Rusty defended.

"Technology is a mixed bag. Just a reminder, no phone usage at the dinner table," Theodore Sava stated. He went to help his wife, Roda, into her seat.

"Yes, Papá," the kids all said in unison as they found their seats.

Dinner was a feisty affair with food being passed and devoured. Kristos adored his parents and enjoyed being with his boisterous Greek family and the love and laughter that surrounded mealtimes. He couldn't imagine how Alexos gave that up to sleep on the ground and fly helicopters in South Korea in the Army. Glancing at his brother now, the once injured, closed-off chief warrant officer was no longer. Now Alexos was a happily married civilian expecting his first child. The joy and confidence radiating from him was a testimony to God's transforming work.

Rusty assisted Mark with cutting up some food. He, too, had come a long way from life-changing injuries to be a father to Mark and a husband also expecting a child.

When would it be Kristos' turn for that kind of contentment? Not that he was discontented with his life, but he wanted more. Was that wrong?

After the meal ended and the dishes were cleared, washed, and put away, Kristos returned to his apartment above the barn. He sat in a recliner, pushing the button for the bottom part to come up to support his lower legs and feet.

Eliza was heavy on his mind and heart. *Lord, I've done all I can to share Your truth, and I'm not even sure why I'm so passionate about her accepting You. Sure, she's cute. I have no clue where she's going or what she wants. She may not even want to have anything to do with me. But You've laid her on my heart so here I am praying, fighting a battle for her soul to be Yours. Protect her and help her to accept You as her Lord and Savior. Give me peace in the waiting. Amen.*

18

Eliza tossed and turned most of the night. Words she'd read in the Bible gave her so much to consider. Jesus was many things. He was the Word made flesh. That confused her. Was Jesus the book she held in her hands? He was a light in the darkness. That she could embrace. He turned water into wine. He told stories and healed people. And He said that anyone who believed in Him would have eternal life. He loved her. Some of that Kristos had said. So why did it seem so new and unusual? She'd been trying to wrap her brain around it all without success. She finally rose early to read some more.

When the time came, she prepared for the day. She still couldn't believe she had to do all this to put on a prosthetic leg. She shouldn't complain. She'd rather deal with a liner, then the rubber liner, the sock, the socket, and sleeve to get the leg on, which she usually needed to prepare ahead of time with a sock and shoe. When she was done, she finished dressing, grateful she hadn't needed to cut off her pants at the right knee and spend her life in a wheelchair. She'd met some of the wounded vets who dealt with that, and many were far more positive about their future than she'd been. She'd been in a downward spiral for months.

What changed?

Kristos.

She hated to admit that meeting him was a turning point. She understood without him even saying it that unless she accepted Christ, there was no future between them.

Did she want a future with Kristos?

None of that mattered until she made a decision for Christ. Without Jesus, all bets were off for anything serious with the handsome horse breeder and trainer. Accepting Christ opened a world of possibilities.

She couldn't make her decision based on that. She wouldn't have followed a boyfriend into the Army. There would have been no guarantee they'd ever see each other. She understood the chain of command. If God were the Creator and Ruler of the world, then she'd be under His command and all decisions and choices henceforth would come through that relationship.

She never realized one could have a relationship with a God that can't be seen but who was apparently still alive.

She combed her hair and checked her roots. She'd need to freshen that up before heading to Mexico. So why had she decided to dye her hair now that she was going to be out of the Army and not worried about trying to maintain that while on deployment? It was a whim. A way to redefine herself. She stepped back from the mirror. Perhaps she should own her heritage and dye it black-brown again.

Would Kristos like that or was he attracted to blondes? It wasn't something she could see maintaining for a long time anyway. She'd make the appointment and decide when she arrived.

She wandered to Ramsey's cage, emptied out the messy bottom into the garbage, and put a new liner in. She changed the water. The blue and yellow monster parrot only fluffed his feathers. When would this thing talk?

I'll talk to you, Eliza, all you need to do is seek Me.

Yeah. God was calling, tugging, reaching…and she was not particularly good at hiding or tuning him out. She'd need to come to some sort of resolution soon as the battle exhausted her.

She'd set those thoughts aside for now. She checked her watch. Her roommate still slept. Eliza headed out to her appointment.

She strode into the office of her career counselor, the one who told her to go out and try something new.

"Good morning, Eliza. I'm noticing a little bounce in your step. New prosthetic or just good news?"

"Both. I'm still not sure what I'm going to do with my life but decided to take a mission trip to Mexico. I leave in less than two weeks."

"Wow. I'm impressed. How do you think this will help with you deciding career goals?"

Eliza shrugged. "No idea. Guess we'll wait and see if it helps with anything."

When her appointment was finished, she decided to call the therapist to set up the EMDR appointment. She wasn't too sure about this kind of treatment, but she was at least making steps toward something that might break the stalemate in her heart. On to physical therapy from there.

Eliza was unsure how her EMDR appointment with Dr. Camilla Rodriguez would go, but she was willing to try it since she had heard from other wounded soldiers how successful their experience with this type of therapy had been. The office was pleasant with little to trigger a PTSD event. Eliza took a deep breath as she picked up the clip board to begin filling out medical papers. She had spent the last several months since the event filling in forms and trying to avoid talking about the moment of impact.

Dr. Rodriguez called Eliza's name and took the stack of forms.

"Sorry about all the paperwork. You know the Army and insurance runs on paperwork." Dr Rodriguez smiled to ease the tension.

"No worries. I'm used to it." Eliza followed the doctor into her private office and was surprised how cozy it felt. Nothing like the military facilities where she had spent hours and hours.

The doctor began to ask a few get-to-know-you questions and reviewed the forms. She came around her desk and sat in the overstuffed chair that matched the one Eliza had sunk into.

"Let me explain what will happen as we go through the Eye Movement Desensitization. Usually your brain will transfer events from your current, right now happening, memory to your long-term memory. Often, when you experience PTSD your brain fails to move the event from the front to the back of your memories. It's as if the trauma is actually occurring again and again when the memory through your senses triggers it. It could be a smell, a taste, a sound, or a certain movement that triggers PTSD."

Eliza tried to take in everything the doctor was saying.

"Does this mean it will be stuck in my current memory forever? If so, why can't I remember?"

"No. In simple terms, it means we need to help your brain get it unstuck. Let me give you an example. Have you every broken a bone or perhaps had a severe sunburn when you were younger?" Doctor Rodriguez asked.

"Yes, ma'am. I fell asleep on the beach once and got third degree burns."

"Ouch."

"Yeah, that took a while to recover from, but I never go without sunscreen now."

"OK. You've just told me about your sunburn but it didn't cause you any pain or trauma right now. Correct?"

"Yes, ma'am."

"Your brain has moved that event from your current thinking to your memories. This process allows you to remember it but not feel the pain. When we do EMDR with your traumatic event it will do the same thing. How does that sound to you?"

Eliza was quiet for a moment. She would have to tell the doctor about an event she couldn't remember but still triggered her.

"I don't remember the actual event. Can we still do the EMDR?"

"Absolutely. I'll ask you questions leading up to the event. We want you to describe in detail everything you can remember before the attack."

Eliza grimaced when she heard attack.

"I mean event. I'll ask you what you can smell, see, hear, taste, touch, and how you are feeling. We'll check in with your body and your emotions. You ready to try?"

Eliza didn't answer immediately. This was a door she was petrified to open, but she knew she had to do it to get healthy. She must try.

"OK."

"There are a few ways therapists do EMDR. Some use lights, or a button you squeeze, or you can just follow my finger with your eyes as I move it back and forth in front of you. I use the simplest method of you following my finger as I ask you questions. Ready?"

"Let's do it."

"First, take a few deep breaths," Doctor Rodriguez said, her tone soft and soothing. She took the breaths as well. "Close your eyes and picture the day before the event. When you have it in your mind, open your eyes and begin to describe it to me."

Eliza opened her eyes and blinked. "Our squad was preparing for a humanitarian mission. Packing the food and supplies into the trucks. We were going to take them to a village about an hour away. We'd made that trip before so we were looking forward to seeing the people who always greeted us warmly. My crew, Spec 4 Cliff Barnes, Spec 4 Bart Clayton, and Private First Class Hal Zarenski were goofing around and telling jokes as we worked. It was a good day. Weather was actually not too awful. Everyone was in a great mood and looking forward to the mission."

The doctor stopped her with a hand. "OK. Eliza, keep your head still. Follow my index finger back and forth with your eyes only. This will cause your brain to move what we talk about into your long-term memory. Remember. You're safe here and can stop at any time."

"Got it."

"Eliza tell me about the next morning, the day you were going on the humanitarian mission."

"The soldier next to my bunk, Private Owens' alarm went off at 0430. It was an hour before chow. I was annoyed because she had set the alarm for so early. It was still dark outside and inside our tent."

"You're doing great. Let's talk about after breakfast. What did you do next?"

Eliza thought for a minute as she continued to watch Doctor Rodriguez' finger slowly go back and forth like the ticking of a metronome.

"Clayton and Barnes were arguing about who could deadlift more weight. Zarenski was finishing a letter to his girl back in Oklahoma. I was packing snacks and drinks for the day."

"Can you smell anything?"

"Stench. The winds are blowing across the latrine area toward the chow hall. It's beyond gross." Eliza squinched up her face, remembering the awful smell.

"What are you wearing?"

"Same thing I wore every day. My combat dress uniform. I remember missing color and swore I would only wear colorful things when I returned Stateside."

The doctor continued to ask questions to help Eliza describe her morning before the squad jumped into the truck.

"I liked the camaraderie with my squad. I loved driving trucks. I'm petite, sure, but when I did that, I felt strong. Important. I belonged with this team, our squad. I loved serving my country this way. We were laughing and joking as we took off on the trip. It was hot and dusty, but we didn't mind. We'd gotten used to the dirt. The other guys were keeping a lookout with their weapons ready through the open windows. The truck in front of us was moving at a good clip and I was able to keep up. Several others followed. We were the second truck in the convoy."

Eliza's breathing accelerated and she clenched her fists, trying to focus on that moving finger.

"You mentioned the kids you'd run into. Tell me more about them. What was it like given you didn't speak their language."

Eliza gulped. "The kids. They would toss a ball around with us. They always wanted candy, and we tried to have something for them when we'd see them. The bigger soldiers would give piggyback rides. We had fun with the kids. I miss them. We didn't need words to communicate. They understood we were there to help."

Eliza's breath came through her clenched lips and her body shook.

"OK. We're going to bring you back to where you are now. Please, in as much detail as you can, describe what you see in my office. Be extremely specific."

"You like the soft neutral tones. They are soothing. The soft browns and blues and greens all make up a unified whole. It's not sterile like some doctor's offices are."

"Excellent. We'll use your senses to help you connect back to this moment. What can you touch?"

"The sofa here is soft and cushy. It's not leather but has a soft texture. I could easily curl up for a nap here."

"What do you smell?"

Eliza paused before answering. "I'm not sure. My deodorant? It smells clean in here. Popcorn? Oh…I can hear it popping down the hallway."

"Good. You're doing great, Eliza. You may have nightmares or recovered memories over the next few days as your mind processes what we did here today. It isn't unusual to remember more details as time passes. Healing doesn't usually happen immediately. Please be kind to yourself and not stress about trying to remember more at this point. It will come when your mind and body are equipped to handle it. How do you feel right now?"

"I'm feeling better than a few minutes ago. A bit shaky. And a little scared."

"That's OK. Very normal. This isn't a one and done therapy. We'll continue to work together and go as far as you can each time. For some it is a quick response and for others it takes longer to see the results. Let's meet again at the same time next week. Does that work for you?"

Eliza nodded and stood. Something felt different but she wasn't healed yet. She'd pray about it and see what God would do.

Kristos was mucking out the stalls when he spied Eliza striding toward Kobbe's office. She must have had clearance from insurance to start therapy. Kobbe had suggested Mandy, a Percheron for Eliza. The gal was petite so he'd thought she might choose the Shetland, but she said no. Mandy was patient and intuitive. Kristos went to get Mandy and led her to the floor with no bridle or reins. For this first session, Kobbe had requested Kristos be present to help with the horse while she worked with Eliza. He'd done this a few times before as had Caden, and it was a nice change of pace.

"Click. Click. Come on, girl." Kristos led the horse out of the stall. The horse came along without him even touching her. "Let's go help someone heal." He'd always enjoyed riding and found it a great place to think through his troubles, so he wasn't too surprised to learn that horses were used for therapy for all kinds of issues. When Kobbe joined the family by marrying his brother, he was more than happy to welcome her using the paddock and horses for her equine therapy business. Horses became a natural biofeedback method for the rider. How that all worked he had no clue, but it didn't matter. Even he couldn't deny the progress he'd witnessed in the few short months they'd been doing this.

Mandy strode confidently by his side into the paddock. Kristos walked the horse around while Kobbe was speaking with Eliza. Eliza still captured his attention, and he wondered if she'd been reading the Bible he'd given her. He caught her eye and she smiled. He grinned in return. He stopped toward the middle of the paddock. "Stay." He stepped away from the horse and walked to the edge of the paddock and waited.

Eliza's anxiety went up at Kristos' presence in the paddock. With Kobbe's encouragement Eliza slowly walked to the horse who towered above her.

"Hi, Mandy. I'm Eliza. I'm hoping we can be friends." The size of the animal terrified her. The large head bent down to observe her. Those eyes seemed to search deep into her soul. The head rose and turned away as if finding her insignificant. She fought back the tears. Kobbe hadn't given much instruction. She said learning how to get the horse do what she wanted, to walk around the paddock in a circle, was a process she needed to figure out herself.

Eliza saw the horse walk next to Kristos without him saying a word. How had he done that? She glanced over to Kristos who was checking his phone. Well, at least she wasn't totally embarrassing herself. She reached a hand to touch the side of the horse's neck and let the hand travel down the soft silky hair. The horse didn't mind it so she did it again. It didn't do anything for the horse but the action calmed her. Eliza could sense the strength of the animal in front of her. Sure, she'd driven trucks that were huge, but they didn't have a mind of their own and while her last truck almost killed her, she had no doubt this animal, if provoked, could do serious harm as well.

Kobbe assured Eliza that the horse was mild-mannered but that horses are hypersensitive to emotions.

Eliza kept petting the neck and moved to do that down the side of the animal. Again, the muscles sent a shiver through her. The horse stepped to the side.

"I'm sorry, Mandy. Did I scare you?" Eliza whispered. The horse's ears twitched. Eliza moved to the side of the head. "Do you want to be with me? How do I earn your trust?"

Mandy tilted her head down. Eliza reached up to touch the horse's face and Mandy held her head still as Eliza continued and gazed into that big brown eye. It had never dawned on her that horses couldn't see anything right in front of their face since their eyes were on the sides of their heads. Interesting.

"Am I a mere speck to you? How are we to get along? Will you come with me if I move?"

Mandy didn't give any indication other than a twitch of the ear. Eliza took a step away from the horse, letting her hand drop to her side. "Come, Mandy," she said. The horse took a small step toward her.

"Good job, girl. Come on." Eliza took a few more steps. The horse waved its head sending her mane rippling along her neck.

Eliza took a shuddered breath. Why was she here? How was this supposed to help her? She thought she'd be riding a horse someone prepared for her. Apparently not the case. She needed to win over Mandy. How did one start a relationship with a horse? What was the point of this?

Eliza turned toward Kobbe who watched from side. "I don't think she wants to come."

"Keep working to gain her trust," Kobbe said.

Eliza turned back to the giant with four legs. Those sharp hooves could trample her to death. Fear rippled through her. *I can't do this. I can't do this.*

Instantly she was sprawled out on the ground with a fire burning next to her. Her truck was on fire! She tried to stand but couldn't. "Help!" she yelled. She thought she heard a scream of pain. Was it hers or from the burning truck?

Sobbing, she stood there before the horse who took a step forward and nudged her. Eliza reached out for anything she could get, leaning her face against the side of the horse's head and sobbing.

The scream from Eliza shook Kristos back to attention. Kobbe warned him that sometimes flashbacks happened with PTSD. Eliza was sobbing and Mandy stepped forward to offer comfort. Good girl, Mandy. Eliza and Mandy stayed together like that for some time. Eliza moved her head away and whispered something to the horse before walking back to Kobbe. There wasn't much conversation there before Eliza strode away, wiping away tears.

Kobbe motioned for him to take Mandy back to her stall. Kristos approached the horse and petted her nose. "You're a good girl, Mandy. Come on, time for a treat, huh?" Not that the horse worked hard at all but he took her back to her stall and gave her a carrot that she gleefully devoured. "Do you want to join your friends outside?" he asked.

Mandy nodded and Kristos opened the door and let the horse go join her friends in the meadow.

Kristos had no doubt there'd been something significant that happened today. It wasn't any of his business. He was no therapist. *Lord, help Eliza with whatever is buried deep inside.*

Eliza drove away from the Mountain Shadow Stables and pulled onto a side road, parked on the gravel, and wept.

Those images. She'd never experienced those before. The event had been a blank in her memory, a time lapse like when you go into surgery and wake up hours later. The world moved on but you've missed some of it.

She was content not remembering but apparently her brain or soul or whatever someone wanted to call it, didn't want to stay locked deep inside. She hoped the psychotherapist and psychiatrist were wrong in diagnosing her with post-traumatic stress disorder. It wasn't a moniker she wanted to own. Veteran, wounded warrior, she was fine with those labels. She'd already been labeled with depression, anxiety, and ambivalence...if that was even a diagnosis.

How could talking to a horse do all that? She hadn't even figured out how to get it to come with her and walk around the paddock. She'd failed her first equine therapy assignment. Would Kobbe even work with her again? She'd left. At least that she could remember. Was Kobbe angry?

She arrived home and went to her room, throwing herself across her bed. Why was she such a mess?

The phone rang. It was her mother.

Sniff. She clicked the button. "Hi, Mom. What's up?" She covered the mic so her mother couldn't hear her shuddered breathing.

"I'm glad I caught you at a good time. I wanted to let you know that the house sold. I packed up some of your stuff and you can get it when you come to visit in Arizona, or I can ship it to you wherever you decide to go."

"Thanks, Mom. Sounds good." Losing the house was something else to grieve.

"Nigel and I decided to elope. We went to Vegas. Can you believe I would ever do something so spontaneous? I'm sorry we didn't invite you. We didn't invite anyone. We'll have a gathering once we settle in our new home. It had been so long, Eliza, since your father died. I didn't want to wait to start life with Nigel. I know you're going to love him as much as I do."

I doubt that's possible. "Congratulations, Mom. I'm happy for both of you. When are you moving?"

"We've already packed everything. My new job starts in a week and we found a place there, a condo, all ready for us to move into. We have a spare bedroom for when you or one of his kids come to visit. Hopefully not all at once."

"Yeah, I hope not."

"Well, listen, I want to learn all about how you're doing but I need to get to work. It's been such a whirlwind. My last day is tomorrow."

"That's fine, Mom. I'm kind of busy here too, another time, huh?"

"Definitely. I love you, sweetheart." With that parting salvo they disconnected the call.

"I love you too, Mom," Eliza whispered.

The tears started all over again.

19

It was late August when Kristos waited by the bus that would take them all to Denver International Airport to catch their flight to Mexico. He'd not seen Eliza on Sunday, but her roommate was there. She'd left before he could ask her how Tornado was doing. He didn't think their relationship was close enough for him to call or text to check up on her. A woman approached, dragging her suitcase toward them. Eliza? Where was the blonde hair? He wouldn't complain, he preferred brunettes. She wasn't wearing her usual jeans which made sense, this trip would be hot. He admired her courage in wearing a skirt, or was it a skort? He couldn't be sure but it came to mid-thigh and her prosthetic leg was in full view. It would be difficult to hide something like that anyway on a trip of this nature.

He breathed a sigh of relief. She was here. Why that mattered to him he didn't know, but it did. He'd been praying even harder for her since her last therapy. She cancelled the next one which concerned him. He couldn't understand the kind of trauma she must be going through and wasn't sure he wanted to.

Everyone got their suitcases loaded in the storage compartment and boarded the bus, flashing him their passports and ID. He had the plane tickets for everyone. They were allowed only one suitcase and a carry-on for the seven-day trip. He hoped everyone brought hats and sunscreen like the packing list suggested. The village they were going to was more remote than anticipated so no chance to run to a store to get supplies.

Once on the bus he whistled to get everyone's attention. "Before we head to the airport, I want to pray for us. Heavenly Father, You have called and led us to this time and place, a trip to serve others and show Your love, mercy, and grace. Give us safe travel and open our hearts to the work You want to do inside us as we serve others. Amen."

A chorus of amens could be heard on the bus. The group wasn't huge, only eight people, four men and four women, but they'd be joining up with another group when they got to Mexico.

"Let's go!" Kristos sat down and the driver put the bus in motion.

Once they arrived at the airport they headed to security. He wasn't able to see Eliza. Did her prosthetic set off the scanner? He never even considered what she'd need to make the trip possible. Her carry-on backpack seemed filled to the brim.

He got the group back together after the screening and they headed to the concourse where their plane would depart. Kristos walked next to Eliza.

"How did screening go?"

She shrugged. "Fine. They did a swab of the prosthetic but otherwise it was OK."

"That bag looks heavy; what did you pack in there?"

"Everything I'll need for the next week for this prosthetic, in case my suitcase gets lost."

"Whoa. That much stuff for one leg?"

"Yes, but at least I don't need to use sunscreen there."

"I can't imagine what you've been through—are going through—in learning to live with that. You realize it doesn't change who you are or the fact that God loves you."

"Maybe so," her soft flat answer concerned him. Was she still struggling with God?

"Have you read anymore in the Bible I gave you?"

"Yes."

"And?"

"I'm still reading it. I brought it along." She trudged ahead of him toward the gate.

Amber, a mom of five who decided to come with her husband's

blessings, stepped up beside Kristos. "Hurting or stubborn?" she asked.

"A lot of both, I think. She's struggling with God."

"The hardest fight for many of us. She's Army through and through."

Kristos frowned. "Why would you say that?"

"Her posture for one and the strength of her stride. She may have lost part of a leg, but she's in shape. Don't underestimate her because of her size or disability. It's going to be interesting to watch what God does on this trip."

"It will."

Soon they were on the plane and Kristos frowned at the seating arrangements. He'd made them but hadn't even considered sitting next to Eliza. Purity and responsibility. He couldn't afford the distraction of the young woman. As far as he understood it, she hadn't accepted Christ and while Rusty had his reasons to marry an unbeliever and it worked out, Kristos was more practical than sentimental and couldn't consider even dating her.

Two lunches together didn't constitute dating, did it?

He frowned.

The flight took off and several hours later they landed in Mexico City. Once through customs and getting their luggage, they were bundled into an old rickety bus that appeared to be painted every color imaginable and barely held together. Kristos wondered if it had the ability to carry them all the way to their destination. A shiver overtook him. Be not afraid, was the Scripture that popped into his mind. He had no reason to fear or any expectation of trouble for this trip. He glanced around and noticed Amber sat next to Eliza.

The bus rocked back and forth as the driver drove fast down dirt roads. The blistering day made the bus a microwave and open windows only brought in more stifling hot air and lots of dust. Many of the team had already put bandanas around their faces to protect them from breathing the dust. Kristos did likewise, and donned sunglasses to keep the sun and dust from his eyes. He glanced at his group who now resembled a ragtag bunch of banditos off to rob a bank. He chuckled at his own silly thoughts as he hung on for dear life. He'd forgotten the treacherous nature of getting delivered to a destination like this and hoped the other team had already arrived.

Eventually after hours of driving, they disembarked in a tiny village in a valley between mountains. The group quickly found spots to relieve themselves as this village had no indoor plumbing. They approached the well for water to wash their hands and faces and cool off. Once finished, several of the village children began to gather around. Soon the team leader for the mission approached.

"Kristos Sava, I presume?"

"Landon, finally we meet face to face."

Landon, the other team leader, began to help everyone get settled in.

"You survived the journey here, let's get your belongings to the building we'll be sleeping in. I've already set up mosquito netting."

The group followed Landon and deposited their bags in a church.

"We're sleeping in a church?" asked Amber.

"What better place? We'll be working next door on the school, which has fallen into disrepair. It's also a central location for the village and surrounding areas for people to come to hear the gospel. Praise the Lord, the church has a generator we can use to show a movie about Jesus to them tomorrow night."

"It's so tiny. How are we all going to fit in here?"

Landon spoke up. "Gals to the front of the sanctuary, men to the rear. We'll divide the area with the pews. The rest we can stack outside until we're done. We'll be doing as much ministry outside as possible, weather permitting."

"Do we have enough bottled water for the week?" Amber asked.

"Great question. We do. We also have tablets to make the well water safer if necessary. Hopefully no one will suffer from Montezuma's revenge during our trip."

The group proceeded to clean up the interior of the church, removing pews and sweeping the wood floor. Soon the bedding was laid out; it was simple and crude but no one complained.

"It's been a long day for you all. We have a meal being prepared by the village women. Come join us for dinner, and we'll get some rest and start the hard work in the morning," Landon said while he patted Kristos on the back.

"Sounds great. Come on gang." Kristos motioned to the group as Landon corralled his team and they headed out for their meal.

Eliza enjoyed the company of the people she was with. It was almost like being back in the Army, being part of a group with a mission and a task to complete. She silently ate dinner and fought the yawns that escaped regardless of her efforts. The ride here had been harrowing. When the meal was finished, they trooped back to the chapel they'd be sleeping in. Eliza was hesitant to take off her prosthetic, but she needed to let her stump breathe. The swelling on the plane and the heat made it uncomfortable. She settled on her mat and put the mosquito netting over herself. She began to take her leg off and found the other women watching her.

Amber was the first to speak. "I'm sorry I'm staring, I'm simply curious. It seems like such a complicated process."

Eliza shrugged and continued. "Not complicated per se but necessary for my comfort. Better than being in a wheelchair, which would have been far more challenging to make this trip with."

Soon the women settled onto their own mats. The heat was stifling and the mosquitos made their ferocious appearance. Having lived in rough conditions at times in the military, Eliza settled into her mat with her bag under her head and drifted to sleep.

She awoke the next morning and began the process of putting her leg on. They had a private room to change in and she proceeded there to prepare for the day. She hadn't done construction before but was capable with a hammer. Once she'd freshened up and put her hair back in a small ponytail, she wandered outside the chapel. She settled on a bench, and over the trees could see the colors of the sky change with the sunrise. The lushness of the mountains and the cool morning air refreshed her soul.

I'm inviting you, Eliza.

She had brought her Bible outside with her. She opened it to John, chapter 1 again:

"In the beginning was the Word, and the Word was with God, and the Word was God. He was in the beginning with God. All things came into being through Him, and apart from Him not even one thing came into being that has come into being. In Him was life, and the life was the Light of mankind. And the Light shines in the darkness, and the darkness did not grasp it."

Who was God? She'd read through all of John and seen Him as the Word, creator, light, life, shepherd, healer, water-walker, miracle worker, teacher, a vine, and a high priest. Jesus was compassionate, He grieved, He warned His followers of the difficulties they would face.

He was betrayed, mocked, and murdered.

He came back to life.

How could one human do all that? He claimed to be God. John, his disciple, claimed Jesus was God.

"Good morning, Eliza." Amber settled on the bench next to Eliza.

"Morning." Eliza sighed. There was so much she needed to process and couldn't focus on that now.

"It's beautiful here," Amber said. "I'm grateful to be here, even if I'll end up working with other people's kids."

"I hoped to work on the school."

"You can do that. I adore kids though. I've taught Sunday School for years at my church and love the passion and enthusiasm of little people."

"Do you speak Spanish?" Eliza asked.

"*Un poco*." Amber showed her finger and thumb with a tiny space between them. "Love doesn't need language." She touched the backpack on Eliza. "Why do you have this? We'll be within moments of the church."

"It has my prosthetic stuff in it and I can't afford to have it lost or stolen. And if I have an issue, I need it with me right then. I'm still pretty new at this, so I'm being cautious."

Amber nodded. "Fair enough."

Silence hung between them as the village stirred to life. Soon they were eating a simple breakfast and starting work on the school. Kids flocked around Eliza and even adults watched her as she worked alongside the other volunteers. She, however, was distracted by the sight of Kristos stripping his shirt off in the heat.

The man was pure muscle and beautiful to watch.

When their break came, one of the little ones stepped forward and pointed to Eliza's leg and asked a question. *¿Qué le ha ocurrido a tu pierna?* The boy pointed to her leg.

Eliza nodded. Instead of trying her rusty Spanish she mimed it. She pretended driving with her hands on an imaginary steering wheel. They had even seen those way out here. Then her hands flew away from the imaginary wheel, and she said "Boom! *Pierna no más.*"

The little boy's eyes grew wide. He stuck out his hand as if he wanted to touch it.

Eliza gently took the boy's hand and placed it on the stump and slid it down to the post.

He took his hand away; soon all the kids wanted to touch her prosthetic leg. She patiently waited for them to satiate their curiosity while drinking her purified water. Soon one of the adults called the kids away. The first little boy turned to Eliza. "*Gracias, muchacha hermosa.*"

"*De nada.*" She gave him a smile and a wave as he skipped away to join his friends.

Kristos strode over. "I didn't realize you spoke Spanish."

"Very little, but enough. My father was of Mexican heritage. It's been a while since I've used it, but I'll admit to trying to brush up a little before the trip."

"Good. We're at the peak heat of the day so we're heading into the chapel where it's cooler to rest."

"*Siesta?*"

"You could call it that. You've been working hard."

"So have you." She was sad to observe his shirt was back on. Together they headed indoors with the rest of the team.

Eliza sat against the stone base of the church, enjoying the coolness against her back. This church was unlike the church she attended in Colorado Springs. No air conditioning. No pews. No microphones.

They both had love and Jesus.

Soon another woman was coming to talk. Eliza frowned. How did she think she was ever going to have time to think during this trip, surrounded by kids and adults 24/7? She sighed. She'd be pleasant. They were all on the same team after all. Until she resolved her skirmish with God, she didn't truly fit in.

20

Kristos caught Eliza watching him a time or two, and it pleased him to think she might find him attractive. It was only the first day and she had worked hard. Being in the Army she was trained to be a team player and to take initiative, not to slack. Some of the others were less motivated to work hard to get the job done. Five days to work was all they had here and the place was a mess. The team was large enough but many of the women chose to cook, provide water, and engage with the women and children of the town instead of participating in the harder physical labor. Eliza was the only one who didn't want the easier task.

After dinner and the movie, Kristos headed outside into the darkness. For the most part, everyone had settled down. Eliza sat outside the chapel, staring up at the night sky. She had changed into lightweight cargo pants but still wore her team T-shirt.

"*Hola,*" he whispered.

"Hola. The night sky is beautiful."

"It is."

"Jesus hung the stars and the moon," Eliza said.

Kristos gazed down at her. "He did." Her face glowed in the moonlight and those lips…He shook his head. This was not the time for romance or even thinking about such things as sweet kisses in the moonlight.

"You still wear your backpack?" Kristos asked.

"I kept it close during the day, and I wore it during the movie. I can't risk it being stolen." Eliza said, glancing up at him.

"I doubt anyone here would..." Kristos stopped and put his finger to his lips.

Eliza sat up straighter. She pointed to the woods behind the chapel. Kristos nodded and grabbed her hand.

"Inside."

"No. We draw attention to the others and possibly put them in danger," Eliza protested.

"Not if it's an animal."

"It's not." Eliza nodded as she stared into the trees.

Kristos was shocked at the moon reflecting off the barrels of—rifles? His pulse accelerated.

"Stay calm," Eliza whispered, clasping his hand. Warmth traveled up his arm and calmed his racing heart. His stomach knotted. Was it fear or eating different foods than he usually did?

Men rushed forward stealthily, while several other guerillas came from the other side as if coming out of nothingness. With their guns, the thugs directed Kristos and Eliza into the woods, and he understood Eliza's concern. If they'd gone inside the chapel, everyone would have been at risk. With the thick underbrush, he was grateful they'd both changed into pants as the air cooled in the mountains. The humidity made his hair curl even more, and he regretted letting it out of his ponytail for the evening presentation of the gospel.

Whatever happened, he'd at least done that. The gospel had been presented. While he hoped he could be a protector to Eliza, he realized when it came to warfare, she was the one with the training. They walked for miles, up steep inclines and sliding into valleys. Where were these men taking them? There was no conversation. Nothing to indicate what might be in store for the two of them. He only hoped they would treat Eliza well.

He leaned closer to her. "Claim you're my wife and they will hopefully leave you alone and keep us together," he whispered.

"*Silencio*," growled a captor to his right.

Eliza glanced at Kristos and gave him a soft smile. If he was to be in danger with any woman, she'd be his first choice. Something about her assured him she wasn't one who would be a needy, weak partner. Whatever happened in the stable during her first equine therapy wasn't going to hold her back now. There was determination in her gaze.

Mosquitos attacked but there was no opportunity to swat at them, constantly grabbing for tree branches to keep them upright. They arrived at a clearing with trucks and cabins. Their captors pushed them into a cabin with no furniture or windows. The door was barricaded from the outside.

Utter darkness wrapped around them.

Eliza dragged Kristos to the wall next to the door.

Men were speaking close to the door with one man giving directions in rapid Spanish. She couldn't interpret the words. Footsteps took the men away from the cabin and silence cloaked the darkness.

"Sit," she hissed.

He obeyed. "What do you think is going on?"

"I have no clue. I couldn't make out the words. Perhaps they think they can ask for ransom? I've heard of that happening before. Or there may be some other evil plot in play. It doesn't matter at the moment. For now, we need rest."

"How's your leg?"

"My imaginary one?" she asked. "It's swollen and desperate to be out of the prosthetic, but I don't want to take it off under these circumstances."

"If I stretch my legs out, could you prop it on them to give a tiny bit of elevation? Would that help?" Kristos offered.

Her heart warmed. She hadn't even thought of that. "It couldn't hurt. Thank you. You may need to help me get it there."

His hand on her knee, helping lift the prosthetic up, was gentle.

"Comfortable?" he asked.

"I'm fine, but how are you going to be? The four pounds of prosthetic might not seem heavy now..."

"I'm fine. Like you said, let's rest so we're ready for whatever comes next. Before we do, can I pray for us?"

"Sure," Eliza said.

"Heavenly Father, we have no idea where we are or why. Calm our hearts. Protect us and give us wisdom and even here let us be a witness of Your love and grace to a lost and hurting world. Be with the team in the village and give them wisdom too. Amen."

"Amen. Nothing is impossible with God, right?" Eliza whispered.

"You've gone beyond the book of John and into Luke I believe?"

"It's also in Matthew and Mark, but not John."

"How?"

"We can talk more later, but now, we need rest," Eliza said. She gave his hand a squeeze and he squeezed back. The hands rested between their bodies and neither released their grasp.

Being connected to Kristos right now kept her grounded and the fear at bay. She'd never been imprisoned before nor feared the dark, so why did she need his comfort?

Did it matter? At least she wasn't alone. Together they'd figure it out. With God, they would possibly survive this. And if they didn't, she had the assurance now that He would welcome her to heaven whenever the day came. Tonight's movie had been her turning point.

She leaned her head back against the rough wall and prayed there would be no creepy crawly things to disturb her sleep.

She recalled earlier in the evening when Kristos preached a short invitation after the movie. Every phrase was interpreted for the villagers. Eliza gave up the fight and surrendered her heart to Jesus. She'd read enough and realized she didn't need to understand everything about God, a task she realized was impossible, before taking that step. Tears formed again in her eyes as she welled up with gratitude for the gift He'd given her.

"Kristos?" she whispered.

"Hmmm? Can't sleep?" His sleepy voice was a comfort.

"I didn't get a chance to tell you that I accepted Christ tonight."

Silence hung for a moment. "That's wonderful. Welcome to the family, Eliza."

"Thanks. You know what's strange?"

"Hmm?"

"Our captors never tied us up. They didn't take my bag, but they might not have noticed it in the dark."

"Small mercies," his hand squeezed hers again and silence enveloped them.

The early morning light gave Eliza enough light from the cracks in the wood to take off her prosthetic and replace her liners and sock with fresh pieces. Elevating it helped. She worried the rubbing would cause a wound or blister. She already sensed one developing on her left foot, but she was grateful she'd chosen sneakers for the evening instead of flip-flops.

Kristos groaned and rubbed his eyes.

"Shhhh, I think the compound is asleep."

He nodded and dragged himself to his feet. He dug into his pants pocket and pulled out a hair band. Pulling his unruly locks back he secured it.

Eliza still wore the baseball hat she'd brought to keep sun mostly off her face. Her hair was also tied up and came through the back. She'd never taken it off last night. Once she was done with her leg, she packed everything and slipped on the backpack. She rose to her feet and moved around, swinging her arms and stretching.

"Are you OK?" Kristos asked.

"Yes. Surprisingly calm. Slept in fits and starts. My stump is OK for now but I'm not sure how it would do if we needed to walk that far again."

"I need to relieve myself," Kristos said.

"Understood. I used the corner over here earlier." She moved him in the direction of that corner.

"I feel weird doing this in front of you," he confessed.

"Don't be. First of all, I can't see much, and your facing way. Secondly, where else would you go, and third, I served in the Army with a lot of men. It's fine."

The zipper was loud in the small room. She should be the one more uncomfortable when she needed to go, especially as daylight loomed. Cracks in the ceiling were also letting in light. There was no hiding from each other in this space. She appreciated his gentlemanly concern.

They both wandered around in circles.

"'Be strong and courageous, do not be afraid or in dread of them, for the Lord your God is the One who is going with you. He will not desert you or abandon you.' Deuteronomy 31:6," Kristos recited.

Eliza stopped pacing. "What?"

"Since I was a child, I memorized parts of the Bible. Those were the words of Joshua before the Israelites would take the land God promised them."

"I don't…I haven't read that."

"How could you? You're getting acquainted with Jesus, but even if this is in the Old Testament and a promise to the Israelites, I believe we can take comfort in it. We are not alone. Christ is with us. He is for us."

"Can you help me learn that verse?"

"Sure…"

Kristos recited the verse and Eliza began to memorize it. She finally grew able to state it herself without help.

"Say it again, Eliza."

"'Be strong and courageous, do not be afraid or in dread of them, for the Lord your God is the One who is going with you. He will not desert you or abandon you.' Deuteronomy 31:6." She found herself encouraged by those words.

"Now, even if we can't talk or sing or whisper, you can say those words in your heart and be encouraged. God hears the cries of your heart even it's nothing more than *help!*" Kristos assured her. Even in the dim light peeking into the room, a grin showed his infectious passion for Christ.

It made him all the more attractive, even if he was disheveled from this misadventure and their crude circumstances.

The door swung open. A rifle barrel appeared, followed by two men. Kristos and Eliza put their hands up and stepped away from the door.

The unarmed man placed a tray of food on the floor and the door shut again. The rough heavy sound of the latch clunking down depressed any hope that they'd be released soon.

"Well, at least they aren't starving us to death," Kristos said.

"They still have other options, like guns, or setting this thing on fire," Eliza said.

"When did you become a Debbie downer?" Kristos asked as he handed her some bread.

"I'm being realistic. Since we don't have a clue as to the why of our capture, I kind of go to worst case scenarios."

"So, shooting and fire are worse than, oh, perhaps rape?" Kristos asked.

Eliza frowned and pulled off some of the bread. "No. That would be traumatic and to live after that would be fraught with pain. Torture wouldn't be fun either, but I can't imagine anything we might have as far as information that would make us a valuable target or asset. Not that it would matter if they believed otherwise."

"Sorry I brought it up, but that's why I hope you'll say you're my wife if they ask. They might leave you alone."

Eliza could only nod. Pretend being Kristos' wife? That would be its own brand of torture.

21

Kristos chewed the crusty bread, grateful it wasn't stale or moldy. The bottled water he was reluctant to trust, but there were worse things than intestinal distress, and dehydration wouldn't help them either. One bottle for the two of them. He took a sip and handed it to Eliza.

Without a word she understood and took only a sip. He would have gladly gulped it down, but if they were both to survive, they'd need to ration it.

"There are no United States military installations in Mexico," Eliza stated.

"Why is that important?"

"Who else would be coming to rescue us? Certainly not the Mexican military. They could care less what happens to Americans."

"Cynical much?" Kristos asked.

Eliza grinned. "As I said before, I'm realistic. Depending on where we are in Mexico, the closest American military would be either Aruba, Curaçao, or Comalapa, El Salvador."

"Would the military even come rescue American missionaries?"

Eliza shrugged. "Perhaps, as I'm still an enlisted soldier in the US Army."

"It's a thread of hope to cling to," Kristos said.

Eliza nodded. "But would the military come for me? I'm not on military assignment. We haven't done anything wrong either that would amount to this capture."

"Fruitless musings. I hope the team is OK back at the village," he said.

"Me too, but I'm more concerned for us here and how to escape if rescue isn't imminent. If the government is good for one thing, it's moving slowly when it comes to things like this. If they even realize we've been captured."

"What else would we be? We disappeared between the common area in the village and the chapel. We didn't take a vehicle and are both aware of the dangers of going into the rainforest."

"Too bad we don't have the satphone with us," Eliza said.

Kristos stopped. "Wait. Remember at the airport, as we were getting on the bus? I took it out of my suitcase and asked you to put it in your backpack."

"Seriously? How could I forget something like that?" Eliza took off her backpack and uncinched the top to dig down. The phone had slipped into an inner pocket at the bottom. She dragged it out and handed it to Kristos, but noise from outside the cabin forced her to put it back in and get the backpack on her back.

The door opened and a man with a gun motioned them outside.

The sun blinded Kristos but he held onto Eliza's hand and gave it a squeeze.

"So, what did we capture here? Two little lovebirds?" the tall man in front of them asked.

"Two American missionaries, volunteering at a small village," Kristos said with as much confidence as he could muster.

"And this little lady? What's in the bag?"

Eliza raised her pant leg. "Liners and socks for my prosthesis."

The man's eyes widened. "Show me."

Eliza took the backpack off, opened it, and pulled out the dirty sweaty sock from yesterday.

"Fine. You may keep your little sack of socks and such."

The man motioned to the armed group around him. "Secure them in the truck."

He turned back to Kristos and Eliza. "We're taking you on an extended trip."

"Why—?" Kristo started but Eliza nudged him with her elbow.

The man sneered. "Listen to the little lady and you might survive this vacation."

The barrel of some kind of weapon was in his back, propelling him forward to a truck. They were shoved into the back of a large enclosed box on a truck bed and the door locked.

Soon the scent of diesel fumes filled the air and with a rattle the vehicle moved forward.

"Too bad there's no air conditioning. This place is like an oven." Kristos wiped the sweat from his brow. Eliza stretched out on the dirty wood floor with her backpack under her head. "Might as well rest. We're headed farther south. Better wait to use that satellite phone when we get to our next destination. Unless we can figure out a way to escape."

Kristos frowned. "Escape? To where? We have no clue where we are, and it's not like we can hitchhike to the next road to wave down a driver to take us to Mexico City. I have little cash. I do have my passport on me though. You?"

Eliza nodded. "And my dog tags."

Kristos gulped. "Hopefully, we won't need those."

"With God all things are possible," Eliza said.

"With God. Thankfully, He is aware of where we are. We're not alone in this. Now could be a good time to pray. Would you like to try?" Kristos asked.

"Sure. Hi God, Eliza here. We're in trouble. You understand the plans of these evil men. Please rescue us and keep us safe. I'd like it if Kristos and I could return to Colorado so I could read Your Bible and grow in my faith. I have so many more needs than this, but if You could help with this, we can deal with the rest later. Thank You for showing Yourself to me so I don't need to be afraid. Vigilant and wise, I hope, but not afraid." She paused. "Oh, Amen."

Kristos grinned. "Amen. 'Be strong and courageous, do not be afraid or in dread of them, for the Lord your God is the One who is going with you. He will not desert you or abandon you.'"

"Deuteronomy 31:6," Eliza said.

Her smile caused his heart to skip a beat. Maybe when they returned to Colorado they could date.

Eliza rose to sit up.

"Can't rest that way?" he asked.

"Nah, these roads are abysmal. Potholes everywhere. I doubt they have any shocks on these old trucks either."

"Sure doesn't seem like it."

"Got any other ideas of what to do now?" Eliza groaned after a particularly hard bump.

"No," Kristos leaned his head back and instantly regretted it when the truck hit another hard bump. "At least they haven't blindfolded us or tied us up." He handed her the water bottle. "Take a sip. We're going to need to keep rationing."

Eliza took the bottle and sipped just enough to get her tongue wet. She screwed the cap back on and handed it back.

Silence settled between them. Kristos noted the fatigue and weariness on Eliza's face; dirt from the road highlighted the creases in her forehead when her bangs were brushed away due to sweat. There were bags under her eyes. Neither of them got enough sleep or slept well the previous evening and yesterday they'd both worked hard outside. He could sense the tightness of his skin from too much sun. He usually went from a burn to a tan so wasn't worried, but dehydration would make recovery harder, and the burn made him sleepy.

Eventually he curled up on the wood floor and dozed off despite the bumps in the road.

Eliza watched Kristos rest and hoped his dreams were good. She was a soldier. She would stand watch. Her mind went back to the day she was last at the ranch and before that beautiful horse, gazing into eyes that plunged her into the depths of pain. She hadn't slept for days after that. She even yelled at Ramsey, begging him to talk to her. He turned his back to her and cleaned his claws.

Livie tried to talk to her as well but Eliza wouldn't discuss it. EMDR therapy had been a revelation, but she wasn't quite sure how to verbalize all that had happened in that moment and since. Had the EMDR made that moment with Mandy possible? It still shocked her when she stopped to think about it.

Getting on a plane to go to Mexico seemed like a good way to escape the pain and maybe finally resolve things with God. Last night it was as if God pushed her into a corner. She had no more excuses. Oh, she could come up with many, but she recognized them for what they were, a smokescreen. She was afraid to give up control of her life to an unseen God. But she did it anyway. The peace that followed was unlike anything she'd ever experienced.

Now she sat in a wooden box on the back of a truck, drenched in sweat, desperate for light and answers. Dust entered through cracks, doing nothing to alleviate the heat.

The rickety truck barreled over rocky mountain roads and through what felt like cooler dense forests. Eliza could rest and not fret. Something about the man who briefly spoke with them this morning led her to believe they would not be harmed. Should she hold out hope that was true? Perhaps. Just because that person didn't intend harm didn't mean his minions or a superior would be kind.

What was the purpose of the kidnapping? She had nothing of value for ransom and she doubted Kristos or his family did either. What political motive could there be? None. Were they a bargaining chip to gain the release of prisoners? Perhaps. That would fail. The United States didn't negotiate with terrorists.

They were forced to wait. Patience. Kristos slept and she kept watch. The bed of the truck was a separate entity from the cab and there was no window to the front. The box they sat in was old, which meant worn wood allowed some light in. She frowned. She dug into her backpack for the jackknife she couldn't take through security but had kept in her suitcase during the flight and retrieved immediately after. She took it out and carefully rose to her feet. She shakily walked to the back of the truck, grateful for her petite stature that almost allowed her to stand upright.

She dragged her hand over the wood. Much of it was rotten and weak unlike the bed of the truck which had been replaced at some point.

Wedging the knife near a screw she managed to break the board loose. She tried the next one and got the one end completely free. Dust, sunlight, and air immediately entered the cramped oven they were trapped in. She moved to the other side and loosened those as well. She set the rotten board down against the wall. She looked out at the space left behind. What time of day was it anyway? She tried to find some way to pinpoint the time and their direction. The lush greenness they were racing through was a sharp contrast to the darkness they'd been trapped in.

I am with you.

Thank You, Jesus.

For some reason she believed she needed to put the board back up. She did and with the handle of the jackknife managed to get it to stay in place. When the door opened, that might dislodge it. While the board could be useful as a weapon, it wasn't prudent to attack until they understood the numbers they were facing and had a plan for escape. Would Kristos be able to fight? He was strong but would he do battle? Some men were wimpy. She didn't think that described the man resting across from her, drenched in sweat. She sat back down as the vehicle slowed. It turned abruptly, knocking her over and waking up Kristos.

She held her breath. The vehicle stopped and the driver turned off the truck and exited. Doors slammed. Voices could be heard but she couldn't decipher them. Kristos sat up and they waited.

Finally, the latch on the back of the truck was disengaged and the door opened with men standing there aiming rifles their direction. Eliza and Kristos held their hands up. A woman appeared and motioned for the men to drop their guns. The woman was older with threads of grey running through her black hair pulled back in a bun. Her dress was colorful with orange, yellow, and turquoise splashed on it. Her wrinkled brow and scowl did not match her outfit.

"*Bienvenido*," she said with stern authority. "Welcome. Come out."

Eliza thought of Jesus calling to Lazarus to come forth out of the grave. Hmmm. She must have been retaining some of what she'd read. Kristos rose. Bending over he extended a hand to her. She grabbed it and together they made it to the back of the truck. He jumped down first and reached to help her down. She appreciated not needing to jump with her prosthetic.

Her pants stuck to her skin and were damp and filthy. The sunshine blinded her. She clung to Kristos' hand. The woman standing before them waved the thugs away. That was the best way to describe them. She doubted they were official Mexican Army, but rather some kind of rogue band of men. Was this woman the leader? The men moved to a distance but did not disappear.

"Come with me." The woman spoke decent English, which meant they'd need to be careful. They followed her into a clean and tidy home with a solid wood floor polished to a shine and leather furniture in the living room. She motioned for them to sit.

"We're dirty," Eliza stated.

"Sit," the woman commanded.

Eliza shrugged and with Kristos following she sat on a sofa. Kristos sat next to her.

Oh, the cool leather and soft cushion were such a relief after that truck ride.

After demanding they sit, the woman rushed out of the room. She left a guard with a rifle standing outside the entrance.

Kristos once again grabbed her hand and squeezed three times. Whatever it meant she appreciated the encouragement it offered.

The air was cooler in this spacious room, with a window partially open, and a cross breeze to another farther away made the draperies flutter. A fan on the ceiling helped circulate the air as well.

Silence hung between them. Who had taken them? Why were they here? Where were they? Questions tumbled through her brain, but her training taught her to stay calm. Eliza closed her eyes as fatigue washed over her. Maybe in this lovely home there was a respite from the anxiety, where answers would come and not be as terrifying as the thoughts she could conjure up.

22

Kristos wanted to close his eyes. Eliza was an intrepid young woman. His admiration for her ability continued to rise. She was a believer, which meant she was no longer off limits. He almost chuckled out loud. As if now was the time to think about dating her. And they had done lunch twice already. They worked steadily together yesterday.

God must have a purpose in them being here at this time. He struggled to remain calm. How would they get out of this?

Eliza's arm went limp and her head rolled to the side. Neither of them slept well the previous night. Her face was flushed from the heat and a leftover from too much work in the sun yesterday. Her T-shirt was dirty. It matched his as they'd all worn team shirts the previous night. What a pair they were.

He surveyed the room the woman had escorted them to. Books on the shelf in English and Spanish. Decorations were homey, giving him hope they weren't doomed to torture or death. How was the team adapting to them being missing? Had they contacted any authorities? Would the mission continue or would they return to the United States due to possible danger? Did anyone in that village have a clue where Kristos and Eliza were?

When would they be alone long enough for him to use the satellite phone hidden in Eliza's backpack? How would anyone track them? Both of their cell phones were left back at the village, so no GPS advantage there.

Thank you, Lord, for preserving us this far and for giving me a capable woman to be going through this with, whatever this is. You are sovereign over it all. You can rescue us. You can show us a way out, a way home. Help me protect Eliza, Your daughter. Help us be a godly witness to You in this trial so those around us would know we belong to You and would see Your power.

What was he asking for? That they could sneak into the night? Where would they go? How would they get there? Eliza couldn't march through the rainforest for days. He wasn't too sure how well he'd do in that event. They didn't even have a clue as to who was holding them captive. They weren't tied up at least, and for that he was grateful. Maybe they'd even have indoor plumbing here. He was certain Eliza would appreciate that. He admired her practical nature when it came to things like that. Not that she wasn't modest. She was. But she wasn't having a meltdown over challenges like where to go to the bathroom and the lack of privacy.

Lord, help us sense Your presence among us. Help us. And give our families peace.

The woman strode back into the room followed by what could best be described as a servant or housekeeper who set a silver platter down with tall glasses with ice and what he assumed was lemonade. Small sandwiches were also on the plate.

Eliza startled awake. He gave her hand a squeeze.

"Eat and drink," the woman said.

"May I use the bathroom?" Eliza asked.

The woman nodded. "Rosa will show you where it is." She sat down as Eliza rose to exit the room.

He missed her presence at his side. *Please don't let them separate us.*

Eliza returned and sat.

"May I also use the bathroom?" Kristos asked. He followed the housekeeper down a hall to a small room. He shut the door. There was no lock. After using the facilities and washing his hands, he splashed his face with some water. He pulled his hair back again in a messy bun. It was filled with snarls that if he didn't work out soon, might force him to cut it short. His mother wouldn't mind. She thought his hairstyle was inappropriate for a good Greek-American man. She feared he would never find a woman to marry with his hair like that.

He grinned. He missed his mother and her delicious meals. His stomach growled. He followed the housekeeper back to the living room and sat next to Eliza.

"Eat and drink," the older woman commanded. The housekeeper left the room.

"I would like to pray first."

The woman waved a hand indicating permission. He held Eliza's hand and bent his head. "Heavenly Father, thank You for this food and for being with us always. Amen."

"Amen," Eliza whispered. She grabbed for a glass and took a sip. She closed her eyes as a soft smile played on her lips. "*Muy bueno*. It's very good." She reached for a plate and put a sandwich on it, bringing it back to her lap.

Kristos grabbed a glass and took a sip himself. He smiled and nodded his agreement. It was refreshing. He grabbed a plate and a sandwich. The baguette contained warm pork and seasonings. He took a bite and chewed. Oh, a slice of heaven.

Eliza bit into hers and nodded. "Eat slow," she whispered.

"*Si*, there is no rush. You Americans always try to go too fast with everything." The woman nodded her head.

Oh, he longed to blurt out a lot of questions but focused instead on the food. There was pleasure in the moment, and he had no clue when they'd eat again. He was sure this woman would reveal her purpose in due time. Pressing could accelerate things in a bad way. If curiosity could kill a cat, it could also eliminate Eliza and Kristos. Getting Eliza home safe was his top priority.

They both finished their sandwich and lemonade, placing the plates and glasses back on the serving tray.

"Rosa," the woman called.

The housekeeper came and grabbed the platter. "Will there be anything else, Señora?"

"Not right now." The woman waved a hand, shooshing the housekeeper from the room.

"I apologize if your journey here has lacked hospitality. Men can be obtuse and brutal, and had planned to only bring one of you, the leader. I'm not too disappointed to find they captured a sweet young woman as well."

Neither Eliza nor Kristos responded. Kristos swallowed hard. He was the target, not Eliza. She was collateral damage should these people not get what they wanted.

The old woman nodded. "I suppose you'll both have to do."

Kristos forbore asking and Eliza remained silent.

"Ah, so you are not going to ask? Hmmm, we will wait a little longer to tell you."

Frowning Kristos finally broke. "Thank you for the food and drink, but why are we here?"

"I'll let my husband inform you when he returns. You may rest here for the time being. Do not try to escape; the house is surrounded by guards and the rainforest has traps and enemies." She rose and left the room, closing the door behind her.

"Sorry, I couldn't wait any longer," Kristos whispered.

"It's OK. She didn't answer anyway, and we have a little comfort for now. We have no idea how long this will last."

"I suggest we rest." He leaned his head back and sensed Eliza doing the same.

When he awoke later, Eliza was leaning against him, still asleep. He surveyed the room again. No weapons to defend himself with. Even traditional tools for a fireplace were missing, so either they had none or removed them for this occasion.

The room was warmer than previously as the temperature rose. He guessed it was mid-afternoon at this point.

The housekeeper entered the room silently and placed a pitcher of water with ice and two glasses. She glanced his way, but her expression told him nothing.

He sat and waited for Eliza to wake up. Kristos was amazed she could even stand being next to him as he struggled to tolerate his body odor from all the sweating, partly from heat, and partly from fear. Eliza however had a faint scent of dirt, sunshine, and woman.

The sounds of commotion outside brought Eliza awake. Trucks were racing around and revving engines. As she sat up, Kristos leaned forward to fill the two glasses with water. He handed one to her.

"Drink slowly."

She nodded. They both understood the precarious nature of their situation. When would they get water again? It wasn't something they could hoard.

Where was their hostess? She hadn't made any other appearance, but the house was larger than most they'd seen in this area so she could be anywhere, even upstairs. She might have left.

The beautifully carved wood door swung open, and a bearded barrel-chested man entered. He wore camouflage and was accompanied by two armed guerillas.

"Ah, my wife told me we had visitors. I hope you've been treated well?"

Kristos nodded, his guard up. Unarmed, untrained, what could he do? He took a drink of his water.

"Hydration is important. We need to keep you both healthy and alive for the moment. Now, why don't you tell me your names and where you're from. Ladies first." He sat in a chair across from them and leaned forward, elbows on his knees and hands clasped as he waited for the information he sought.

"Specialist Eliza Torres, United States Army."

Their captor's eyes grew wide. "I'm impressed. What's an Army Specialist doing in Mexico?"

"On leave to help rebuild a school," Eliza stated in a strong, steady voice.

The man nodded. He focused on Kristos. "Your turn."

"Kristos Sava, Colorado Springs, Colorado, United States of America."

The man squinted his eyes. "She is Hispanic, but you are not."

"American, sir. She is my wife." Kristos took a sip of water.

"Fair enough. Mr. Sava and Specialist Torres-Sava, you will be my guests for a while. I cannot keep you here but will do what I can to make you comfortable." He motioned for a man behind him. "Carlos, take their picture, please."

The man allowed his rifle to hang from its strap and pulled out a phone and snapped a few photos. Kristos stared into the camera but didn't smile. He wasn't sure what Eliza did.

"You are probably curious as to why you are here and not working hard to rebuild that school. My name is Santiago Gutierrez, and my brother Eliud Perez was captured by your FBI in the United States. They lie and say he smuggled drugs into your fine land. Now why would we want to do something like this? You are what we call leverage. They release my brother, and I release you both. Since I obtained a double bargain, I can kill one of you to prove my sincerity if your government will not cooperate. The question is, who would I kill first? The woman or the large man who appears to want to protect her as if she were a fragile flower?"

Eliza stiffened next to Kristos. "I am no fragile flower," she hissed.

"Any volunteers?" he asked.

Kristos and Eliza both kept quiet.

Santiago tilted his head. "Interesting. I wonder why neither of you will volunteer?"

"The United States Government does not negotiate with terrorists," Eliza stated in a firm tone.

Laughing, Santiago shook his head. "I am no terrorist, and neither is my brother. His arrest was a misunderstanding." His face lost the friendliness as he frowned. "Enough. Take them away, men. Carlos, send the photo and our demands."

Kristos had finished his water. He placed the glass on the tray and Eliza did likewise.

"I would like to use the restroom before we go anywhere, and I'm sure my wife would as well."

"Fine," Santiago motioned for Eliza to go first. Kristos remained seated. When she returned, he was allowed to go. When he exited a man nudged him with the barrel of his rifle toward the door. Eliza was no longer inside. An old, mud-covered pickup truck was parked out front and they were put in the open bed. This time the guerillas put handcuffs on them, attaching the other end of each to a side of the truck. They were on opposite sides. Wherever they were going, they were going to be dealing with the dust, wind, and heat for the ride. Both sat facing each other.

Eliza was stoic. She'd never seemed timid to him before, but this situation brought out a steel will buried deep inside her. He understood she had some burdens she carried and hoped they wouldn't be a problem if this thing went on too long.

A truck followed them with more armed men. How could they even consider the two of them to be this valuable?

Barring a miracle, both would be dead soon.

Lord, help us.

23

Eliza sighed as she tried find a comfortable position on the metal truck bed. Kristos didn't appear to be enjoying the ride either. At times, the tall trees of the rainforest around them blocked the sun. She thought they were heading farther south. She wasn't well acquainted with Mexico. Were they headed toward the Atlantic or Pacific side of the country? What did it even matter? Only it gave her mind something to ponder instead of worrying about being tortured or killed.

They'd only been gone one full day. It already seemed like longer than that. It was too soon to hope that someone somewhere had rallied a rescue operation. Even if they had, how would they find them? Would the military come in to help them escape? She never had any interest in being in a black operations situation, much less one where she was an object to be acquired and saved. How else would they ever get free?

She longed for conversation but the truck was loud and the windows were open in the cab so their captors would be privy to anything they said. She tried to be content with waiting until they were alone again. She hoped they didn't separate them. It wasn't like they were dangerous armed prisoners.

Drugs and human trafficking were the crimes Eliud was accused of. It was good he was captured but apparently their little cartel wasn't big enough to get him free on their own. Or so inept as to get caught. She was glad the man was in prison and did not want to be exchanged for someone like that who held no regard for the lives he ruined in pursuit of money.

Hours later they arrived at another compound. There was a charming home and some smaller ones around it. The landscaping was lovely. In another situation she'd have enjoyed vacationing here.

But this was no vacation.

One of the men removed Eliza's handcuffs and dragged her off the truck with Kristos following. Eliza rubbed her aching wrists. The Mexican kidnappers yelled slurs in Spanish and used their guns to push Kristos and Eliza forward as they followed another man down a walkway around to the back of the house. There sat a smaller building with bars in the windows. The man opened the door with a key and shoved them in. There was a small bathroom in one corner. She hoped there would be running water.

There was one twin bed, two wooden chairs and a small table and a small sink. A box sat on the table along with two plastic glasses.

"Get inside. We'll bring you some food. The water is drinkable and there are plastic cups over there."

She stepped farther into the room to allow Kristos to follow her. The door slammed shut behind them. The click of the lock spoke the finality of their situation. She frowned. "First dibs on the bathroom." She rushed to the small space and closed the door. At least there would be a tiny modicum of privacy here.

When she exited, she went to the sink to wash her hands. She shook off the dampness. Kristos handed her a glass of water before he entered the bathroom. Eliza sipped it. It tasted good. She walked around the small space. The windows with no glass were a nice touch but contained metal bars. There were shutters that could be closed from the inside. Might help with bugs or if the weather got bad. She set her glass down on the table and lowered herself into a chair. She tugged off her backpack and rolled up her pant leg on her right leg. She pulled off the prosthetic and began to peel the layers down to her stump to let it breathe. The stump was red from the heat and sweat. Too bad she hadn't packed anti-inflammatories in her bag. There were some in her suitcase, but how far away was that by now? She leaned back and let the prosthetic stand free.

Kristos exited, grabbed the other glass, and sipped. He peeked out the windows before joining her on the other chair. "At least we aren't bouncing around in that truck. There's one guard I can locate, but he's farther away from our hut. Can you get out the satphone?"

Eliza opened the bag and dug for the phone buried at the bottom. She pulled it out and handed it to Kristos. "Will they even be able to locate us?"

"Guess we'll find out." He dialed and spoke to someone on the other end before hanging up. "We'll try again soon to make sure they can track us."

"Who was it?"

"My brother Rusty. He was aware we'd been taken and contacted the feds. We'll call back to make sure they got our signal."

"Not sure what they can do about it. They have no authority here."

After another call, they settled into silence. Eliza let her mind wander to her time with Mandy. Why had she run? Why couldn't she continue to stare into that horse's eyes? Those big beautiful brown orbs that turned on a projector inside Eliza, showing her a scene she'd not recalled before. It had been horrible. As if she could sense the heat of the flames and the force of the blast pushing the air from her lungs. She couldn't breathe.

"Eliza? Are you OK?" Kristos asked.

"Huh?" Eliza blinked rapidly. She wasn't in the barn with Mandy or being blown up. She was here with Kristos and while captured, they were relatively unharmed by their adventure so far.

"You're breathing accelerated, and I thought you were having a heart attack—or saw something that terrified you."

A shiver overtook her body. "Nothing more than a horrific memory."

"I'm sorry."

Eliza turned to focus on him. Kristos was tall, strong, handsome, and a gentleman through and through even if he currently appeared worse for wear. "It's not your fault."

"Do you want to talk about it?"

"Not especially."

"There's nothing else to do to pass the time. The guys in the truck you drove. Were you close to them?"

"Cliff Barnes, Bart Clayton, and Hal Zarenski were the best. Zarenski was a Private First Class and Barnes and Clayton were both E4s. They were like big brothers to me, but all the guys were since they towered over me. Initially, I got hazed, but over time I won their respect. We played cards, frisbee, even basketball. I was surprisingly fast and could shoot a basket if I could find a spot between all those long arms and big hands." She chuckled at the memory. "They treated me like one of the guys but respected that I was a woman."

"Nothing romantic between you and any of them?" Kristos asked.

Eliza shook her head. "Not that they didn't try. I wasn't open to that. I couldn't envision a way forward if the relationship broke up. I thought someday if they were stationed elsewhere and friendship developed well enough it might be worth the risk, but not on deployment. I'm not a roll-in-the-hay kind of gal."

The memories of their faces that last day flitted across her memory and the tears came. "I can still see them that day, joking around and on the trip before the event. I can't wrap my mind around the fact that they don't exist anymore. That I can't pick up a phone and give them a call to check on how they're doing. That we can't laugh and joke. Maybe it's good that I lost my leg and can't go back. I would be searching for them and expecting to find them."

"Have you ever cried over their deaths before?"

"No." She hadn't wanted to acknowledge to herself the finality of their passing. It's like they vanished as much as her leg did, although she understood there was something for the doctors to remove initially. Now that she pondered it, it crushed her. She wished she could have died with them. Sometimes living was too painful, aside from losing her leg.

"It's OK to cry."

She did. She let the tears flow. Her head throbbed from the heat, the dust, the bumpy ride, and her sorrow. The lost time she'd spent spinning her wheels trying to figure out what would be next. The days and nights lost in a haze of alcohol to numb the pain deep inside she couldn't explain. So much time wasted. It had gotten her nowhere.

She sighed. "You realize the US government will never release this Eliud dude. Eventually they will kill us."

Kristos nodded. "Yeah, I've considered that. I'm at peace with where I'm going, and I'm grateful you're headed there too. Still, I'm praying God finds us a way out of this mess without either of us needing to be delivered home in caskets if we even get that much."

Eliza shivered again. The day was brutally hot. Even with the shutters open there was no breeze and the stagnant air weighed down on her. The thick musty smell assaulted her senses. Her red and swollen wrist throbbed. Her stump ached. Everything hurt.

"Heaven sounds nice though. I'm not afraid of dying anymore—although I do have a healthy fear of the process it might take to get there. I'd avoid that if I could." She sighed.

"I agree."

"We must be away from significant civilization given the number of cans of fuel on the truck with us during the drive. No close gas stations," Eliza said.

"We haven't seen anyone so far other than the thugs that brought us here."

"Yeah. Makes you wonder if there isn't something bigger going on."

"Listen, you need to rest your leg. Why don't you lie on the bed for now. There's nothing else to do at the moment," Kristos said.

Eliza nodded. "Can you help me over? I'm missing a leg."

Kristos rose to help her hop to the bed. She collapsed on the mattress, which was surprisingly comfortable.

"You may regret this, Kristos. I may not be willing to get out of here any time soon."

"It's fine. I've slept on stable floors with my horses, but at least then there was hay to soften things. Rest. I'll keep watch for now, not that there's anything to see."

Eliza rolled to her side where she could see Kristos and closed her eyes. In seconds, she was out.

Kristos watched Eliza sleep. Even though she was sunburned and dirty, she was adorable to him. He longed to join her in the bed but didn't dare. He rose and paced the small room, stopping to stare out the windows, hoping for clues as to where they were as well as to catch the slightest hint of a breeze. It didn't help. *Lord, please help us out here. Free us and keep us safe so we can continue to honor and serve You with our lives. Help me protect Eliza should the need arise. I love and worship You alone.*

He grabbed a comb out of his back pocket and began to work through the snarls in his curly hair. When he finished, he dampened it with some water and managed to pull it back into a bun. He splashed water on his face, hoping it would cool him off. He finally pulled off his shirt, since Eliza was sleeping, and used water to clean off his torso a little and then ran the shirt under some water to try to clean it. He rung it out and placed it over the extra chair to dry. He leaned back in his chair feeling a little fresher and resting his head against the wall of the cabin, he drifted to sleep himself, hoping help was on the way.

24

Long days passed. Even keeping a tally, it was hard to grasp the length of time. Eliza grew antsy. The sound of tree frogs at night provided a comforting song to sleep to, but the other bugs that crept into their little space were a nuisance—especially the mosquitoes. Keeping the windows closed provided relief from bugs but left them suffocating from the weight of heat. Occasionally, the engines of trucks rumbled in the distance. She was tuned into the clumping of boots headed to their cabin, signifying either a delivery of food, or a possible end to this imprisonment.

They'd done well in passing the time. Kristos would share Scriptures with Eliza and help her work to memorize them. He taught her some of the older hymns and even some newer worship choruses. She enjoyed listening to his voice. They'd tried to keep any noise down to avoid notice from the guard. Kristos told her how Paul and Silas had been in prison and singing praises to God and God miraculously opened the doors and they walked out free.

She doubted that would happen to them. Even if they could walk out, where would they go?

Her stump improved, and she put the prosthetic on during the day and they marched around the small room challenging each other to sit-ups, pushups, trying to stay strong. The food they'd been given was adequate. Kristos called his brother on the satphone again to learn what was up but while they were aware of their location, there was no news as to when or if a rescue had been planned.

She'd learned how the Bible mentioned not knowing the day or the hour of the Lord's return and that they needed that same kind of readiness for their souls as they did for the physical rescue they longed for.

"'Be strong and courageous, do not be afraid or in dread of them, for the Lord your God is the One who is going with you. He will not desert you or abandon you.' Deuteronomy 31:6," she quoted.

Kristos had been gazing out the window. "What?"

"That was the first verse you taught me. You take disciple-making seriously. You've not let this time go to waste. I appreciate that. While I would like to be able to read the Bible you gave me, I'm getting the Cliff Notes version."

Kristos grinned. "Can I tell you a secret?"

"Why not? Who would I tell?"

"I'm dyslexic. I struggled in school and that's why I dropped out of college. I've done a lot of audiobooks of the Bible to help me as I read it."

"Sounds like it takes effort."

He nodded. "And discipline. I'm grateful for it now when there's no access to a Bible. God brings up those passages and lessons to my memory. Having you here to share them with helps."

"I'm in seminary without books," she joked.

"Kind of. Listening to my dad's and other sermons over the years and doing audiobooks on subjects surrounding theology, helped me retain the information."

"That helps for now, but what if we're here for another week, a month, a year, or several years? What if our caretakers left and never returned?"

"'Finally, brothers and sisters, whatever is true, whatever is honorable, whatever is right, whatever is pure, whatever is lovely, whatever is commendable, if there is any excellence and if anything worthy of praise, think about these things.' Philippians 4:8."

"You've mentioned that one before," Eliza groused. The thought of being there for years depressed her.

"Let's try it since it's Paul's prescription for gloomy thinking. What is true?"

"We are in Mexico. In prison," Eliza stated, crossing her arms as she sat in one of the chairs.

"We have fresh air, sunshine, running water, indoor plumbing, a bed, we are fed three meals a day…"

"There's not a lot of creativity there; it's getting boring."

"Nevertheless, we are fed and we are not abused. They kept us together. Going through this alone would be harder."

"Yeah, I guess you're right."

"We both love the Lord and put our hope in Him. Now, what is honorable?" he asked.

"You letting me sleep on the bed alone."

"And the fact that they've not harmed us. What about right?"

"Right? Right is not giving into the government demands which results in us staying here forever."

"Come on, Eliza, you can do better than that," Kristos challenged.

She sighed. "Fine, right is you never coming on to me, and our talking about God, the Bible, and singing songs."

Kristos grinned and it gave her a tingle all the way to even her phantom toes.

"How about pure?"

Eliza frowned. "We've not had sex so that's pure, right?"

Kristos nodded. "I think that qualifies. What about lovely?"

"I know what it isn't—you or me at the moment in our filthy, stinky clothes and hair."

"I'll agree with you but there is loveliness here. How about fresh water? Sunshine? The trees out there?"

"OK, you win on that one. What's next?"

"Commendable," Kristos answered.

"You not taking advantage of me or treating me as helpless."

"I could say the same for you. You've handled yourself well through this crisis."

Eliza shook her head. "Except for my negative-Nelly thinking."

Kristos chuckled. "God understands our weaknesses and gave us each other so we don't stay there for long. Guess I'm commending

God, who is also pure, lovely, honorable…"

"What's next?"

"Excellent and worthy of praise," Kristos said.

"I guess you nailed it on the last one—only God is truly all those things. He provided for our needs, including our need for each other. I'm glad that if I had to get abducted it was with you by my side."

"Thanks, Eliza. I could say the same for you. I'm glad you decided to come to Mexico, not only because you are here with me now, but because you submitted yourself to Jesus."

"For those things I will be grateful. This situation I'm having a harder time with, but you have helped. We aren't as bad off as we could be."

"Exactly."

"Don't you think we'll get sick of each other if we're here for years?"

Kristos shook his head. "I hope we don't need to find out, but as for me, I doubt I could ever get sick of you."

Eliza's face grew warm.

As supper was brought, Kristos tried once again to engage the soldier in conversation. For days there had been no response. Tonight was different.

"Hurricane coming." He handed Kristos a box containing food.

"How close to the coast are we?" Kristos asked.

The man didn't smile or answer. He backed up and locked the door.

"Hurricane? Did he say hurricane?" Eliza asked.

"He did. It felt like we drove straight up the mountains so we shouldn't worry about flooding or anything like that."

"High winds and heavy rains can still cause landslides and make roads impassable."

Kristos set the box down on the floor, finding the chair, he sat and began to rummage through the contents. "Crackers, some fresh fruit, dried fruit, bread, and peanut butter, jelly." Kristos frowned. "No knife to cut any of it. No silverware of any kind, not even the plastic spoons."

"At least we saved some of those. We'll make do. It's better than nothing."

The wind picked up and for once a breeze began blowing through the room. Kristos ran to peer out the window but couldn't see much of anything beyond the trees. The sky had grown darker. "Eliza, come and look."

Eliza was soon next to him. "Oh boy, yeah this isn't going to be your average storm. We'll need to close the shutters, but I wonder if those will hold. They only have that little hook and eye set up."

"We'll deal with that when we need to. For now, we need to be ready. Grab the satphone, please," Kristos asked.

Eliza fetched it for him and handed it over. "What's the point?"

"My peace of mind." He dialed. "Hey, Rusty? Any news?"

"The feds aren't telling me anything except the news this morning was that Eliud Perez was killed in prison. The only trade they could make now is with a dead body. How are you doing?"

"We're enjoying our luxury mountain resort and Eliza is the best vacation companion ever, but there's a hurricane bearing down on us from what we've been told."

"I'm sorry I don't have better news. We're continuing to pray. Love you, bro."

"Ditto." The call disconnected and Kristos shut the phone down and they stashed it back in the bag.

"What news?" Eliza asked.

"Eliud Perez was murdered."

"Oh." She slumped into her chair. "We're doomed." Eliza deflated like a popped balloon.

"Not necessarily. We can't be held accountable for what happened over there. He was killed in prison, not by the government," Kristos said, needing to somehow reassure Elisa.

"Much of policing in Mexico is corrupt. They'll believe the death was intentional and instigated by the US government."

"Conspiracy theorist?"

"Not usually, but let's consider that our chances of surviving this kidnapping drastically decreased."

"Life is terminal," Kristos said matter of factually.

"I know we all die someday. We often don't have any say in the how or the when."

"Hey, what's gotten into you? Why are you all of a sudden so on edge?"

"Oh, you're Susie Sunshine, aren't you?" Eliza mocked then shook her head. "I'm sorry. I guess I held this elusive hope that the US military would send someone for us, but with the storm bearing down, that's unlikely and with the news of Eliud's death, we won't have much time after the storm subsides before we're eliminated as collateral damage."

"Hey, sweetheart. It's going to be fine no matter what happens. Our eternal destiny is secure, and in the meantime, we have the Lord and each other," Kristos reminded her.

"And food, water, and shelter," Eliza added.

Kristos nodded. Had he just called her sweetheart? She didn't protest. The more time he spent with this remarkable young woman the more he found he wanted to know about her.

"We'll keep the windows open for now, but the minute things appear like they're getting nasty, we'll close them."

"Sounds like a plan." Eliza settled back into her chair, took a deep breath, and released it slowly.

Kristos came to sit next to her. "The other day you mentioned you had a pet. What is it?"

"A blue-and-gold macaw named Ramsey. I got him free from a guy being deployed. Thought it would be fun to own a bird. The guy told me the bird would talk, but it won't. It only squawks."

"Do you let him out of his cage? Does he try to bite you?"

"Nah, he's tame. He'll sit on my arm or the chair. He likes it when I preen the pinfeathers he can't access. He's friendly enough but won't talk no matter how much I try to tempt him with special treats."

"Do you still give him the treat?"

"Yeah."

"So, you reward him for not talking."

Eliza leaned her head back as she groaned. "Why didn't I think of that? I wanted him to like me. Now what do I do?"

"Maybe the guy lied and he really can't talk. Or what he has to say isn't fit for your ears." Kristos grinned.

Eliza chuckled. "If that's the case, I guess I need to let it go and accept Ramsey the way he is, a big messy noisemaker who occasionally lets me pet him."

"How big is he?"

"He's about three feet from top of his head to tail and weighs around three pounds. His cage is taller than I am."

"You like big birds and I like big horses."

"Yeah, I guess so."

"Did you have any pets growing up?"

Eliza shook her head. "No. My dad was an over-the-road truck driver, and my mom was a nurse. I think they believed taking care of me was more than enough to deal with."

"Where are your parents?"

"Dad died when I was thirteen. Complications from diabetes. Mom just got remarried. She sold our house in Nashville and is moving to Arizona."

"She just got married? Have you met the man?"

"No. Apparently, Nigel is wonderful. I hope he is for my mom's sake. They were going to wait and have a big wedding but decided to elope instead."

"You didn't get to be there for the wedding?" Kristos asked, he couldn't imagine not being there for a family wedding.

"No, but that's OK. I'm sadder about losing my safe place to land—that house in Nashville. I'm in no position to purchase a house, so that wasn't an option but it makes me feel like I'm—"

"Homeless?"

Eliza nodded. "Mom and I were close until I went to the Army. I guess my leaving the nest left a void in her life."

"Only natural. She'd been a widow for many years. That had to be tough."

"It was, but we had each other. I still miss my dad."

"Who are your closest friends?"

"My high school friend Rachel. We used to talk daily until I entered the military. She's married and has two kids and still lives in Tennessee. I was close to some of the men in my squad, but women in that arena are harder to come by for friendships. How about you?"

"What about me?"

"Friends?"

Kristos grinned. "I have three friends from high school. Michael, Jeremiah, and Peter. Michael's getting married this fall. Maybe you'd be so kind as to be my plus one?"

"Hold the bus, you have a friend named Jeremiah?"

"And he is not a bullfrog."

They both chuckled as the wind picked up.

"Maybe it's time I closed this window. We can keep the other one open for now." Kristos rose and closed the window shutters. "Just seems so wrong to have these on the inside of the house but with no glass windows and bars I suppose it makes sense. Someone planned ahead or there have been others before us."

Eliza shivered.

"You cold?"

"No, just wondering what happened to those others."

"Try not to let your mind go there. Now back to your willingness to be my plus one? I'm handling the horses for that so most of the time I'll be busy. But not too busy for a dance with you."

"He's one of your best friends, but you're not standing up as a groomsman?"

"Oh, I am that, but on the end because I'll be transporting the bride so I can't be up there ahead of time."

"If we get out of here, I'll think about it."

"Promise?"

"Yes." Eliza grinned at Kristos and his heart did a flip flop. He hoped for the sake of his own purity that they weren't trapped here for too long because even dirty and bedraggled, Eliza had released a tornado of desire in his own heart.

"Who's your favorite horse?" Eliza asked.

"Zena. She's an old mare who I volunteered to take when she lost her usefulness to the previous owner. I can still ride her, and she's got a lot of wisdom behind those eyes. I can tell her anything and she'll love me."

"I'm sure your mother loves you," Eliza offered.

Kristos grinned. "Yes, but I can't tell her all my secrets, fears, and dreams."

Eliza raised her eyebrows. "Can you tell me?"

25

liza waited for Kristos to respond. Her pulse accelerated and she'd been tapping her foot, the real one, for a few minutes since he'd shut the one window.

Kristos walked toward the window again. "The temperature is dropping and it's starting to rain. We must be on the edge of the storm. I've noticed our guards have abandoned us to seek shelter."

He was avoiding her question. "I can't blame them. Too bad they couldn't have let us join them in the comfort of the big house."

"Nah. We're better off here where no one gets trigger happy and decides to play chicken with their bullets."

Kristos closed and latched the shutters but opened one up again. "We haven't checked the light in here. Does it work today?"

Eliza went to the switch on the wall by the door. She flipped it and the light went on. "Guess we're good. I'm glad the one in the bathroom works, it's a tiny space, but still."

"Agreed." He closed the window. This was something they had done at night, but this was different. It was daytime and would likely be at least a day or more before they could open them again.

Or before anyone would come to bring them food. Or release them. Or kill them.

Eliza had never been fond of storms, but since the event, storms were at times more challenging. There was medication at home to help her calm down. At home. Not that it mattered. It would have been left at the church when they were kidnapped anyway.

Kristos came to sit next to her on the bed. He put an arm around her. "I wasn't avoiding your question. At some point I will share more with you. Right now, it doesn't seem helpful. You're scared and so am I, but God is aware of the past, present, and future. He doesn't promise to deliver us from this but He is with us. Remember the story from the Old Testament about the three men who went into the fiery furnace that we shared with our missionary team?"

"Because they wouldn't worship an idol?"

"Right. But what happened?"

"They trusted God whether they would be burned alive or survive."

"Can you imagine? A furnace like that your chances of dying are 100 percent and yet, God was there with them, and they didn't burn or get singed." He let his arm drop. "No matter how dreadful things get, He is with us and our home in heaven is waiting. Nothing can happen to us that He doesn't permit. Not that He wants them to happen, but He always has a plan to use events to bring honor and glory to Himself."

An otherworldly energy emanated from Kristos when he talked to her about the Bible. She hadn't put her finger on it until now. Even with the dim lighting, he glowed with the love of Jesus. Covered in dirt, yet he was radiant—beautiful even. Was Kristos human? Could he be an angel?

She kept her musings to herself. "Do you want to rest for a while?" Eliza patted the bed.

"Nah, you can rest. I might stretch out on the floor if I get bored or tired. It might get noisy later so catch some zzzz's while you can."

Eliza stretched out on the bed, leaving her prosthetic on. She turned her back to the room to face the wall and closed her eyes.

Boom! Crack!

Eliza screamed as everything around her was on fire. Was that Hal calling from the truck? How had she been thrown? Her heart raced and she tried to rise but a hand on her shoulder caught her attention.

"Help. Someone! The guys in the truck! We need to get them all out," she pleaded as she fought him.

"Eliza. Tornado. It's Kristos. You're safe. It's only a nightmare."

That smooth voice brought her back to the present. She dripped with sweat. Kristos helped her sit up. Foot finally on the floor, she shook as he wrapped his arms around her and drew her close to his chest.

"You're OK, we'll be OK." He rubbed her back gently and her breathing slowed.

She sucked in a shaky breath and sat up. The room was darker. "Did you turn out the light?"

Kristos shook his head. "We lost power, which likely means no water either. Thankfully that one plastic container was handy to fill. I did that while you rested, just in case."

"Good thinking. No flushing then either."

"We'll be out of here soon so don't worry about that. We had a crack of lightning close by. The storm's become pretty nasty out there. Was that what startled you?"

Eliza shrugged, not that Kristos could see that. "Maybe. It was horrible. If this is what healing is like I'd rather go back to amnesia."

"It must have been horrible. I'm sorry you went through that."

"Thanks. Me too, but then, I never would have met you or Jesus."

"Jesus would have found a way."

"No excuses, right?"

"What?"

"Your dad preached about all people being without excuse in knowing God because creation itself testifies to Him."

"Yeah, no excuses. But I agree, your life wouldn't be the same if you hadn't met me. You wouldn't be stuck here in the mountains of Mexico. I'd be here all by myself and you could be who knows where."

"Or dead. There's no reason for me to have survived that explosion. I should have died with my team."

"Would that have been a better outcome?"

"Definitely not. I didn't know Jesus. I'd be in hell. I escaped my own fiery furnace I guess."

"We could play the what if game if you wanted. If the guitarist hadn't been sick, I wouldn't have been at that bar the first night we met."

"If I wasn't hungry for Mexican food and Gabby brought me, then I wouldn't have been there. If I hadn't been trying to numb my pain with beer, I might not have had the guts to come check you out."

"If you weren't so cute that guy wouldn't have tried hitting on you," Kristos offered.

"And you might not have had a beer bath."

They both chuckled.

"I hate beer," Kristos said.

"I gave up drinking, but I admit I have really wanted to drink a few at times."

"I'm glad to hear you stopped. I'm not opposed to a drink, but just don't see a need for it. I've tried it but didn't like the taste."

"That's cool. I can appreciate that. So, lots of ifs went into our meeting," Eliza said.

"Yup. And now look where we are." His dry tone made her chuckle.

She grabbed his hand and gave it a squeeze. "I'm glad that if I must go through this, you're here with me. I was afraid they would separate us."

"I feared that too, but I prayed God would allow us to stay together."

"I'm glad He gave you your request. You did pray for rescue, too, right?"

"Of course. We've both prayed that."

Another crack of lightning lit up their dark space and shook the ground beneath them. Kristos held her close as she shivered in his arms.

She gulped. "That was close."

"Yeah."

"I don't think either of us are going to be able to get back to sleep at this point. How about some food?" Eliza broke away and slowly moved toward the small table where the box was. "There were raisins in here, right?"

"I think so. I had a cracker earlier. They're stale but it's still sustenance."

"Yeah." She came back to sit on the bed next to him and pried open the box of raisins. "These were never my favorite food, but something a little sweet sounds good."

"What will you want to eat when you're free to do so?" Kristos asked.

"Probably fresh fruit. Pineapple sounds yummy."

"That's a good one. How about the main course?" Kristos asked.

"I don't think it's good for us to play this game. It makes it hard to appreciate the simple fare we have."

"I agree." Silence fell between them as the storm raged outside.

Kristos awoke on the floor and his body ached. He rose to stretch and check out the window. The worst of the storm had passed. There were trees down and it continued to rain. The chilled muggy air forced him to close the shutters again. He prayed the storm wouldn't create mud in their dirt floor prison. It was a wonder this poorly constructed hut stood against the winds.

Maybe now they'd get electricity back and regular meals.

He peeked out the other window, which allowed him a view of part of the house. It was still dark out. There was still no guard. No lights on in the house, and no cars or trucks visible on the side like there had been in the past. He closed the window again and found a chair. He sat down and thought about the last ten days more or less.

By now, the team would have returned to the United States, unless they were forced to leave immediately in the wake of their disappearance, deeming the mission unsafe. Would they bring back his stuff and Eliza's?

What a silly and materialistic thing to even be thinking about. The contents of a suitcase?

Were his parents worried? He was tempted to try the satphone but resisted. He didn't want to wear down any battery, and there was no clue as to how long this ordeal would continue. Eliza was a trooper. He was nearing the end of his tether with this extended imprisonment. He wondered if she was as well.

What was the worst thing that could happen? Well, he could think of two: they were killed, not the worst thing as they'd go to heaven. But if they were abandoned here with little food and no running water? They wouldn't last very long, and that could be a less appealing way to die.

Morbid thoughts to be sure. He wasn't even certain about what day of the week it was.

Kristos silently paced as Eliza slept. Sure, she was filthy and had a body odor, but she had been more resilient than he'd anticipated. Loneliness pierced his soul.

A lone owl's hooting mirrored the hollowness he experienced inside. He recognized that superstition in this culture meant death was near. Sobering thought. As if every breath he took wasn't a gift from God. Yet, agitation ate at him. He'd been gone for a week or so on mission trips before, but it finally hit him, this was the longest he'd been away from his family.

Was he homesick? Perhaps. He longed to confide in Zena as if she had the power to help him. He imagined his mom setting a table with all her wonderful food on a Sunday night and the laughter and sometimes spirited debates that took place among him and his siblings. Here he thought he was so independent, even from a younger age taking care of his siblings and the barn and property.

Was he too connected to his family? Alexos had gone all over the world in the Army. Rusty took people on adventure trips, climbed mountains, rescued people…And what did Kristos do? He played with horses.

Kristos worked hard but he'd never been far from his family. Even on mission trips he'd often texted or sent photos at times to his mom or one of his siblings or even his friends. Now, other than fifteen-second conversations with Rusty on the satphone, there had been nothing. No hint of whether they missed him or were worried.

Did his life matter at all? He'd been part of seeing Eliza come to know Jesus but was there more than that? Did raising horses honor God? Was he missing out on something bigger?

Why was he filled with all this self-doubt now? A crisis of faith? A dark night of the soul?

It was as if he'd tumbled into a deep dark hole and not even Eliza could reach him here. Was that what her PTSD did to her?

Was this his defining moment? His trauma experience that he'd need to recover from?

Kristos grabbed a stale cracker and nibbled on it slowly. He followed that with a few sips of water. He again paced the small room.

He leaned his head against the bars that kept them from escaping. He was physically and emotionally trapped. When had this much ever been required of him?

I don't think I can do it, Lord. I don't know what to do. I'm going crazy in this tiny hut and am desperate to move outside. That's where he'd always find his solace, with the horses or out on horseback. He did his best thinking in those moments. While Eliza had been a trooper through it all, he wearied from trying to keep both their spirits up. There was comfort and safety in sharing Scriptures, but he longed for more in a relationship.

If he was this lonely now, with just one woman for comfort and conversation, how would he do as a husband? Would he be able to lead his family with the strength of his father, Theodore Sava? The man had been a rock. Unshakable through the trials and challenges that come from raising a family, working a farm, and then being called to pastor a church. Kristos realized he took for granted that it was easy for his father.

Maybe it wasn't and he was believing in a delusion. Had he been so wrapped up in his horses that he missed the struggle his father faced when Rusty fell off that cliff, or when their mom had breast cancer? How about when Alexos was injured and almost died? Life hadn't been rosy, but for some reason Kristos had failed to register the hurt and anguish those moments had to have caused.

So here he stood, his head leaning against cool wet metal bars, trapped and helpless to escape while caring for a woman he deeply admired. If he couldn't lead in this moment, would he ever be good enough to lead as a husband and father?

Was that why he hung around the horses? They didn't demand nearly as much from him as this trial did.

You can do all things through Christ who gives you strength.

Kristos looked up to the heavens. It was almost as if a voice had spoken out loud to his heart. Tears flowed down his cheeks. *Help me, Lord. I'm not as strong as I look. I can't do this anymore. I'm scared.*

No matter how much I quote those verses and pretend the bravado, I'm terrified. I'm trying to trust You. I know You see me. See us. I know You have a plan, but I'm stuck here in this moment, blind to the bigger picture and I can't stand it.

Again, the voice...*My strength is found in your weakness.*

Kristos didn't understand. How did being weak and falling apart after almost two weeks of this imprisonment enable God to be strong? *I'm not trying to disparage You, Lord. I know You are strong and capable of rescuing us, but in this moment, I struggle to believe You will do that for us. Help me trust You. I can't do this anymore.*

The moon peeked out from behind some clouds and the brightness caught his attention. It was almost as if God said, "I'm here." As if God were the man in the moon. He chuckled at his own corniness. He could imagine his brother Rusty laughing along with him. The moon disappeared behind the clouds shrouding the world and the cabin in complete darkness once gain.

A deep peace washed over him, and he sat in a chair near the window, trying to think about his family and pray for them. He realized he'd been so focused on their situation he'd not even prayed for anyone else other than him and Eliza. How self-focused this misadventure had become for him. Instead, he interceded for his family, the people he knew who had challenges, the group who was no longer in Mexico but enjoying their lives and clueless about what was going on with him and Eliza.

Sounds of Eliza stirring caught his attention.

"Kristos?"

"Over here."

"Is the storm over?" she asked.

He paused before answering, thinking she might be referring to his middle-of-the-night meltdown with God. While he had peace right now, it was something tenuous and fragile. "Either it's over or we're in the eye of it. It's raining and cool but pretty mild as far as wind goes."

"I thought the eye was sunny and just like a regular day?"

"If that's the case, we're not there. As far as I can tell, it's pre-dawn perhaps? Where we are in this is beyond me," Kristos said.

"You sound, different. Are you OK?"

"It was a rough night for me."

"How so?"

The darkness was a cloak of safety. She'd been honest about her struggles so why would he hide his own? Just to look good to her?

"I'm tired of this. I'm struggling to trust God to rescue us. I miss my family, my horses. I'm struggling with whether I'm doing enough in my life that would have value. Do you know this is the longest I've been away from home? I couldn't even move off the property but built that apartment for the convenience of being close to the horses."

"What's wrong with that? It's your job. It's a practical solution."

"Sure it is, but I'm realizing I haven't really cut the apron strings as it were. I'm so connected to my family I'm questioning who I am apart from them."

Eliza sighed. "You and I have the opposite problem, huh? You're too close to home and I've no home at all to return to. I guess if I had a choice, I'd prefer what you have. Unless your family is filled with jerks then I recant my wish."

Kristos chuckled. "I'll admit my older brothers used to razz me and my sisters can be annoying, but none of them are jerks. They are actually pretty cool people, and I'm glad God put me in this family."

"Siblings are a gift. I think I've always been more of a loner as an only child. I've traveled far from home to find myself…and I'm still working on that. You have a home, a family to turn to, a job…even Rusty's been able to talk to you on the satphone, at least for a few seconds. They know you're alive. I don't know if my mother is aware, or my roommate, or even my best friend Rachel. Do they even miss me?"

"I'm sure they would if they knew."

"So, you doubt God will help us escape our prison? No happily-ever-after for us? Not like Paul in prison and the doors just fell open? Not even the hurricane broke down the walls, giving us a chance to escape. We're doomed?"

"Kind of where I was at."

"Are you still there?" she asked.

"Not necessarily. I'm more at peace, but I'm shaken that I would even get to so dark a place."

"What, Kristos Sava is an actual human being with emotions?" Her joking tone took the edge off the comment.

"Yeah. I can't be some live action hero from the movies ready to rescue us. I'm clueless and helpless right now to do anything more than pray and wait."

"So, we wait. I remember my mom's response whenever I would say 'I had no choice.' She'd come back with, 'You always have a choice.' Pray and wait seems like a good combination and has been working rather good so far."

"How about the manner in which we wait. We've been praying, reciting Scripture, singing songs, conversing, and working out. We've functioned well as a team. The other choice would be to scream, yell, bemoan our fate, be nasty to the people bringing us food and tear each other down," Kristos suggested, fully realizing how close that came for him only a few hours prior.

"Got it. We'll stick to our current method of waiting. Do you think the team returned to the States without us?" Eliza questioned Kristos.

"Whether they left the next day or left as scheduled, it's pretty safe to say we missed our flight."

"Yeah, silly question. It's not like I had time to get to know them all either. One day. We had one night and one day on site."

"You were a hard worker. I was impressed." Kristos complimented her.

"Thanks." Eliza smiled, her heart warmed by the compliment. She rose from her bed and put on the prosthetic. She hated that the process took so long.

Kristos sat in shadow as the sun hadn't risen yet. The rainforest was eerily silent. There had been something in his tone of voice that sounded as though he hadn't completely emerged from his inner darkness. She could relate. She'd been there too many times herself.

Only no one had been there for her.

She could be there for him at least.

She rose and, in a few steps, found herself standing before him. The sky lit up just enough for her to see the dark shadows under his eyes and marks left by tears washing off some of the dirt that seemed to accumulate on them no matter how hard they tried to keep clean.

She placed her hands on his shoulders and he turned his focus to her.

"I'm sorry you had to go through a rough night," she whispered.

He swallowed hard and gave a slight nod of his head.

Suddenly, it was as if something changed inside her. She'd always found this man attractive. They were friends but she wanted more. She reached up and caressed the scraggly beard. His eyes closed as he leaned into her palm.

What would it be like to kiss this man?

She bent her head to softly brush her lips against his. What started out as an attempt to comfort quickly changed when he returned the kiss with passion. She pulled away, pushing herself from his arms that had found their way around her waist. She took a step back.

Whoa. She'd been playing with fire and would likely be the one to get burnt. Her heart pounded and she blinked rapidly. She'd never experienced anything like that before.

He reached out a hand for her to return but she shook her head.

Eliza stepped back toward the bed and frowned. There wasn't enough space in here to escape the heat that had blazed between them.

Kristos rose. "Eliza…that was—"

"A mistake. I shouldn't have. I was wrong. I'm sorry." She turned to look out the other window but wasn't able to focus on anything. *Calm down. Slow your breathing.* She clenched and unclenched her fists in an attempt to calm herself. To master her own desires. Oh, did she desire this man.

"I don't think it was a mistake," Kristos whispered. "That had to be the most amazing kiss I've ever experienced. Are you saying you felt nothing?"

Eliza refused to answer. She didn't want to lie. Confessing the truth, however, would only open them both up to temptation they'd regret later.

No one will know.

I would.

"Eliza?"

"We can't do this. It was wrong of me."

"It was just a kiss," Kristos defended, his voice soft, pleading...and sad.

"I wanted it to be so much more than that," Eliza said, her voice shaking. Tears had started to fall. Everything in her wanted to experience more of that passion. The touches. Tenderness. Love.

She was filthy, wearing dirty clothes, and rank with body odor no matter how many times she tried to wash herself off. They were all alone out here, but God still saw. She'd stand before Him someday to give an account of her sins. *Lord, forgive me for wanting Kristos this way.*

"It's a natural and normal thing between a man and a woman..." Kristos said.

"Yes it is, but best within marriage," Eliza stated firmly.

"It won't go further than this—kissing and hugging."

She finally turned to face him. "Really? And if one of us can't say no? All I wanted was to offer you comfort. I like you. A lot. But that... that was too good. We're in a potentially dangerous situation. We can't be going down that road. It's like driving over an IED, and we'll both burn up and destroy everything if we even try to make the trip. Not today, but eventually."

Kristos had a slight grin. "I was that good, huh?" He took a step closer.

She punched him in the shoulder. "Let it go."

He sighed and silence lapsed between them again. Kristos went to the chair and sat.

"Do you have one of those crackers?" Eliza asked. "I'm a little hungry."

"Sure." Kristos handed her one and tried to seal the package again, like it would matter.

Eliza took a bite of the stale cracker and sat on the edge of the bed. It was going to be another long day.

26

Several more days passed and still no visitors to the little prison shack. Eliza was losing hope. Tension sizzled between them if they accidentally touched. She would jump back. Kristos' frustration over the wall she'd erected between them was palpable. She was stubborn. She'd drawn her line in the sand and he didn't argue her out of it at least. They'd avoided talking about it as well.

"No offense, Kristos, but this place stinks from the toilet, from us, and we're running out of water." The electricity had not come back after the storm. "Even with the windows open it's horrible. There's hardly any breeze and it's brutally hot again."

Kristos wiped his brow with his arm. "Don't need to tell me. I'm aware of how dire things are. There's nothing I can do to make it better. We've been praying this entire time but unlike Paul and Silas in prison, God has not chosen to open that door or loosen these bars. Trust me, I've checked them all several times a day." Frustration flowed from his words. His shoulders slumped as he sat down.

"We're barely eating or drinking enough to stay alive. It's only natural we'd be getting testy. I'm sorry to complain. You've been encouraging and supportive through this, this, whatever this is." She held her arms out and dropped them to her sides. "God, I'm grateful we can see the sunshine. It reminds me You are always here, even when I can't see You."

Kristos smiled. "That's the spirit, Eliza."

"Don't you want a turn?"

"Sure. Heavenly Father, I thank You that even here, doing nothing,

You love us and call us Your children."

"Oh, I like that. Jesus, You died for my sins long before I ever acknowledged You; thank You for Your gift of salvation and for company on the journey."

"Eliza, you've learned so much since we were abducted."

"I had a great teacher." She walked over to take a tiny sip of water. She would love to drink it all, but who knew how much longer it would be?

She set the glass down and returned to the chair. They'd given up working out when they started rationing food and water.

Silence settled between them. The sounds of the rainforest had returned after the storm. Sounds of birds singing and wind moving through the trees. Monkeys howling. The Mexican tree frogs continued to serenade at night.

Mosquitos still made their way into their little hovel but had been scarcer. Eliza didn't have the energy to scratch any more. She strode over to the door and banged on it with her fist. "Let us out! Come on!" Bang! Bang! Bang! Her wrist was captured before she could hit the wood again.

"I want to go home…" Tears began to flow. "I don't even know where home is anymore." She turned and found comfort in Kristos' arms as they enveloped her and held her tight as she sobbed. She hated crying and hated even more that a man she admired would see her this weak. She was an American soldier after all.

"Shhhh. It's going to be OK, Eliza," Kristos whispered.

"Don't lie to me. You have no clue how this will turn out."

"True. God does and I'm putting my hope in Him. Even if my end is not what I would desire at this time in my life, as long as He is glorified, I will rejoice. Remember, I've struggled too."

"Why do you sound so depressed as you say that?" She tilted her head back to gaze up at him and his bedraggled beard. His eyes held dampness.

"Because I don't cherish the idea of dying of dehydration and starvation here in this prison. I keep wondering if I should have fought our captors sooner, but I'm not trained for that and it's just not in my nature."

"We can't second guess our choices. I kept watching for a moment of weakness to exploit and escape but I'm not as good a warrior as I once was given my peg leg."

Kristos gave a small grin as his eyes met hers. "You're turning into a pirate now?"

Eliza pulled away from Kristos even though she enjoyed the contact.

"Pirate Tornado at your service. Too bad I didn't have a hook for an arm instead of this leg."

"You wouldn't be able to tie your shoes then," Kristos commented.

"I'm sure I'd figure out a solution."

"So, Pirate Tornado, are you also captain of this ship?"

"Unfortunately, yes. Seems Captain Santiago is AWOL, so that makes me the highest-ranking person here."

Kristos went to sit down. A rock sailed through the window between the bars and landed at his feet. "What?"

Eliza went to the window and tried to keep out of sight while checking out the jungle.

He picked up the rock. "There's a note attached." He unfolded the paper.

"And it says?"

"Hold tight, lay low." Kristos' eyes grew wide. "Best to hit the floor, Eliza." He pointed to a spot to the side of the door, so they'd be out of the way if someone came busting through guns-a-blazing.

Were they about to be rescued? Had God heard their prayers? Eliza grabbed her backpack, shrugged it on, and settled next to Kristos on the floor.

She focused on her breathing to slow her heart rate down. Kristos clasped her hand in his and squeezed. *Oh, please don't let this be a false alarm.*

Time ceased to exist days ago and even now Kristos had no way to measure the moments between them sitting against the wall and the subsequent nothingness that hovered over them like an oppressive force.

He recalled a verse from Psalm 32:7. "You are my hiding place; You keep me from trouble; You surround me with songs of deliverance," he whispered.

"What?" Eliza hissed.

"God brought that verse to mind. The Holy Spirit can do that, helping us recall Scripture when we need it most."

Eliza nodded. "Let's say it together."

Kristos had no issue with that.

"You are my hiding place; You keep me from trouble; You surround me with songs of deliverance."

"Psalm 32:7," he finished alone.

Once again silence reigned. His pulse throbbed loudly in his ears, picking up speed. No noises came from the rainforest either. It was as if the earth held its breath in anticipation of what was about to unfold. After weeks of listening to the constant noises of the rainforest, it was eerie to hear silence.

And yet, nothing happened. He closed his eyes for a moment. He was so tired of their misadventure, but grateful for the woman by his side.

An explosion shook the earth and the door to the tiny cabin smashed open. A man in camouflage held a rifle. "Come, now." He motioned for them to follow. Sounds of gunfire filled the air.

They rose.

"Friend or foe?" Kristos asked as he pulled on the man's arm.

The man had grabbed for Eliza and held on to Kristos, dragging them out of the building.

They started running for the rainforest.

Eliza pulled back, stopping the man. "Answer the question."

The man turned and shook his head. "Friend."

They picked up the pace, running into the rainforest where there was no path, only dense underbrush for them to trip over. The sounds of gunfire followed them. They reached some rocks and the man shoved them behind a boulder. "Stay."

What was going on here? Who was fighting who and were they being rescued by good guys? Where were they going?

"Duck down," Eliza said as she dropped to her good knee. Kristos followed suit. The man fell, wounded. "Help him," Eliza said as she grabbed his rifle.

Kristos did as she bid and dragged the man behind the rocks.

"Go," the man said. "Leave me."

"Fat chance," Eliza said. "Kristos, do you think you could drag or carry him?"

Kristos took a quick glance at the man. "His arm was hit. I'll tie it off and we'll limp along with him. Are you good, Eliza?" He removed the bandana around the man's neck and tied it around his bicep. He jerked the man up to his feet and put an arm around him.

"We can't stay here long. We don't have enough ammo to defend ourselves. Let's go. You take the lead so I can cover us."

"Which way?" Kristos asked the man.

"Keep going straight. There's a clearing up ahead and a chopper will be meeting us."

Kristos moved as fast as he could and sounds of brush and twigs breaking behind him alerted him to Eliza following.

Finally, they found the clearing but there was no helicopter.

"Now what?" Eliza asked.

Kristos was already making his way, with his burden, to a section of bushes around the clearing. "I sure hope there's no poisonous stuff here. What am thinking? We're in the jungles of Mexico. Of course, there are a bijillion nasty creatures."

They crawled into a cluster of bushes and dropped to their knees.

The man grabbed for something. "I had a radio. Must have lost it. Hopefully, the rest of the crew will be here soon."

"We have no way to contact the helicopter?" Eliza asked, gun hidden in the green leaves but aimed toward where they had come. "How do I know which are friend or foe?"

"I'll need to identify. Your friend here can keep a lookout to prevent an attack from another direction," he whispered.

"Can do," Kristos responded.

Silence settled around the rainforest once again. There were no longer sounds of pursuit. Gunfire ceased. They waited. Kristos was barely able to breathe. His heart rate accelerated even as he tried to remain still. Who was rescuing them? Were they safe? They were at least out of that wretched prison hut.

Kristos kept scanning the area but there were no sounds of pursuit.

"Did your team abandon you?" Eliza asked the man.

"They might not have survived. This was our rendezvous point. Either that or they were captured."

"I didn't think anyone was even on the property to fight. We hadn't seen anyone since before the hurricane," Kristos whispered.

"Now would be a good time to tell us who you are and where you come from," Eliza said.

"Manny. Is all I can tell you."

"Guns, battles, you rescued us so you must have heard about us somewhere along the way. Was this a political rescue or a drug cartel war we got in the middle of?" Kristos asked.

"Nothing to do with Santiago or fighting him. You were the mission. Rescue and return to the US."

Eliza glanced at Kristos and raised an eyebrow.

He shrugged. "I think we need to trust him, Eliza. He was willing to let us go ahead without him and gave you his gun without hesitation."

"Fine. So now what? Are we safe? Where do we go from here, wherever here is?"

"I believe if we continue down the mountains, we'll come to a road. We can't stay here," Manny said.

"I'm all for moving on, but suggest we take it easy," Kristos suggested. "We haven't had much to eat or drink the past few days and unless we find a water source soon, we'll be in trouble." He stood up and assisted Manny to his feet as they freed themselves from the tangle of leaves and branches that had been their hiding place.

"You are my hiding place; You keep me from trouble; You surround me with songs of deliverance. Psalm 32:7," Kristos recited to himself, but Eliza and Manny heard him too.

"Yes, but I'm not quite ready to sing yet," Eliza said as she gave him a soft smile. "Let's go."

27

Eliza struggled to keep up with Kristos. The rainforest had resumed the signs of life with birds singing and animals moving through the underbrush. She'd spied sloths and parrots of all kinds, even a blue-and-gold macaw like Ramsey. Eliza moved her backpack to her front, then draped the rifle on her back so her hands were free to help her grab onto trees with the uneven terrain. Hours had probably passed and there'd been no pursuit.

"I need to rest," Manny said.

"Fine." Kristos settled the injured man on a log and waited for Eliza to make it into the little area. "How are you holding up, Tornado?" He grinned as if this were a minor lark they had embarked on.

"Not well, I hate to admit." She sat down and pulled up her pants leg to check her prosthetic.

"You—um—what?" Manny asked.

"Cat got your tongue? It's a prosthetic to replace the leg that was blown off overseas."

"Do you need to change the liner or sock or whatever?" Kristos asked.

"I don't have anything clean at this point. I'm afraid if I take it off, I'll never get it back on again."

"But that could hurt you."

Eliza nodded. "I don't think we have a choice. You can't carry both of us down the mountain."

Kristos sat on a boulder, leaned his head forward, and was silent. His head popped up and eyes wide he grinned. "Eliza, the satphone."

"Oh, yes!" She took the backpack off and rummaged for the phone and handed it to Kristos.

He turned it on and dialed. "Hey. We escaped with some help, but we have one injured and no idea where we are."

Silence.

"Three of us. No. No clue. Manny was shot in the arm. We have a rifle and some ammo."

More silence and he shut the phone down.

"Soooo?" Eliza asked.

"We'll see if they can find us but not likely. The connection was rough so I'm not sure they were able to locate us. So now what? Do we keep moving or try to sleep?"

"I vote for sleep," Manny said.

"As long as we have some daylight, I think we need to keep moving," Eliza said. "I'm exhausted too and while I realize we're not in much danger from wildlife here, I'd like to find some water at least."

"We won't be able to get far but I'm game. Come on, Manny, let's move," Kristos helped the man up. Even with two functioning legs the rescuer struggled to stay on his feet.

"Just a little farther," Eliza said as she pulled her pant leg down and rose. "Keep your eyes and ears open for sounds of water. Hopefully, we'll run into a river somewhere. Especially after that storm."

They walked on until it grew too dark to see well. Collapsing on the ground, they each leaned up against a tree. Eliza placed the rifle across her lap, but it was still strapped to her torso.

"Lord, rescue us, please," Kristo prayed out loud.

"Amen," Eliza responded. She leaned her head back as her bones melted into the tree and jungle floor. Her mind slowly shut down like a long hallway with a series of lights, each set going off one at a time until there was nothingness.

She startled awake a few hours later. The moon played peek-a-boo through the tall umbrella canopy of trees. She found a spot to relieve herself and returned to her tree. Kristos stirred and opened his eyes.

"You OK, Eliza?" he asked.

"I've been better. Was there something you didn't tell me earlier after that call?"

He shook his head. "I wish there were more. Rusty gave the phone to the authorities, but I'm not sure who. They were not forthcoming or seemed aware of any rescue."

"It's possible they can't acknowledge it if it's a black ops situation. Or they may not want to worry us if this is something worse." Eliza closed her eyes. "I'm so thirsty, hungry, and tired."

"Me too," Kristos offered. "Let's get a little more rest before morning. Manny here is growing warm. I'm worried his arm is infected. We need to find help soon or a way to get him to help. Whoever he is, he rescued us, and we owe it to him to help if we can."

"I agree on all counts." Eliza closed her eyes again and descended into darkness.

Dawn burst through the trees with a shaft of sunlight hitting Eliza in the eye. She blinked wildly. She nudged Kristos with her prosthetic foot. "Time to get going."

Kristos rubbed his eyes and yawned. He stretched his arms out and groaned. "Are we late for an appointment?"

"You could say that. Wanna check, Manny?"

Kristos rose and took a few steps over to their sleeping rescuer. He put a hand on the man's forehead. "He's burning up."

"Great. All the more necessary we find water and a way down the mountain as soon as possible."

Kristos rousted Manny and dragged the man to his feet. "Let's go."

Manny groaned and opened his eyes but didn't protest any more. They continued to stumble in a direction they hoped would take them to water and safety.

Eliza struggled to stay on her feet. Her stump ached and every step was an irritation. There was no point in dawdling here in the rainforest. It's one thing to tell a kid to stay put if they get lost, but did anyone even know where to search for them at this point? What happened to the rest of the rescuers back at the estate where they'd been imprisoned? If this were a military operation, she'd be going back to save her friends.

But she was leaving the Army, and this was not her mission. At this point, her mission was to find water and possibly transportation to a place they could get help for their sick compadre. She wondered about Manny and his tight-lipped response. Was he part of a black op that went wrong? Or was he with another possible enemy? Either way he was a human being in pain. Friend or foe they needed to get him help. He'd been cooperative at least.

Funny how the rescued party now became responsible for the rescuer.

Kristos was having to do far more than navigate through the rainforest, keeping this man upright. The man was relying increasingly on Kristos' waning strength to keep them both up and moving forward.

He heard something. He paused. "Shhhh!"

Eliza stopped next to him. "Water. We're near water." She slowly moved forward toward the sound and Kristos and the barely conscious Manny followed.

They arrived at the banks of a river and Eliza was on her knees scooping up water to drink.

"Take it slow," Kristos warned. He and Manny also knelt to get some refreshment.

"I'm tempted to immerse myself. I'm so tired of being filthy." Instead, Eliza splashed water on her face. "Ah…"

Kristos grinned. He proceeded to splash water on his face as well.

Manny sipped and sat back. "I don't think I can go on."

"You will and shall. We can stay close to the water and hopefully it will take us to a village of some sort," Kristos said.

"As long as that village is not connected to Santiago," Eliza said.

"We don't have any choice. We need food and he needs medical care. Moving forward is our best option." Kristos helped Manny to his feet. "Let's go."

They started off again, now following the river. They rested at midday, each enjoying a siesta. When Kristos awoke, he went to the river to drink. Soon Eliza was by his side.

"Do you think Manny is going to make it?" she asked.

"I hope so."

"I'm so hungry. I don't know if some of the berries we've seen are safe for us or not. If we don't find something soon, I'll shoot an animal and somehow, we'll get it cooked to eat even if we need to tear it apart with our bare hands."

Kristos chuckled. "Manny has a lighter. You have your pocketknife and the gun. Do you want to keep going in hopes of finding a village or go hunting?"

"Let's go a little farther before we try that," Eliza said.

"OK." Kristos headed back to Manny and hefted the almost unconscious man to his feet. Thankfully the man was smaller than average, but he was growing heavier as the day went on and he would drag his feet.

The river curved and they followed it to find a road and a bridge that crossed the river. A rough road on the other side seemed to head down the mountain.

Kristos stopped. "River or road?" he asked.

Eliza frowned. "River. I don't want to be far from the water and while that path looks like it might go down, we don't know for sure."

"I'll trust you on this." They continued to move forward.

Rounding another bend, they found a small compound of houses. They stayed behind the trees to watch for any sign of life.

"It's afternoon. They could be taking a siesta," Eliza suggested.

"Let me go poke around." Kristos left Eliza and Manny and ran behind a building; he peeked in a window. No one was there. He went to another crude home, and again, empty. He managed to get through the entire area without finding anyone around.

He rushed back to Eliza and helped Manny up. "No one is around. The place is abandoned, or they all left for some reason. Let's get this guy in a bed and see if we can find some supplies to make dinner."

They found a hut toward the edge of town that appeared the least used and placed Manny on the bed. Kristos ran to fill a bucket with water and brought it back to help cool their patient.

Eliza scouted out the food. She returned to the hut. "There's not much here but I did find some rice at least. Every place is dusty. No one has been here for a while. I noticed an old truck out back."

"Yeah, I saw that too. I didn't check it out though," Kristos admitted.

"Would you try to get a fire going and cook some rice? I'll go check out the truck."

"You know much about old trucks?"

"Enough to be dangerous. I drove them in the Army, remember? I'm not a full-fledged mechanic but I have some skills." Eliza took off.

Kristos managed to get a fire going and using some water from the stream got it boiling in an old pot and dumped in some rice. He wasn't the best cook and rice wasn't something he'd ever tried, but once he got it boiling he put the lid on and let it stay on the side of the fire. Some of the water boiled over. He found some potholder type things to use to hold it and an old wooden spoon to stir. Too bad there weren't any seasonings, but beggars couldn't be choosers. Or was that squatters couldn't be picky?

Thank You, Lord, for bringing us this far. Heal Manny and get us to civilization and back home. Keep drawing Eliza to You so that all she's learned here in the mountains won't be lost when we return to our regular lives.

28

Eliza longed to bathe in the cool river but with no clothes to change into she settled for washing her hair. She finger-combed it and returned to the cabin where there was now smoke coming out of the small stack on top.

Water dripped onto her shirt but she didn't care. Her stomach growled. She entered the cabin and checked on Manny who was out cold.

Kristos glanced over. "Well?"

"The truck starts. There's not a lot of fuel, but it should get us a ways down the road."

"So, morning or tonight?"

"We have food, water, and shelter for now. Let's wait until first light and get some much-needed rest. I'm not sure how bright the lights are on that thing and I'm unfamiliar with this dirt road. I want clear vision and light to drive."

"Can you hand me the satphone again?" Kristos asked.

"Sure." She dug in her backpack and handed it over.

Kristos flipped it open and dialed. "No one is answering." He paused. "No voicemail either."

"What did you expect? That like 911 someone would always be on call?" Eliza asked.

"Well, yes. That's exactly what I'd hoped for." He flipped it closed and turned it off, handing it back to Eliza.

He went to check the rice, almost forgetting to use the potholder. While most of the water was gone, it didn't seem overly soft, but was edible. He put the lid back on.

"Dinner?" Eliza asked.

"Almost. I hope. I'm not a great cook."

"Neither am I. I've no cause to complain since I assigned you the task."

Kristos grinned. "I'm not sure how we'll get sustenance into Manny."

"We'll figure it out."

Soon Eliza and Kristos were sitting at a crude table, eating hot rice with their hands.

"It's actually mushy so I guess you succeeded," Eliza said. "Thank you."

"I'm glad it worked. It doesn't taste like much but it helps. I'm thinking I'll smush some with the spoon and use the extra water and try to get it past Manny's lips. That way he gets water and a little bit of food," Kristos suggested.

"I'll help."

Together they sat Manny up. He didn't even open his eyes although he groaned. Eliza coaxed his mouth open, and Kristos worked on getting some of the mush into the man's mouth. Eventually Manny would swallow, and they would repeat the process. When the food was gone, they let him rest on the bed.

"I'll go retrieve some bedding from another hut and bring it here. I'd like it if we all stuck together," Kristos said.

"I agree."

Kristos scrounged two mattresses that were worse for wear but it was better than sleeping on the dirt. He brought them back and closing the door to the small cabin, they placed them on the floor and reclined. Eliza had rinsed out some of her other socks and liners from her bag and had them draped on a chair.

"Going to change in the morning?"

"That would be the plan. Night, Kristos."

"Night, Eliza."

With that she closed her eyes. *Lord, You brought us this far. Freedom, food, and water, and a safe place, I hope, to rest. Preserve Manny so he might know You. Give us rest and safe travel tomorrow. I adore You, Jesus.*

Eliza awoke the next morning and changed her sock and liners and reattached her prosthetic. There had been some rubbing and she'd likely need to go without it for a day or two to let the stump heal when she returned home. That was a small price to pay for safety. She handed Kristos the satphone.

He opened it, turned it on, and dialed. He shook his head. "Out of order signal."

Frowning, Eliza put it back in her bag and settled the bag on her back. "That doesn't sound right. Something fishy is going on."

Kristos put a hand on each of her shoulders. "Listen, Eliza. We've made it this far, haven't we? Scripture says, 'This I know, that God is for me.' He is with us. He will not abandon us. We need to cling to Him even now. A little easier perhaps when trapped and there is nothing else to do but think and ponder and worry. Now we're on the run, seeking help, and have no clue which way to go. We still need to seek God and He will lead us to safety."

"You don't know that."

"What is our ultimate safety, Eliza?"

She nodded. "Our home in heaven."

"Right. We persevere in hope that we survive down here, but even if we don't, God is still good. He is still merciful. He is still on His throne and worthy of our praise, worship, and obedience."

"You're right. We cling to Him and lean on each other. My turn to make the rice." She headed out to get the water. Heating it up like Kristos did, she added the rice and let it continue to boil for a little before putting a lid on and removing the pot from the heat. Kristos had gone to the river and returned with water dripping off his unbound hair and beard.

"Oh, that felt so good." He pulled back the wet hair and rebound it with his hair band.

They sat to eat and tried to get food and water into Manny who, again, was barely able to open his eyes. Eliza went to wash the pot, lid, and spoon in the river before returning it to the hut. The fire was put out. She walked to the truck and did an outward inspection before getting in and starting it up. It chugged to life. She put it in drive, pulling up to the hut. Together they managed to get Manny in between them on the middle of the bench seat. There was no crew cab in this old thing.

It was uncomfortable to wear the backpack, so she reversed it and gave the rifle to Kristos. Her bag wasn't so full it got in the way of the steering wheel. Kristos shut his door, and they moved forward down the dirt path through the rainforest.

Due to the warmth of the day they kept the windows down.

"So much for washing our hair, huh?" Eliza joked.

"I pray we can soon find showers or baths. I hope they have a lot of hot water and soap because I'll be in there a long time," Kristos said.

"Me too."

The narrow dirt path they followed was filled with ruts and incredibly bumpy. Sometimes Manny would tip over to lean against her but Kristos was quick to get him upright again. There was a sense of déjà vu as she drove, even though this was through a rainforest instead of a desert. There were likely no land mines planted on this path. She found her breathing growing rapid. Sweat dripped down her face but that was simply from the heat, wasn't it?

"You sure you don't want me to drive?" Kristos asked. "After all, you're probably a better shot."

"How sad is it that we anticipate threat and danger instead of hospitality and comfort?" She stopped the truck. "You can drive if you wish." She got out and came around and Kristos did as well, taking the driver's seat. Eliza was happy enough to relax for the moment but that feeling of dread wouldn't go away.

"Better?" Kristos asked.

"No. It's like I'm afraid someone is going to open fire on us at any moment. There's no real foundation for that."

"There isn't? We were held captive, and Manny here was injured in the gun battle. Who knows who is connected to who around here. We haven't a clue where we are. I'm so turned around with everything. I think we're heading south but are we really? Have we traveled more toward the Gulf of Mexico or the Pacific? Where did our help come from? Is Manny a soldier, and if so, for who? He wears no dog tags. No identification whatsoever."

"Nothing adds up. And the satphone? Could we just not get a signal?" Eliza asked.

"I don't understand either. I'm grateful for water, food, rest, and now transportation. Oh, and that grizzly bears don't populate the rainforest in Mexico."

The rumble of the truck's engine and the rattle of the vehicle was their only sound for some time as they both watched and waited for whatever would come next.

"We won't get in trouble for taking this truck, will we?" Eliza asked.

"Medical emergency, I hope not."

"Is it sad that I miss my phone and the maps feature?" Eliza asked.

"Not sad at all. I was thinking something similar. It's hard not knowing our location, isn't it? Since we don't even have a paper map, it's like we're driving blind with no clue where we'll end up."

"Or how good the gas mileage is on this old thing; it showed only half a tank. I hope that's plenty to get us where we need to go." Eliza said.

"Just keep praying."

So, Eliza did. *Lord, we may not know where we are but You do. Help us get to safety and home. I understand my true home is with You and that paradise will never compare to the world we live in now. I can't imagine a life without fear, loss, heartache, trauma, loneliness, and pain. Kristos told me all about it and I look forward to reading more when I can. In the meantime, thank You for the shade of these trees and for sustaining us so far. Give us guidance and wisdom as we move forward and help us honor You in all we do.*

A fallen tree blocked the path. Kristos stopped the truck. "Should I keep it running?"

"You can turn it off. It started easily enough, and I don't want to waste fuel. Do you think between the two of us we can move that?" she asked.

"Let's go find out."

Kristos turned the truck off and exited the vehicle. Eliza stepped out as well. Her stump ached as she started to move again so she took it slow. They got to the tree, and it was larger than she first thought.

"Too bad we don't have a chain saw." Kristos said.

"We're back to hoofing it?" Eliza said.

"I guess so." Kristos sat on the log facing the truck.

"Now we're not near water. That bucket would be hard to carry with us." At least they had the forethought to fill a bucket and put it in the back of the truck. "Of course, that depends on how much survived the bumpy road." Eliza strode to the back of the truck.

"Well?" Kristos asked.

"We can each drink some and hopefully we'll find more water before too long." She grabbed the cup they'd taken and filled it up. She went back to the truck and climbed in to give the water to Manny. He was no longer burning up but getting cooler. Eliza frowned and checked his pulse.

"Kristos?"

"What?"

"Come here." Eliza set the glass down on the dashboard.

Kristos crawled in on the driver's side. "What's up?"

"Check his pulse. I can't find one."

Kristos put two fingers to the man's neck and then tried his wrist. Finally, he rested his ear against the man's chest. He sat up. "He's gone."

"What do we do?" We don't want to leave him here, do we? But carrying him with us isn't possible either. There's no shovel to bury him."

"Best we can do is lay him out on the truck bed and hope someone finds him. We can let people know and maybe they'll come back for the body. He never told us his last name or who he worked for."

"OK." Eliza grabbed the glass and got out of the truck. She drank slowly as tears began to roll down her cheeks. It wasn't as if she hadn't seen dead soldiers before. She had, and it was heartbreaking in war. This was a different kind of battle, for survival, and they just lost their rescuer. Did Manny know Jesus? He wore a cross around his neck, but then from what Kristos had told her, many people did without truly having a relationship with God. Some people clung to religion and its practices instead of to the person they purported to worship. By the time they could pause and even ask about it, Manny wasn't coherent.

She wiped away a tear and walked to the back of the truck. The gate was still down from when she got the water for Manny. Now the man was stretched out in the back of the truck. Kristos had taken Manny's hat off his head and placed it over his face.

Eliza dipped the cup in the water and handed it to Kristos who sipped slowly before handing it back to her. She dipped it in again and drank and then refilled it for Kristos. He drank as well.

"More?" Eliza asked.

"Sure."

They both drank one more cup of water and there was barely anything left. Eliza had to tip the bucket to get the last two cups out.

"Hopefully, that holds us for a while." She'd repositioned her backpack and strapped the gun around her.

"I guess we should set out. Since this is somewhat of a dirt path, we can anticipate it will lead us somewhere habitable." Kristos wiped his brow.

"Let's get moving. Rest in peace, Manny. And thank you for your help." Eliza went to shut the passenger door to the truck. Kristos did the same on the driver's side. They hoisted themselves over the thick log and set out walking on the path. The sounds of their feet hitting the dirt held a steady rhythm to the sounds of the wind in the trees and the birds singing and flitting about. The buzzing sound revealed the jungle's constant state of life.

29

ristos was sad over Manny's death but grateful for not having to carry him on their journey. They marched in silence for a long time.

"During my Army boot camp, we walked, marched, or ran everywhere in formation and with a cadence. A kind of chant that helped pass the time," Eliza said.

"I've heard about that. Why? Do you want to walk to a cadence?"

"Not really, it was a memory. On assignment we didn't do cadence, especially in a war zone. You don't want to advertise your position."

"Walking quietly is probably better?" Kristos asked.

"I think we can talk like this, softly, without attracting undo attention, but yeah, silence is safer so we can listen for anything or anyone headed our way."

Silence reigned as they walked and listened.

Kristos tried to figure out what day it was. They had arrived in Mexico on a Monday and set to work on Tuesday and were kidnapped that night. After that he couldn't figure out the number of days they were in the cabin. With the storm and lack of food, they'd stopped counting. How long had it been? Well over two weeks at least. Or was it three? And this was day three of their freedom.

Some freedom, not knowing if they were hunted or if someone was trying to rescue them.

"I'm thinking Santiago won't expend energy to find us given that his brother is dead," Kristos stated.

"He might not be trying, but if he did, he'd imprison us again on principle and make some other demands. He has power and was itching to make others stand up, take notice, and fear him. He's a mere man. Controlling with fear might gain him temporary power and reward but eventually that too will end as someone else strives to take his place," Eliza said.

"You're right. Hopefully, that means anyone we meet might be predisposed to help us."

"I believe the chances of that are in our favor."

"We should be on the alert," Kristos suggested.

"Agreed."

Silence once again hung between them. Kristos considered his petite companion. She was small but mighty. Practical and not one to fall apart in a crisis. She was a trained soldier and understood when to take charge and be proactive. He admired her strength. So why did she fall apart on day one of therapy with Mandy? Obviously, there were deep wounds tucked away. Hopefully, she'd find a way to be free from the trauma of the past.

What about the trauma of the present? While they'd not been tortured, their imprisonment and this journey were still a difficult challenge. Would either of them have survived without the other?

What would happen when they returned home? Would they still want to see each other or would putting this event behind them mean distancing themselves from each other? He hoped it had brought them closer.

"We make a good team," he said.

Eliza nodded. "I'd say so."

"There's a spot up ahead. Let's rest for a while before continuing on," Kristos said as his own energy waned.

"OK. The sun appears high in the sky from what I can tell. Is it noonish? I would have thought it later given how long we've been traveling." She settled down, stretching her legs out.

"Yeah, noon I suspect. I would have thought we'd have found people by now."

"Or that river again at least. I'm parched," Eliza said.

"It could be worse."

"How?"

"It could be freezing cold."

Eliza chuckled. "Given our attire, that would be worse. I'm glad I packed my cargo pants, though, it's been cool at night in the mountains. I'm afraid my mission T-shirt however has seen better days." She tugged at it, smeared with dirt and blood from Manny's injury. "I doubt it will ever come clean. Would you be offended if I burned it first chance I got?"

"Great idea. We'll have a bonfire at the ranch and ceremoniously burn them in triumph of surviving this."

"I anticipate roasting some marshmallows as well."

"Of course. No smores?"

"Nah, I prefer my chocolate without the graham cracker."

"Fair enough. We'll plan on that as soon as we can after returning to Colorado."

Eliza sighed. "I realized that not once have I worried about what kind of job I'll seek when I get out. I'd love to help out Kobbe though. After all this, sitting in that office and getting things straightened up and doing the books sounds like a slice of heaven."

"Even being around the horses?"

"Did I offend Mandy when I left last time?"

"Nah, she got to join her friends in the pasture. I'm sure she'd welcome you again."

"It's like her eyes can see deep into my soul."

Kristos nodded. "It's biofeedback. Horses are acutely attuned to the emotions of people near them. When there's a connection they respond positively."

"I'll need to try again when we return. I even avoided Kobbe's phone calls after that. Not a very mature response."

"Don't beat yourself up over it. Recovering from trauma can be messy from what I understand."

"Life's been pretty easy for you?"

"I wouldn't say easy. I've worked hard for what I have. Nothing remotely traumatic until this. I wouldn't have survived it as well without you."

"And God. Don't forget God. He's been with us every step of the way." Eliza reached over to grab his hand and squeeze.

"Yes. How about I pray for us before we continue?"

"Sounds good."

They bowed their heads but kept holding hands, a comfort to Kristos' soul. "Heavenly Father, You are fully aware of where we are and where we need to be. You understand our human frailty. Our thirst, hunger, and fatigue. Give us the energy to continue and provide wisdom for whatever lies ahead. We desperately need You with us every step of the way. Amen."

"Amen." Eliza rose from her spot and pulled him up as well. "Shall we continue?"

"Yes."

She released his hand and he grabbed it again. She didn't pull away. They were in this together, and the physical contact gave him hope.

Peace filled Eliza's soul as she continued walking while holding Kristos' hand. She held it while sitting and it was terribly forward of her to grab it. When he didn't pull away, a completeness and security surrounded her. She was wanted. Not desired but wanted. Who would desire her in this state of mess and stink? Kristos had his own unique odor as well, but it didn't seem so offensive to her as her own. Maybe it was because she'd grown accustomed to it?

This was a man who honored and protected her—physically, emotionally, and spiritually. If there was a positive outcome from this misadventure, it was the depth and breadth of her knowledge of Jesus and God and the Holy Spirit. She hungered to read more, to learn, and grow in her faith.

Would she someday be good enough for a man like Kristos to want to date? Or even marry? He didn't find her prosthetic a problem. Could he still be romantically interested? He'd never done more than give a hug or hold her hand. He wouldn't even sleep with her in the twin bed in the prison hut, and the floor had to have been terribly uncomfortable. Kristos never complained. Despite everything he remained a gentleman his mother would be proud of.

Eliza hadn't thought about her mother for a long time. Had someone informed her of what happened? Was the Army aware or was she now AWOL? She hoped not. She needed a medical retirement not a dishonorable discharge. She'd lose her benefits if that were the case. She let out a shuddering breath. It didn't pay to worry about it now. That was something to deal with when she returned to Fort Carson.

The day wore on with no sign of anyone, but this wasn't a major road, only a dirt path overgrown with weeds. It had been a long time since anyone traveled this way by car or truck.

Sounds of rippling water caught her attention. She squeezed Kristos' hand and let go. "Running water!" She rushed toward the sound, and around a bunch of trees she spied a rickety bridge over a creek.

Eliza pulled her backpack off.

"What are you doing?"

"I put the cup in here." She dragged it out and offered it to him.

He waved her off. "Ladies first. If you give me the satphone I can try again."

She handed that to him and rushed to the water to fill the cup and slowly drink the cool refreshment. She filled it again and drank and set it aside so she could splash her face with water.

Kristos came to drink and handed her the satphone.

Eliza put it away and waited. Kristos drank and then drank again. He filled it a third time and splashed his face with it. He closed his eyes and sighed.

"What is it?"

"The phone is dead. I turned it off every time, but the battery won't power up."

"At least people are aware we were rescued and alive. Now we only have a connection to God. That doesn't need a battery."

Kristos handed her the cup and rose before helping her to her feet.

"We need to stay connected to the source of power."

Eliza grinned. "And stay close to the Living Water."

"Creek or road?" Kristos asked.

"Creek, although I fear it might be slower going."

Together they headed the direction the creek flowed. Soon they found themselves climbing a bank to a bridge high over the creek. When they reached the top, they found a paved road.

"Now what?" Eliza asked.

"Why don't we rest here and hopefully someone will come and give us a ride."

"Sounds fair, but we still have no food, and if we wait too long, we lose the opportunity to find some down the way."

"You want to hunt?"

"If we need to, yes. Are you any good with a rifle?"

Kristos grinned at her. "Yes. I can hunt. I'm not as good a sharpshooter as you."

"There's a flaw in our plan to wait."

"What?"

"It's afternoon, more of a siesta time. The Mexican culture isn't as rushed as we are."

"Are you saying you want to take a nap?" Kristos asked.

"Not at all. I'm suggesting we keep following the river. At least we'll have water and we can feed ourselves if we need to."

"OK, lead the way." Kristos motioned for her to cross the road first and he followed. He helped her down the steep incline back toward the riverbank where they stopped to drink before traveling on in convivial silence.

30

Dinner was subdued although Kristos bagged a pheasant-like bird that they cooked and enjoyed. Their little fire was enough to keep some of the mosquitos away, but they were so full of bites already it made little difference.

As he stretched out on one side of the fire, he put his hands under his head and gazed up at the stars. Psalm 8:3–4 popped into his memory. “When I consider Your heavens, the work of Your fingers, the moon and the stars, which You have set in place; what is man that You think of him, and a son of man that You are concerned about him?” he whispered.

“That’s humbling,” Eliza said from the other side of the fire.

“We are so small when you consider the vastness of the universe, yet I am convinced God is fully aware of where we are and what we need.”

“I’m growing in that faith, and obviously we endured some hardships on this journey, but we’re still here, and doing well.”

“As well as can be expected. I wonder how our families are doing with our absence? Rusty was aware of what happened and apparently so was the federal government.”

“Maybe we made the evening news,” Eliza said. “I’m sure my mother is beside herself, but what can any of them do about it?”

“If I know my family, there are prayer chains going and prayer meetings taking place on our behalf.”

“What’s a prayer chain?” she asked.

“I guess that would seem an odd thing. It’s a group of people committed to pray for the needs of the people in the church. One person calls and gives the request and then that person calls the next. Now they send out a church email."

"Sounded like a game of telephone. The first person says, 'Pray for Kristos and Eliza as they were kidnapped in Mexico.' Then person two gives the message, 'Pray for Kristos and Liza as they're napping with kids in Mexico.'"

Kristos interrupted. "Then the third person says: 'Pray for Krist and Liz as they nap with Mexicans.' Like why would they need prayer for that? I guess the email process makes more sense at this point."

They both chuckled.

"Good night, Kristos. Sleep well."

"You too, Eliza. Sweet dreams."

The night passed uneventfully, and they awoke to drink at the stream. Kristos managed to catch a fish. It wasn't big but at this point neither could eat very much anyway. He cooked it and they had a few bites and drank more water before putting out the fire and moving on.

Kristos now carried the gun, which was only fair since Eliza lugged her bag with her prosthetic stuff in it. He was grateful she'd kept it on her person. What would they have done had she not been able to walk? She was slight enough he could have carried her but still. Just one more thing to be grateful for even though he was certain she had blisters. He had them. Both wore regular sneakers, but they weren't designed for this kind of use. Still, branches and stones scraped their arms. Was there any part of him that didn't ache, hurt, or itch? Even his teeth screamed for a toothbrush.

The rainforest changed to have an ethereal aspect. He'd heard of cloud forests but never expected to step into one. The humidity was suffocating. They labored on and soon the cloud-like atmosphere evaporated and they were back in what they'd grown accustomed to, a regular rainforest.

As the creek took another turn it widened and another bridge was ahead. They climbed up the embankment to the dirt road as a motor bike sped their way. Kristos waved his arms and the biker stopped. It was a young boy.

"*Nosotras estamos perdidas.* We are lost. Is there a town nearby? *¿Hay algun pueblo cerca?*" Even though her Spanish was halting, Eliza was able to communicate to the young man.

The boy motioned for her to get on the back of his bike.

"No. *Mi amigo va conmigo.* My friend goes with me."

The boy shrugged and spoke so quickly but pointed in the direction he was headed.

Eliza turned to Kristos. "I guess we go that way."

The motorbike sped on down the dirt path, and leaving the water behind, they followed him. The bike was soon out of sight. They walked and walked. Soon a vehicle approached from the direction they were headed. Kristos brought the rifle around to the front of his torso and clung to it.

The truck stopped and an older man exited. "Are you Americans?" he asked in broken English.

"*Si, señor,*" Eliza said.

"I am Alberto, come with me. Many people search for you."

"I'm Eliza and this is Kristos. *Gracias.*" Eliza and Kristos got into the cab of the pickup. Alberto turned the vehicle around and drove a ways until they came to a small village similar to the one they had been doing work in when they were kidnapped.

"Food and clean clothes we can help," Alberto said. "And bath." He plugged his nose and smiled. They exited the vehicle.

"*Muchas gracias,*" Eliza said. "Thank you so much."

"Come this way, my wife, Anna, will help."

They followed the man into a simple hut not much different from the one they'd been trapped in.

The man spoke quickly to his wife who rushed forward. "Tsk, tsk, tsk. Eliza and Kristos, I am Anna. Let us clean you up. You may borrow clothes until yours are clean and dry. Let me get water for bath." She motioned them to sit at a crude table and proceeded to put out bread and cheese on the table. She poured them glasses of water and set them down. "Eat," she instructed.

Kristos didn't need any further encouragement.

Eliza felt like a new woman although the dress she'd been given practically swallowed her up. Even the rougher fabric was a refreshing respite from her filthy T-shirt and undergarments. Her hair brushed out she had been surprised at how gaunt she appeared when she glanced in the crude mirror.

She emerged from the room and Kristos took his turn. She sat out on the front porch where Anna motioned her to go. Maybe it was her Army training, superstition, or an abundance of caution, but Eliza put her backpack on once dressed. Until she was home, she didn't dare risk being separated from it. She watched the quiet village as little kids rushed over to check out the newcomer to their neighborhood.

Albert came from around the house and shooed the kids away. He sat down in another chair. "They are curious."

"Yes."

"When your clothes are clean and dry, I will drive you to city, to the police."

"Where is the closest United States Consulate?" she asked.

"Over a day's drive to Merida."

"That is where we need to go. No *policia*." Eliza's spirits drooped. Over a day away to finding a way home and safety. Due to the drug cartels' control over many in the police force she didn't want to risk going there.

Alberto nodded. "I will find a way." He rose and went inside. "Anna!" he called and spoke with his wife in rapid Spanish.

He rushed out of the house. "*Adios*, Eliza." He rushed to his truck, started it, and headed down the road with a cloud of dust behind him. She hoped he wasn't bringing back trouble.

Kristos soon joined her on the porch, bringing a glass for her. "Anna says this is horchata. In spite of several trips to this country I haven't tried this."

"Oh," Eliza took a sip. "It has been so long." She drank some more and closed her eyes, savoring the cool refreshing flavor. She opened them to glance over at Kristos. The shirt he wore was too big for him and the pants too short, and held on tight with a belt. "Aren't we a pair?"

"I appear foolish but, you look delightful."

"Thank you. It is good to be clean at last."

"Was that Alberto who drove off?" Kristos asked.

"Si. I mean, yes. I have no clue why. We are pretty remote here from what I can figure. I asked about the US Consulate, but he said it is over a day of driving to get there."

"And then he left?"

She nodded. "I told him no police."

"I wonder where he went?"

Anna came outside and fanned herself. She pointed to their glasses. "You like?"

Eliza grinned. "I love. Gracias."

The woman beamed.

"Where did Alberto go, Anna?" she asked.

"To find cousin who flies planes. He might take you to Merida."

"That would be wonderful," Kristos said.

Anna turned to leave. "I prepare dinner."

Eliza jumped up. "May I help?"

Shaking her head, Anna responded. "No. Rest. You have been on long journey. You are a guest."

Eliza sat back down. "It is odd to sit in comfort after all this."

"I don't care if I sleep on a floor again tonight, I will sleep well." His bright eyes and ruddy cheeks gave him a glow. Or was it the slowly fading light? Her stomach growled. She sipped more of the sweet rice milk made with fresh cinnamon.

This is what hope tasted like. She grinned. Maybe by tomorrow they'd finally be safe and headed for home.

31

The next morning Kristos arose early to find his clothing folded in a neat pile. He went to the bathroom, closed the door, and changed out of the ill fighting nightshirt he'd been given. The hospitality of this family was beyond what he could have hoped for.

Alberto returned at some point during the night, but Kristos failed to hear the man enter the cabin. The truck was parked out front, and it gave him hope that today they'd be one step closer to home.

Kristos folded up the nightshirt and brought it out to set it where he had found his clothing. Eliza still slept on the padded area they had made for her. He watched her with her beautiful dark hair. He was grateful she'd let her natural color shine through. It suited her. Those pretty lips were turned up in a smile. He hoped she was having happy dreams. Could they include him?

He moved out to the porch. The light was growing brighter beyond the treetops. He savored the quietness of the moment. The heavens tell of the glory of God; and their expanse declares the work of His hands. *Lord, You have brought us safe thus far and even though we endured fear and anxiousness, we never forgot You were with us. Thank You for protecting Eliza and myself. Continue to provide for our safe journey home and help us be a witness to Your glory and grace when we share our journey. We couldn't have made it this far without You and each other. And if Eliza is to be a life mate, Lord, make that clear and help her be open to that. Show me the way to winning her heart. If we can endure this together, we can handle marriage. Only if it is Your will, Lord. I love her. I think I might have fallen in love with her that first night. You were aware all along what we both needed. She got the best gift when she found You. Help her to continue to grow in You, Lord. Amen.*

The door opened and Eliza emerged dressed in her own clothes, clean but still some stains remained. She smiled and it was as if the sun had doubled in brightness.

"Good morning, Kristos." She stretched and yawned.

Yes, he could get used to waking up with her for the rest of his life. "Morning, Eliza."

"I'm wondering why you rarely call me Tornado? The guys in my squad did and it was my nickname in high school as well."

Kristos shrugged. "I know your squad and school mates probably liked to play off your last name and you being a tiny, passionate storm. While I can understand how apt the description is, I like Eliza. Reminds me a bit of *My Fair Lady*, although I can't think of any way I'd ever want to transform you."

"Given this leg I doubt I could dance all night either."

"How is it feeling?"

"Still hurts, but I can't realistically deal with that until we get home."

"We could give you respite on the flight and have a wheelchair at the airport."

"It would help but I hate to inconvenience anyone."

"After all we've been through that should be the least of your worries, but it speaks a lot to your character that you put the needs of others before yourself. You realize though it's OK to ask for help."

Eliza nodded.

"We could try dancing at my friend Michael's wedding. I'm working the horses but you could come, bring Livie, and after I do all the things a groomsman is required to do, we could try dancing together."

Eliza bit her lip. "I was never much of a dancer before I lost my leg but as long as it's a slow dance…maybe?"

"Is that a yes to coming as my date?"

"If we can make it back, a definite yes." Her smile caused his heart to flip. She'd said yes to the wedding dance and being his date.

It gave him hope.

Anna opened the door and stepped out with two steaming mugs. "Coffee? I'm making breakfast but it will be a few more minutes."

"Gracias," both Kristos and Eliza said in unison as they each grabbed a mug. Anna returned inside.

Eliza sipped. "I originally didn't like it black but being in the Army you learn to adjust. It's been so long I wonder how my body will react to the caffeine."

Kristos took a sip. "It's strong. I suggest you sip and make it last. I don't need to accompany a hyper Tornado to the consulate."

"Ha, ha, mister funny guy. You might only have a nervous wreck on your hands."

"Whatever happens, we'll get through it."

They sipped their coffee, enjoyed a nice simple breakfast, and soon were on their way in the old truck.

"My cousin, Tácito, has an airplane and can fly you to Merida airport. You catch cab to consulate."

"Wonderful. I hope they take a credit card. Do you have any pesos, Eliza?" Kristos asked.

"Some. Hopefully, it's enough."

They said their goodbyes and were soon on the road to the tiny plane that awaited them.

"Gracias, Alberto," Kristos said.

"Safe travels, mi amigos. Be well." Alberto jumped back in his truck to head for home.

Kristos and Eliza waved farewell and headed toward the hanger. A tall lanky young man came to meet them.

"*¿Eres Tácito?*" Eliza asked.

"Si. ¿Eres Kristos and Eliza?"

"Si."

"I take you to Merida. Come."

He led them to the little plane, it looked as if only two people would fit, and assisted Eliza into the front passenger seat. Kristos jumped in the back.

Soon the rickety airplane was in the air. The sound was too loud for conversation.

Kristos marveled at the scenery during the hours the tiny airplane flew over the rainforest and then had a view of the Gulf of Mexico. He wondered what this would cost them. They had barely anything on them at the moment. Surely this man would not fly them for nothing. When they finally landed at the airport, Eliza was assisted out and then Kristos.

Leaning into Eliza, Kristos whispered, "What do we pay him? We have nothing."

Eliza turned to Tácito. "*¿Qué te debo? Nosotras no tenemos nada.* We have nothing."

"No es nada." Tácito mimed using a rifle. "Alberto give me gun."

"Gracias." Kristos said as he ushered Eliza toward the hanger to figure out where to go from there to get transportation to the consulate.

"I forgot about the gun. I must have left it in Alberto's pickup," Kristos said.

"It worked in our favor. Come on." Eliza led the way toward a bank of vehicles resembling cabs. She came to the first one, "*¿A cuánto dinero llevarnos US Consulate?*"

The man gave an amount and thankfully it was sufficient to get them there. They climbed into the cab and clung on as it sped through the streets of Merida and came to a stop in front of the consulate.

Eliza paid him as they got out. "Gracias."

Kristos grabbed her hand and they headed past the grey posts protecting the white building that looked to be made of concrete. A guard greeted them.

"We are seeking help to get back to the United States," Kristos stated. The man nodded and ushered them in the door. They were searched and then taken to a seating area. Through a window they could catch a glimpse of a courtyard and the pole bearing the United States flag.

"I think we're not far from Cancun. Too bad we can't take a side trip. Only problem is I forgot my swimsuit," Eliza joked.

"Some other time. I think we've overstayed our welcome in Mexico."

"You call this a welcome? OK, I'll grant you the first twenty-four hours were fine. After that, it wasn't the trip I anticipated."

"I agree 100 percent."

"I hope we're not in trouble," Eliza said.

Another guard appeared and smiled. "Far from it. Follow me." They entered an elevator and when it opened, they followed the guard down a hallway. He opened the door to an office and ushered them in.

A woman dressed in business attire rose from her desk and strode toward them as the officer departed.

"Kristos Sava and Specialist Eliza Torres. You are an answer to prayer. Come, sit down. I am Consul General Dorothy Ngutter. Can I get you anything to drink?"

"Water, thank you. It's a pleasure to meet you," Eliza said.

"Yes, we didn't quite expect this," Kristos added.

"I didn't expect either of you. We are all overjoyed to see that both of you are OK." She walked over to a small fridge and pulled out some bottled water. She brought them over.

Kristos and Eliza both took the water and in unison said, "Gracias."

The Consul General grinned. "It is fine to speak English here. I need to make a few phone calls, so sit tight. I need to let others know you've shown up here. After that I want to learn about what happened."

Kristos opened his bottle and sipped the cool water. Eliza did the same, raising her eyebrows. He shrugged. What was going to happen next?

Eliza leaned over and whispered. "I want to go home."

"Me too."

The woman soon returned to them. "Now, why don't you tell me your story? Then we'll figure out how to get you back to the United States."

After retelling their harrowing adventures, the Consul General made arrangements for a flight and transportation back to the airport after an invitation to stay, shop, and rest were rejected by both Kristos and Eliza.

"I appreciate your offer, Consul General, but we want to go home. Maybe someday we can return and enjoy Mexico, but for now, we want to get home. I don't care if we land in Denver at two a.m."

The Consul General smiled. "Then go and be well." She stood and shook both their hands. "It was a pleasure to meet you both. Godspeed."

She walked them to the door and an officer escorted them to the courtyard they'd spied earlier. They were put in a comfortable sedan with tinted windows and dropped off at the airport. They were checked in and through security without any hassle and soon were on a jet bound for the United States of America.

During their layover in Mexico City, they used vouchers the Consul General had given them for two hotel rooms since their layover was so long.

"I realize it's pricey, but I need to stop and buy new clothing. I cannot stand wearing any of this anymore," Eliza said.

"Fair enough, there are shops here, I hesitate to go farther…"

"Afraid we'll get kidnapped again and miss another flight home?"

Kristos chuckled. "Maybe."

They both visited a few shops and Eliza bought some new clothes. Kristos even purchased some items. They ate a satisfying meal and checked into their hotel. They parted at their doors.

"Sleep well, Eliza," Kristos said. He put a hand on her shoulder and drew her close, placing a kiss on her forehead.

"You too, Kristos." Eliza entered her room and made a beeline to the bathroom.

After a scented soak and washing her hair, she put on a simple short set she'd purchased and climbed into bed, making sure to set her alarm. After days together on the run, it was odd to be alone now for the first time. She missed the sense of strength and security she derived from being close to Kristos.

He wanted to dance with her at a wedding. The thought made her warm. She hugged her extra pillow. *Thank you, Lord, for bringing us this far. You are faithful and worthy of my devotion. Help me not lose the lessons I gained during this time. Help me live life fresh and new because that is what You have made me. Wake me in time to prepare for our flight home. I love You.*

32

Kristos managed to call home before going to bed. He wanted a welcome home for Eliza as well as for him.

He dressed in his fresh clothes that morning. He'd trimmed his beard the previous night. He hoped Eliza liked it. He left the razor behind as he wasn't checking a suitcase. Just a plastic bag with his dirty clothes.

He joined Eliza in the lobby, and they headed for the airport. After they passed through the security check, Eliza and Kristos grabbed a bite to eat before boarding.

"Did you sleep well?" he asked Eliza. "By the way, that outfit becomes you."

She wore a pretty top with a skirt. She'd even purchased some sandals.

She blushed at his comment. "Thanks. After how many days in cargo pants I longed for something looser. I don't often wear skirts and am still not quite comfortable with people seeing my prosthetic leg, but at this point comfort won out. You don't look so bad yourself."

He'd donned a button-down short-sleeved shirt with a fun pattern and cargo shorts. He was practical enough to realize these would still be useful when he returned home, even though jeans were his normal go-to. Much like her, he was desperate for something different.

"We're going to arrive in Denver looking like we're returning from a relaxing vacation," he said.

Eliza chuckled. "Well, I guess we had lots of days to relax and do nothing in the hut, but…I wouldn't call it a vacation. I didn't realize how much I valued my freedom until it was taken away."

Kristos nodded. "You're returning a new person, Eliza, not just because of the events of the past weeks. But the spiritual transformation in you is stunning."

"God and I needed to skirmish a little over who would be in control, but I believe He's shown me now, repeatedly, that He is truly in charge. For that, I'm grateful. My surrender wasn't an act of defeat but of gratitude."

"Well said."

"Re-entry into our world is going to be odd. I've returned from deployments before, but even though I was serving in the military, I had food, water, and a purpose."

"We had a purpose all along, Eliza. We were to love and worship God and support and encourage each other. We succeeded in both. It's a microcosm of what the church is supposed to be like."

"That makes sense. I'm glad God stuck me with you during our misadventure."

"Stuck? Seriously?" Kristos nudged her with his elbow. "Do you want to remove your prosthetic and ride in a wheelchair? I could carry you into the airplane."

"No. I might take it off while we fly. It felt great when I took it off last night, something I didn't do much during our trip in case we needed to leave quickly."

"Let's go wait to board." Kristos held her hand as they walked to the terminal; Eliza refused to have a cart drive them there.

When it came time to board, their names were called first.

"What?" Kristos asked.

She shrugged. "They called us, let's check it out." Eliza rose and dragged him to the counter.

"This is Eliza Torres and I'm Kristos Sava. You called our names?"

The flight attendant smiled. "Yes. You get to board first. We want you to be comfortable. We're glad to see you're safe and sound. You were upgraded to first class. Enjoy your flight."

They glanced at each other, grinned, and headed down the jetway to the plane.

They were seated comfortably side by side.

Just as we should be—maybe forever, he thought.

They held hands through the flight even as they rested.

Upon landing in Denver, they were allowed to disembark first. Kristos grinned at Eliza. "I could get used to this."

"Don't let it go to your head." She elbowed him and grinned. His heart did a little flip. It seemed to be doing that a lot.

They made their way to the tram that would take them to baggage claim and the lobby for pickup.

They sat down with their bags on their laps.

Eliza sighed. "I'm hoping the Army didn't consider me AWOL."

Kristos put his arm around her. "I'm sure it will all work out OK. Who knows, Ramsey might talk to you now."

"That would take a miracle." At least she smiled.

"That's my girl. We've seen plenty of those already, so why not more?"

They exited with the crowd but stepped out of the way once they reached the main area where the restaurants were.

"Restroom first. Do we need to call a cab to get home?" Eliza asked. "I hadn't even thought that far."

"Someone will be meeting us to bring us at least to my parent's home. We'll get you back home too."

She nodded and they parted at the restroom.

When Eliza stepped back out of the bathroom she searched for Kristos. He walked her way. He still took her breath away much like the first night she'd met him.

"Ready?" he asked.

"For a ride home? You bet."

They strode past baggage claim and stepped outside. Kristos waved as a car pulled up to the curb.

"It's my brother Rusty and his dog, Lola." Kristos opened the door and slid into the back seat after her.

"Hey, bro. Can't wait to hear about your adventure. Eliza, it is a pleasure to meet you."

"Nice meeting you, Rusty." Eliza settled back into her seat.

"I won't besiege you with questions. I'm sure you've got a lot of decompressing to do. Relax till we get to the ranch."

Kristos began asking questions about people Eliza didn't know, so she tuned out.

After about an hour ride they were pulling into the driveway toward the ranch. News trucks were waiting.

"Sorry, I didn't realize they'd be here," Rusty said. "I also apologize for the issues you had with that satphone."

"Don't stop. We don't want to talk to them right now, as for the phone, you couldn't predict it would be flaky," Kristos said.

A police officer stood guarding the gate of the Sava ranch, which was normally left wide open but was now closed to keep the press out. Eliza tucked her face toward Kristos who wrapped her in his arms in case people were trying to take photos through the windows. They managed to get through the crowd and made their way to the house. Eliza pulled back to check who would be there.

No one. The porch was empty. Her heart sank. What did she expect? She had no one here but her roommate and Kristos had friends and family.

"I wanna go home," she said flatly, trying unsuccessfully to hide her emotions.

Kristos turned to her. "Hey, we've gone through all this together, what's another few hours?"

"Hours?" she squeaked out.

The car continued to drive around the house and down another road. "We're meeting at Alexos' home," Rusty said.

Soon they arrived at a clearing filled with cars. Rusty pulled up to the front of the house and parked. People began pouring out the front door yelling, "They're here!"

Kristos got out first and helped Eliza out the door. He whispered to her. "You're beautiful. Don't be intimidated, Tornado."

She straightened up at the mention of her nickname. She was a soldier. She had overcome so much. She could endure a few more hours. If she could sit somewhere and rest.

Her mother rushed forward. "My baby!"

"Mom? When did you get here?" Eliza asked. Kristos was getting enveloped by members of his family. At least that's who she suspected they were.

"I came as soon as I was contacted by Captain Jane Sava. She's married the man who brought you here. She was able to find me, and I flew out immediately. The Savas gave me a room to stay in while we waited for any word from you. Rusty updated us when you called. And we prayed. A lot."

"I didn't think you were religious, Mom," Eliza said, stunned.

"I wasn't, but being around this family changed everything for me. Even Nigel has come to know Christ. He returned to work after a few days of being out here waiting for word. He's flying in tomorrow so you can meet him."

"Eliza!" Livie came rushing her way and enveloped her in a big hug. "I'm so glad you've made it back. Ramsey is missing you, but I've been trying to take good care of him." Livie held her arms out straight, hands on Eliza's shoulders. "Tornado, you look gorgeous. Apparently spending a few weeks with that handsome cowboy has done some good." She smiled and winked.

"Will I get to meet this paragon?" Eliza's mom, Joy, asked.

"Sure, as soon as he's free from his family." Eliza pointed to the crowd around the returning hero. As she spoke, Kristos glanced over to her and broke free to head her way.

"Eliza, would you do me the honor of introducing me to this lovely lady?" His smile tickled her heart.

"Kristos Sava, this is my mother, Joy Torres Lloyd."

"May I give you a hug?" Joy asked.

"Certainly." Kristos enveloped the smaller woman in his arms. He winked at Eliza. Once he released the hug, Joy fanned herself.

"My, how did you stand being alone with him for that long and not fall in love?"

Kristos raised an eyebrow as he turned to Eliza. "I think the question should be reversed, except I think I began falling in love with her from the moment we first met and she doused me with beer."

"It was an accident," Eliza protested. Still, he took the pressure off her and proclaimed to Eliza's mother that he was—in love? With her?

"I'm going to steal her away for a few moments longer, then we'll feast."

Joy shrugged and waved them away. Kristos grabbed Eliza's hand and drew her to the porch.

"Everybody gather around," Kristos called out.

Great, now the attention would be focused on her as well. Her pulse increased and her palms were damp. At least all the faces were friendly.

"Many of you haven't met my traveling companion, Specialist Eliza Torres. We want to thank you for praying for us and in time we'll share our story, but today, can we pause for a moment and thank God for bringing us home?"

Pastor Sava stepped up. "Let me pray that prayer, son." The man turned toward the crowd after stepping behind Kristos and Eliza and putting a hand on the shoulder of both.

Eliza shivered. This was all too new.

"Heavenly Father, we thank You for bringing Kristos and Eliza back to us safely. We pray You will help them heal from the days they were held captive, suffered through a hurricane, and wandered through the rainforests of southern Mexico. We praise you for calling Eliza to be Your precious daughter and helping her grow in faith during this trial. We pray You would heal any emotional and physical wounds from this. From this father's heart to Yours, heavenly Father, I am grateful." He stopped and squeezed their shoulders. "And the people all said..."

The crowd joined in unison, "Amen!"

A shorter woman stepped forward. "Let's eat! We have everything set up in the backyard."

The crowd began to move around the side of the house.

Kristos turned to Eliza. "Bathroom is down the hall to the right. There's a door leading out the back through the kitchen."

"Thanks."

Eliza headed to the bathroom. She was no hero and didn't need recognition. They survived. She wanted to go home and sleep in her own bed. She would be polite but wished Kristos hadn't sprung this surprise on her after all they'd been through.

"The Army is aware of everything so you're not in trouble," Livie said, walking with her toward the backyard where everyone was gathered.

"Thanks, Livie. I want to go home."

"But your mom is here. She's sweet. So is the entire Sava family. I can understand why you would be drawn to a man like Kristos. He comes from good stock as my mamma would say."

"He is pretty special," Eliza whispered. But when the dust settled, would he still want her? Was she ready for all that might mean? She blinked back the tears that threatened.

Kristos walked Eliza toward Alexos' car. Big brother was going to take both her and Livie home since he could get on post.

"Are you OK?" She'd been quiet since they'd returned.

"Not really," she sighed. "I just wanted to go home. While I appreciate all of this. It was too much after all we've gone through. I'm tired. I'm sore. I'm exhausted. I'm sure you are as well."

"Can I call you tomorrow?" Kristos asked.

"I'd rather you didn't. I need some time."

His heart sank. "I thought that now we were past all this, we could finally date each other. Exclusively."

"I never promised that, did I? We've been joined at the hip for weeks and while I couldn't have asked for anyone better to go through this ordeal with, I need some space from you and all the memories. I need time."

"You can't be alone forever, Eliza."

"Maybe not. But you can't always have someone to cling to either. You have your family. They are always there for you. Me? My mom will leave in a day or so and I'll be alone again. I can't jump into a relationship right after all we've been through."

"But I thought…" Kristos whispered.

"You thought wrong." Eliza turned to walk to the car where Alexos and Livie awaited her and without glancing back she got in and left.

Why did it seem like he'd just lost something precious?

33

"And the great news is that our local hostages from Mexico returned to Colorado Springs yesterday. News cameras caught footage outside of the road to Mountain Shadow Stables, the business Kristos Sava runs," the male newscaster said.

Video showed the car but there were no good images of either of them, only a jaunty wave from Rusty. Photos of both Kristos and Eliza appeared on the screen. At least they used her military photo. Not that it mattered. She wouldn't be in the Army too much longer.

"Reports say—"

Eliza clicked the television off. Why had she bothered to turn it on this morning anyway? Guess she had her fifteen minutes of fame. After caring for Ramsey and eating a light breakfast, she headed out the door. Seemed her return created a huge need for everyone on post to see her.

She attended several meetings and was medically examined. She connected with her command. They were grateful for her return and placed her on quarters for some R&R. Her commander gave her permission to leave only for meals and appointments.

Eliza drove to dinner that evening to meet her mother and new stepfather, Nigel. Her mom had suggested a family style restaurant with pure Americana food. Eliza wasn't sure when she'd want to eat rice and beans again. Not any time soon.

"Oh, Eliza!" Her mom gripped her in a bear hug when she entered the restaurant. Mom released her. "Eliza, sweetheart, meet Nigel."

Nigel was a tidy older man, not big and broad like her father. Instead, he was the type to wear a suit and tie to work. Now he wore khakis and a short-sleeved button-down shirt. At least he didn't have a pocket protector in there.

"Hi, Nigel. It's good to finally meet the man who has made my mom so happy."

The man beamed. "She's been bragging about you since the day we met. You are everything she described and more."

The hostess came to seat them, and Eliza slid into a booth across from her mom and Nigel. They placed orders for water and soda and began to peruse their menus. Eliza made her choice quickly and set the menu aside.

"So, Nigel. Just what did my mother say about me?" she asked.

Nigel set his menu down and a soft smile made her realize why her mom had fallen for the man.

"She told me how brave and determined you were. We were both worried and praying for you when we learned you'd been kidnapped in Mexico. The fact that you're sitting here now looking as beautiful as you do, only affirms her boasts of you. We are so glad you returned safely."

"Thank you for the prayers. I'm not sure about bravery. I doubt I could have survived all that without Jesus and Kristos. It was definitely a time of testing, and I hope I've emerged a better version of myself than I went in with."

Mom grinned. "Oh, dearest, I'm certain you have. It has been some time since we got to be together face to face, but there is a new softness to you that makes you even more beautiful. I'm sorry you had to go through that but grateful God was able to use it to draw you closer to Him."

Eliza asked more questions about her mom and Nigel's new life in Arizona and how they'd come to faith when they spent time with the Savas during Eliza and Kristos' captivity. God had used this trial for His glory in so many ways.

When it was time to part, Eliza turned to her stepfather in the parking lot. "Nigel, I wasn't too sure how I'd feel about you, but even though you don't need my approval or blessing, I want to say welcome to the family."

Nigel became teary-eyed. "That means a lot, Eliza. Would it be too forward to give you a hug since you're my new stepdaughter?"

"That would be wonderful."

The hug involved her mom as well and not that anyone could ever replace her father, there was a sense of completeness in being in the protective arms of both her mom and stepfather in this moment. Another blessing.

She finally had a few moments to call Rachel.

"Hey, Rachel. It's Eliza."

"I was worried sick about you. Why haven't you called before this? Your trip was over almost four weeks ago."

"You didn't hear the news?"

"What news?"

"Maybe it was only the local news. Anyway, Kristos and I were kidnapped on our second day in Mexico. We only returned yesterday."

"What? Oh no! Oh! Are you OK?"

"I'll be fine. Tired, worn out, but grateful God never left or abandoned us while we were there."

"I wish I had time for you to tell me more…" Little kids screaming in the background grew in intensity.

"You need to go take care of the kids. We'll talk soon." Eliza hung up, deflated. She had been so close to Rachel, but she didn't have time to tell her about how Jesus changed everything for her. Livie was her new confidant and was happily dating another enlisted soldier.

Several days passed since they'd returned from Mexico and Kristos missed Eliza terribly. He walked into the barn and headed to Zena's stall.

"Hey, girl." Zena nudged his shoulder. "I can't wait to see Eliza tomorrow. I'm gonna marry that gal if she'll have me after all we've been through. She's seen me at my worst and didn't hate me. What do you think? Do you need to meet her?"

The horse nodded.

"Great, I hope to have you meet the next time she comes to the barn. Even though Kobbe chose Mandy to be her horse to work with, which is fine. You keep my secrets and Mandy can keep Eliza's."

The horse whinnied and went back to eating.

"I'll see you tomorrow. Thanks for listening, Zena."

He left the stall to find Kobbe leaning against the open barn door. Her arms were crossed. She turned his way but didn't move.

"Hey, Kobbe." He strode her direction.

"Heard you talking to Zena."

"Did you hear what I said?" Kristos asked.

Kobbe shook her head. "I thought you would want to know that Eliza will be coming out this week on Tuesday."

"Great."

"Yeah. I hope that even with the trauma you both went through, Mandy can help."

"What trauma? Are you saying that being with me that long is traumatic?" Kristos grinned.

Kobbe chuckled. "Being with any Sava boy for that long and no one else would be traumatic for any woman."

"Does Alexos know that?"

"I would think being with me right now with cravings and wild pregnancy hormones, I'd be the one who is creating the trauma."

"I doubt it. You love each other and are a good match. You're going to be great parents."

"Thanks, Kristos. It's great to have you back. Caden did well in your absence though, I must admit."

"Are you saying I'm replaceable?"

"Never. Have a good night. See you in church tomorrow." She gave him a wave and strode away to the little motorized cart she used to get from their home to the barn.

"Night." Kristos watched her depart and headed up the stairs to his home. He entered and looked it over with fresh eyes. Would this be enough for someone like Eliza? He had a spacious set of rooms and magnificent views from the windows. He was out of danger now and could focus on his deepest dream, other than freedom. The dream for a family.

For the first time in forever he had a face of the lovely young woman with whom he could envision sharing his adventure. Eliza might be struggling with trauma, but she was still the strongest most resilient woman he'd met, other than his sisters-in-law, Jane and Kobbe who both had gone through painful times. Was Kristos part of Eliza's happily-ever-after? He hoped so.

34

On Sunday morning Eliza twirled around her barracks in a dress. A dress! After Kristos' appreciation of her skirt on the return trip, she decided to stop hiding her leg. It was as much a part of her as her previous one was and in time, she would get one that would look a little more like a real leg than this one that was more obviously a prosthetic. She'd even bought new dressy sandals.

Ramsey whistled when she stopped. "Oh, you silly bird. I wish you would talk. I could always ship you off to Mexico." She wagged a finger at him and he squawked.

Livie came out of her room. "Wow, look at you, girl. Trying to reel in that handsome cowboy?"

"I guess I'm getting brave enough to try something more feminine than camo for a change."

"You'll knock his socks off. I'm ready to go if you are."

"Yeah. I am." She picked up her purse, Bible, and a notebook, and they headed for church.

Entering the building, people kept stopping Eliza to tell her how they prayed for her, how pretty she looked, and how they hoped she was doing well.

"It's almost like you're famous," Livie whispered.

Kristos strode forward to greet them. "Morning, ladies. You're both stunning. May I sit with you?"

While he spoke to them, he'd kept his eyes glued to her and her face grew warm. "Sure."

They found a spot to sit.

"Did your mom and stepdad make it home OK?"

Eliza nodded. "Yes. They left yesterday. They were disappointed I didn't have more time with them to go sightseeing, but Rusty hooked them up with some tours."

"Great. Wanna do lunch? We could go to your favorite restaurant, Hernandez Hacienda."

Eliza chuckled. "Yeah, for all our time in Mexico we didn't get to sample a lot of the food, did we?"

"Considering they eat more than rice and beans, bread and water, you're right. Lunch then?"

"Sure."

The service started and Pastor Sava asked that Kristos and Eliza stand as he prayed over them once again thanking God for bringing them home safely.

The service continued after that. Now when they sang the songs, Eliza had a deeper understanding of what they meant. Pastor Blake recited Deuteronomy 31:6. She didn't even need to write it down. This verse about not being afraid, how God goes with you, and how He will never leave you had been pressed into her heart.

Eliza swallowed hard and Kristos grabbed her hand and squeezed. Glancing at him, she witnessed some moisture in his eyes. She blinked back her own. God had certainly not abandoned them.

When the service ended, they strode to the back of the church to once again be overwhelmed with good wishes and prayers. One elderly woman whispered in her ear. "Nab that one. He's one of the good guys." With a sly wink she was gone.

"What was that about?" Kristos asked.

Eliza chuckled and shook her head. "I need to get Livie home. Her boyfriend will be off duty soon and they have a date. See you in a little bit."

He nodded and grinned. "OK. Stay in that outfit. I like it."

Her face grew warm. She smiled and nodded. His compliment warmed her heart. Eliza headed home and dropped off Livie. She paced her apartment and refreshed her lipstick. She'd even bought some perfume. She hadn't used it at church but maybe now? Far better than how she'd smelled while in Mexico. She headed out to the restaurant and parked. Kristos was at her door in an instant, helping her out.

"Thank you, kind sir."

"Did I ever tell you I like you better as a brunette?"

"No, but I'm glad. Going blonde isn't easy to maintain with hair this dark."

They walked hand in hand to the restaurant and were soon escorted to a seat. They placed their orders.

"This was the place we first met," Eliza said.

"Yeah, and while I thought you were cute, I wasn't too sure I liked you. I hate beer—the taste and the odor. Took forever for my guitar to not carry that scent. I almost sold it."

"Seriously?"

"I needed to take the strings off and clean the inside and let it dry. It's not good to let an acoustic guitar get wet."

"Wow. It was an accident. I'm so sorry."

"I understand. You've come a long way since that day."

"It wasn't that long ago. Think you can come to like me now?" Eliza asked.

"I think I more than like you, Eliza."

Their conversation was interrupted by the meal being delivered. The server departed.

"Let me pray for us." Kristos grabbed both her hands. "Lord, You proved Yourself faithful. You protected and provided even when at times we might have doubted it. Thank You for returning us here. Let our conversation glorify You. Thank You for this food and this lovely woman. Amen."

"Amen." Eliza picked up her fork. "You realize that lying to God might tempt him to strike you."

"How was I lying?"

"Lovely woman?"

"But you are. You've been adorable, sweet, feisty, fierce, resilient, courageous, honest, and absolutely beautiful."

"You never called me that when we were in Mexico."

"The woman you are inside is beautiful regardless of what you wear or how bad you stink. By the way, I love your perfume."

"Thanks. I'll admit I thought you were cute when I first saw you. Now that I am better acquainted, I view you differently."

"I hope it's in a good way."

"Oh, definitely. You're handsome, even when your beard grew scraggly and your hair was all matted. Oh, and you stunk. I will never underestimate the power of a good deodorant for myself or you."

Kristos chuckled as he cut his meat. "Are we a mutual admiration society?"

"Something like that." Eliza grinned. For the first time in her life, she could admit she had fallen head-over-heals in love. With Kristos.

"I'm glad to hear it. I'm wondering if we could date, exclusive like. You be my girl and I be your guy."

"Maybe that would work." But would it?

"I'll be honest. What I want to do is ask you to marry me, but I haven't purchased a ring yet."

Eliza's eyes grew wide. "Marry you?" Her hand went to rest over her heart.

"Yup. Silly idea?" He kept his eyes on his food and his lips were pursed.

"I don't know. It's a little too soon."

"Why?" Kristos questioned. "We were together every day for weeks and I still like you. Some people don't ever spend that much time together before they marry. I think we got a head start on things—especially knowing we work well together as a team."

Eliza paused before answering. "I don't want to get married until I'm done with the Army. That could come soon. And I have a lot to figure out and I need to do that on my own for once. On the other hand I don't want to be engaged and wait a year to get married. It was hard enough to not want to sleep with you when we were in Mexico. Especially after that kiss." Her face grew warm and she hoped her tanned face hid that.

"But—"

"And another thing. How do you feel about my leg? You've never seemed bothered by it and you've been helpful, but does it, well, put you off?" She set her fork down.

"It doesn't bother me. Your leg isn't you, Eliza. I've fallen in love with your heart and your mind. I couldn't even think about dating when you weren't a believer, yet God led me to continue to pray for you every day. For your salvation and healing. I still pray for you. After all we've been through, I desire you even more. That's why I wouldn't let myself sleep by your side even when there was only the one bed and my alternative was a hard nasty floor."

"I don't want you to ask me yet."

"Why?" Kristos raised his eyebrows.

"We need to wait a little longer. We've been through a difficult time together and while that bonded us, we need to be wise. Waiting won't hurt anything. I want to hear clearly from God that you and I are to be together. I'm not sure I'm ready to be dependent on someone."

"I don't want to take away your independence. I want interdependence. That's what God designed. However, I hear what you're saying with the waiting. I've been schooled. The student becomes the teacher. Fine. We'll wait. You'll need to let me know when you hear something on your end, because I believe I've heard on mine. It can't be a yes until you feel confident God is leading you to a life united with mine. I'll support you and your decision."

"Thank you for understanding. I don't want to lose you, so I can say yes to dating you, since that was your first question."

Kristos grinned. "Great. You're not my fiancée—yet, but I'll be thrilled to have you as my girlfriend." He leaned forward. "Does that mean I get to kiss you?"

"No. I'm not sure when I'll be OK with us doing that…but I don't need desire clouding my judgement." She set her fork down and took a drink of water.

Kristos frowned. "I was hoping it would help make the decision easier, but I'll accept your decision."

"Don't get all grumpy on me. If I do decide to marry you, I want to do that with no regrets or the temptation to do more than kiss you.

Even if I were to marry someone else, I wouldn't want them to be upset that I went further with you than they would think is good."

"That's a lot of ifs," Kristos grumbled.

35

liza walked with Kristos to her car after lunch and she relished him holding her hand. When they came to the door, both turned to face each other.

"I'd love to have you come meet the family tonight," Kristos said. "I realize you met some of them the day we returned, but we usually have everyone together for dinner on Sunday evenings. They already love you because you brought me home unharmed. Will you come?"

Eliza blinked a few times. Family? His family was large. She was an only child. She didn't understand how this could possibly be good. "I'm not sure."

His star-like eyes captured her attention as he pleaded. "I promise to introduce you to Zena afterwards."

"We've already met briefly." There was a promise of far more than that, as if hypnotized she nodded. "What time?"

He told her when and opened her door.

"See you later, Tornado." He shut her door and stepped back as she pulled out of her spot and drove back to Fort Carson.

She entered her barracks and let Ramsey out of his cage. The bird came to perch on the arm of her chair. She agreed to date Kristos. He wanted to marry her. Marriage meant being part of this group of people.

At one point during their imprisonment, he described them all to her and his affection for them all came through loud and clear. Now, he wanted her to love them too. Their meeting upon returning to Colorado was a blur of names and faces. And lots of hugs and smiles. No family was that perfect though.

Her mother had stayed with them and spoke highly of Theodore and Roda Sava and the gang. One of his teen sisters wanted to join the Army after high school and she understood that scared Kristos. She'd tried to reassure him that it could be a good thing.

Not that she was a great example, but she survived. Her training helped her keep her head most of the time during their captivity and escape.

She struggled to realize the entire escapade was real. It was as if she travelled to Mexico with a hard heart, rebellious and fighting with God. That Eliza was left behind and a new Eliza returned.

Unfortunately, the trauma of the past hadn't been erased and some new trauma emerged. She never would have survived without Kristos and his grasp of Scripture and ability to use it to encourage them both.

She took a brief nap and put on more casual attire. She brushed out her hair, pleased that the healthy sheen she was used to had returned after some good shampooing. She touched up her makeup and headed out to Sava Ranch. Why was she thinking about doing this?

This was for Kristos. She owed him her life—physically and spiritually. His explanation of the gospel, his constant faith, were all part and parcel of her being able to take that ultimate step of surrendering her life to Jesus. Before that she'd felt unworthy of a man like Kristos Sava.

She still questioned whether she was good enough. She was beginning to understand that she was loved by God. And Kristos claimed he loved her, and she thought she was in love with him. Kristos' family had been kind when she met them after she'd returned from Mexico, but once they got to know her better would they still like her?

She parked her car and Kristos came down the stairs from his apartment above the stables.

"Eliza." He rushed toward her and gave her a hug. She sighed and relaxed in his embrace.

"You seem surprised I came."

He shrugged. "Well, I'm totally aware my family is a handful, and they can be noisy and boisterous. I was afraid you'd cancel."

"I thought about it. They were all nice to me when we returned, but after all we'd been through..."

"I understand. You needed space. To be honest, so did I. As much as they needed to love on us, I need time to myself. Thankfully they haven't pushed for the story."

"Will they tonight?"

"I doubt it. I hope not. I realize we gave the bare bones of it to the Consul General in Merida, but with all the chatter on the local news stations right now, I don't want to talk about it."

"I can relate."

A mutt came running to greet them.

"This is Obadiah, the family dog and welcoming committee. He's usually kept inside when Kobbe's working which is why you haven't meet him yet. You met my brother Rusty's dog, Lola, the one who looks like a fox. I mean the dog, not Rusty." Kristos gave her a quirky smile. "Lola is a support dog." He started leading them to the house, holding her hand.

"Oh, right, the traumatic brain injury?"

"Yes."

"Seems we all carry trauma with us somehow," Eliza said.

"Life can be hard. I don't know how I would have made it through our time in Mexico if it weren't for God—and you. You have no idea how much of a blessing it was to have you with me through all of that."

"I think I was more of a burden at times," Eliza murmured.

"Not at all. You helped me focus on God when it would have been easy to wallow in fear. Your struggle and God bringing Scripture to mind helped me cope better. Helping you grow in your faith as well as provide comfort, gave our time together a deeper purpose beyond survival."

They managed to make it to the front porch.

Kristos paused. "Ready?"

Eliza took a deep breath and slowly released it. "We've been through worse."

"Yes, we have. Come on." They entered the home together and Kristos led them to the dining area.

Eliza was surprised at how many chairs were around that table. She counted eleven.

"It's a lot, isn't it? Just think, by next year there will be two more Savas to join the bunch bringing the number to a lucky thirteen."

"You don't believe in luck," a tall man with military posture said as he stepped in. "Hi, Eliza. It's a pleasure to meet you again. I'm Kobbe's husband, Alexandros or Alexos if you prefer."

"A pleasure to meet you, sir."

"Call me Alexos."

She nodded. He was a superior officer, could she do that even though he was no longer in the Army?

More people flooded into the room. Roda bustled in with food. "Hi, Eliza, I'm so glad you could join us tonight. Find a seat. We'll be eating in a few minutes." She set her dish down and rushed out again. Another woman brought out more food.

"Hi, Eliza. I'm Jane, Rusty's wife. We met the other day, but I expect it would be hard to remember everyone." She turned toward another room. "Rusty, Mark, dinner."

The reddish haired man bustled in with a little boy who beamed with delight. She'd recalled seeing Mark and being entertained by his enthusiasm for life and his intrigue with her prosthetic leg.

Mark waved. "Hi, Eliza. How is your robot leg?" His father helped him into a seat with a booster.

"It's doing well; thank you for asking." She truly didn't mind his curiosity and admired his willingness to ask questions instead of stare. Kobbe arrived with more food. Kristos pulled out a chair and helped her get seated and sat next to her.

He whispered in her ear. "You're doing great."

"You had doubts?"

Theodore Sava strode in with his teen daughters and soon Roda brought the final dishes and sat down as well.

"Let's pray," Theo said. "Heavenly Father, we thank You once again for sparing Kristos and Eliza and bringing them safely home. Bless this meal and the beautiful hands that prepared it. May our conversation glorify You. Amen."

"Amen," was heard around the table, with Mark giving an enthusiastic one. Eliza relaxed and began to fill her plate as the dishes were passed.

Kristos was struck by the realization that even though he dated girls in the past, he never invited any of them to family dinner on Sunday. Oh, they sometimes joined in meals at other times but never this semi-official family gathering of the clan. In recent years he lamented that he was an adult and there was no mate by his side. Having Eliza here was a comfort and joy. She laughed at jokes and the family kept the banter to safer topics, avoiding the trip to Mexico.

When the meal was finished, Eliza offered to help with the cleanup and his mother declined the offer.

"Kristos told me he promised to introduce you to Zena. She's a beautiful horse and I don't want you to get home too late," Roda said as she shooed them out of the dining room. The rest of the family dispersed, and Kristos led Eliza back outside. The sun was starting to descend, but it would be some time before it became fully dark. They walked over to the barn.

"So? What did you think?" he asked.

"They are utterly delightful. Thank you for convincing me to come."

"I'm glad you liked them."

They strode into the barn. The large doors were still open but the horses were in their stalls. The air flowed through, relieving the barn of the lingering heat of the day. Holding her hand, Kristos dragged her to the final stall.

He made a clicking noise and the head of a large Percheron appeared.

"Eliza, this is Zena." He reached up to pat the horse's nose.

"Hi, Zena. She's beautiful, Kristos."

"She is a sweet old lady. Aren't you, girl?"

Zena nodded and gave a soft whinny.

"So, this is your confidant, huh? I need to see therapists and you have Zena."

"Well, that may be true, but I found I also need another woman in my life to talk to as well…you."

Eliza wasn't sure what to say.

Kristos turned to her and a hand came up to her face and brushed her hair back. The warmth of that hand, even with the calloused fingers, gave her a sense of connection and safety. She gazed up at him in the shadowy barn.

Zena nudge him closer to Eliza, which made her giggle. Kristos grinned.

"I think she approves," he said.

"Of what?"

"Us. This." Kristos leaned down.

Eliza pushed him away.

"Aw, come on, Eliza. It's just a kiss."

"It's not a kiss like my grandma used to give me, or even my mom. No. There is no such thing as 'just a kiss' from you, Kristos."

He stepped back and dropped his arms. "I don't know what you want from me, Eliza."

"Some patience and a little understanding. How about this. Until you can feel comfortable doing that in front of your family—we shouldn't be doing it at all."

"You play dirty, Eliza," he groaned.

"I'm worthy enough to be your wife someday, I'm worthy enough for you to respect this now." She grabbed his hand and led him to the door of the stables. "I think it's time I go home."

Kristos didn't say another word as he walked her to her car and closed the door behind her. He didn't even give a little wave as she drove away.

She obviously frustrated the man and that saddened her, but if he couldn't respect her boundary on this, much like the men in her unit needed to, then any potential future between them was closed.

While the tears flowed as she drove home, she was even more resolute in maintaining her stance, no matter how charming her singing cowboy was.

36

Two days after the Sava family Sunday dinner, Eliza returned to Kobbe's corral at Sava Ranch for equine therapy. Anxiety thrummed through her. Would she have a breakdown like last time? So much had happened since then. She hadn't experienced too many flashbacks during her trip to Mexico, but since returning she had times when she couldn't sleep well, waking up thinking she was still on that cot in that prison, hungry, thirsty, and so filthy. She would get up and shower in an attempt to wash off the filth and bugs.

Kristos had called several times, but she let every call go to voice mail. She needed space to think and heal without him.

An involuntary shiver overtook her.

Was Kristos going to be here today? She partly wished for that, but also didn't want him to see her fail.

She sucked in a deep breath before getting out of the car to head to the stable. She walked in by Kobbe's office. Kobbe came out to greet her.

"Ready? Mandy is already in the ring waiting for us."

Eliza nodded and walked by Kobbe's side. Kobbe opened the gate and entered with Eliza. Kobbe took a seat. Mandy raised her head at their entrance. Eliza strode toward the horse slowly, speaking softly. "Hey, Mandy." The horse stared as if sizing her up.

"I'm sorry I ran out on you last time. I'm not sure how you opened that door to me seeing those images, but I was scared. Actually, terrified." Eliza continued talking softly and the horse's ears flicked forward indicating the animal listened.

Eliza stepped up to Mandy and caressed the horse's neck. "You're so soft and beautiful. Will you be my confidant? Will God use you to heal me? I don't understand." Tears pooled in her eyes. Mandy's head came down to nudge her shoulder.

Petting the soft head, Eliza finally rested her head against the large chest of the animal and rested there. Mandy remained still but made a small sound. Eliza looked up but continued to pet the horse. "You are so big, powerful, strong, beautiful…I can understand why Kristos loves you." The horse turned her head to look down at Eliza, once again that brown eye seeing deep into her soul.

"I'm supposed to connect with you so you will follow me around this corral. Can we be friends?" She continued to caress the horse. Mandy's tail swished back and forth.

It dawned on Eliza that her trying to get this horse to trust and follow her was much like God trying to call her to Himself. He was patient, loving, kind, surrounded her with people and love and she kept spurning Him, digging in her heals to avoid following where He might lead.

Why had He never lost faith in her? Never stopped pursuing her? She was nothing special.

What made her give in? She wasn't completely sure. Was she going to be spending weeks and months like this, trying to get Mandy to move and follow her?

She took a few steps back away from the horse.

Eliza lowered herself to the ground. Mandy was a huge horse and could easily trample her, but she didn't seem dangerous for all her strength.

Eliza couldn't sit comfortably on the ground with her prosthetic. She groaned as she tried to position her legs.

Mandy considered her for a long time. Eliza waited. Had God grown tired of waiting for her? No flashbacks overtook her now as she surrendered to the wait. Mandy took a few steps toward Eliza, dropping her large head down to the tiny woman. Eliza reached up to pet the horse but remained silent. Mandy nudged her shoulder.

"If you want me to get up, I might need your help." Eliza reached up to grab the horse's mane and with a tight grip struggled to her feet. Mandy remained still. When Eliza was upright, she patted the horse. "Sweet Mandy. Thank you. Wanna take a walk with me?"

The horse nodded. Eliza stepped forward and Mandy followed. Eliza kept a hand on Mandy's neck, stroking the silky soft hair, sensing the controlled power underneath the flesh. Mandy might be a large Percheron draft horse instead of a sleek racehorse, but she was even more impressive for her gentleness.

"Come with me, Mandy," Eliza whispered as she took a few more steps. She continued to talk to the horse, telling her about some of what happened in Mexico. And they kept walking.

"Eliza?" Kobbe called out.

"Hmm?" Eliza had forgotten all about the therapist on the sidelines.

"We can end now if that's all right with you."

Eliza strode toward Kobbe and Mandy followed even though Eliza was no longer touching or talking to the horse.

Kobbe grinned. "You may not be aware but you and Mandy slowly moved around the course at least three times. You did it. You got her to follow you."

Eliza turned to give Mandy as much of a hug as possible and wept into the horse's neck.

"Thank you, Mandy," she choked out.

"How are you feeling?" Kobbe asked.

"Fatigued, not physically but emotionally. Wrung out. But heard and accepted. I'm not sure how else to phrase it."

"That's understandable. Shall we schedule another appointment for next week?"

Eliza smiled as she patted Mandy's neck. "Yes. I'd like that a lot."

Mandy nodded and the women chuckled.

"I guess Mandy approves of that plan as well," Kobbe said. "We'll see you next week."

"Bye, Mandy," Eliza said as the two women headed through the gate. Mandy stood with her head over the rail and whinnied.

Eliza turned and petted the horse's head. "Yeah, I love you too, Mandy. Thank you." She turned and walked away with a weight lifted from her shoulders she hadn't realized she'd been carrying.

She drove home with a smile on her face, experiencing a deep peace. God had been patient with her. Out of devotion she would trust and follow Him, much like Mandy did her. And listen to what He wanted to tell her. She entered her quarters and settled down to open her Bible. The book fell open to Jeremiah 31, and she read these words: "The LORD appeared to us in the past saying: 'I have loved you with an everlasting love; I have drawn you with unfailing blessings.'"

He certainly had, and for that she was grateful.

But what was she to do about Kristos?

Her phone beeped indicating a text.

Bonfire tonight out behind parents' home. Friends coming. Wanna burn those stinky clothes?

She was ready—ready to put that past behind her and step into her future. Would Kristos would be a part of that?

She texted back. Yes.

Kristos had the campfire blazing. Michael, and Jeremiah and Genna, as well as Peter and Holly were due to arrive soon. Eliza agreed she would come too. Perhaps not the most traditional bachelor party but the guys all decided it was time to do something different. The wedding was only a week away.

The guys and their girls all arrived at the same time.

"Where's Eliza?" Michael asked.

"She said she would be here." Kristos tossed more wood on the fire. Skewers were on a nearby table with marshmallows, chocolate, and graham crackers for any who wanted it.

"I look forward to meeting her. She seems to have blossomed since you returned from Mexico. At least from what I saw on Sunday morning. Quite the transformation," Jeremiah said as he pulled up a chair to sit next to Genna.

"You're noticing other women?" Genna teased as she nudged her boyfriend with her elbow.

"I missed that," Michael said. "How do you think she changed?"

"She appears softer, prettier, dressed more feminine. I think before it was as if she was keeping the world at bay and not letting anyone in. Now she appears more approachable, vulnerable. Like a wall has been demolished and the outer shell fell away to reveal someone new."

Genna grabbed Jeremiah's hand. "You're talking about the soldier?"

Jeremiah nodded.

"I agree. She seemed—happy," Genna said.

Kristos nodded. "She accepted Christ before our kidnapping. I think she left a lot of her old self in Mexico." He paused as he scanned for her arrival. "I think I did too."

"In what way?" Peter asked.

"I always wanted a wife and family but I don't think I realized how much I needed someone who was there for me, by my side. On my team. Challenging and supporting me as we work toward a common goal. I've been single too long. I didn't think I needed a wife but now I believe my life would be poorer without one—especially if it's Eliza."

"Here she comes," Michael said as he rose to his feet.

The other men stood, too, as Eliza entered the backyard and made her way toward them.

Michael stepped next to Kristos and nudged him, whispering, "Just don't propose at my wedding dude. That would be poor form."

Kristos grinned. "Not to worry. I'll be too busy transporting your bride to be wooing anyone that night, much less proposing."

Eliza strode toward the group. She would finally meet the men who called Kristos friend. And their girlfriends. Another hurdle that would take her one step closer to deciding if this was a relationship God desired for her.

She wondered briefly how her Army buddies would have reacted toward Kristos. Spec 4 Barnes, Spec 4 Clayton, and PFC Zarenski would have teased him and quickly become buddies, she was sure. Especially after they learned how he helped her through their captivity.

OK, Lord, here goes.

She stepped into the circle around the fire. "Hi, everyone, I'm Eliza."

Kristos came to stand by her side and gave her a side hug. "I'm so glad you came."

Introductions were made and everyone sat around the fire.

"I brought my clothes," Eliza said, holding up a paper bag.

"I brought mine as well." Kristos grabbed his bag. "Everyone, part of what Eliza and I wanted to do after we returned to the States was burn the clothes we wore every day for the weeks were held captive."

Michael cleared his throat. "I'd like to pray before you both toss those in the fire."

Kristos nodded.

"Dearest Jesus, we thank yYou for this group of friends and the freedom we so easily take for granted here. We are grateful You brought Kristos and Eliza back safely. Although I'm sure there is much we don't know about their captivity, we do know You were there with them and that they depended on You. You were the one who freed them and brought them back to us. We ask that You would continue to use those events and their relationship with You to reach others with Your love, no matter where they go or what they do."

Amens chorused around the campfire.

"Thank you, Michael." She stood with her bag and so did Kristos. "Are you ready for this?"

"Most definitely. One, two, three."

They tossed their paper bags on the fire and flames quickly licked up the bags, revealing the clothes inside that were quickly burned.

Kristos put his arm around Eliza while they stood and watched it go up in smoke. Eliza sighed. If only the hard times were so easily erased from life.

"God uses fire to purify us. Make us stronger. Burn off the chaff,"

Genna said looking to Eliza. "I can't imagine any of that was easy for either of you."

Eliza sat and Kristos followed.

"Not easy at all, but our captors only intended to take one person. I'm grateful Kristos came outside to talk to me that night. Although that meant he was in the same difficulty as I was, we weren't alone and he taught me so much Scripture and about God over those days. He was able to use God's words to comfort us and encourage us. I was too new in the faith to understand much. It would have been much harder to endure any of that alone."

Kristos held her hand. "Don't forget, Eliza. You ministered encouragement to me as well. It wasn't all one way. God gave us each other to be a help. I couldn't imagine emerging from all that as well as we have had I been alone."

The warmth of the fire mirrored the warmth inside her at Kristos' words and the understanding of his friends.

Soon the clothing was gone, and Kristos put more wood on the fire. He brought out his guitar and sang some songs while they laughed and roasted marshmallows.

"How do you like yours, Eliza?" Kristos asked.

"I can roast my own. I like it torched!" Eliza put her skewer toward the flames and after dancing around them and the coals a bit it caught fire. "Yes!" she crowed, pulling it out, blowing on it, and soon stuffing it into her mouth. "Perfect!"

Kristo laughed as did others in the group.

She had lost her buddies in an explosion, but here around this fire, there was safety, music, and new friendships.

God, You truly are so good to me.

Seeing Eliza interacting with his friends warmed Kristos' heart even more than the fire did. There had been something freeing in burning the clothes.

More cathartic was watching Eliza fit in with his friends and their ladies. When the night was over and the fire had died down, Kristos walked Eliza back to her car as the other couples were leaving.

"I'm glad you came," Kristos said as he held the door open for her.

Her soft smile made his heart flip. Soon. Hopefully soon she'd relent to becoming his wife.

"Thank you for the invitation. I really enjoyed it. And just so you know, when you're ready I believe God is telling me yes." She slipped into her car and he closed the door with a huge smile on his face.

Oh, Eliza, am I ever ready.

37

The Friday afternoon of Michael and Bridget's wedding day arrived. Kristos had previously transported the enclosed white carriage to the main house. From there he would deliver the bride to the ceremony site and then return both bride and groom back to the main house where the reception would be held. The farm had their own large wagon for taking attendees back and forth from the venue which was out near a back pasture. As a precaution they'd erected a tent in the event of rain.

The October colors of the aspens were beautiful although most of the trees in that area were tall evergreens.

Kristos loaded up his two favorite geldings for the job: Adonis and Ajax. They were brothers and a well-matched set visually and size wise. They were uniformly silvery gray. He'd bedecked their manes with some ribbons and flowers to match the coral color the bride had chosen for the wedding.

"Come on, boys." The horses stepped into the trailer with little fuss.

Caden was hired for the day to help with horses from the host ranch in pulling the other large open wagon with benches. "Thanks for hiring me for this job, boss. I've not had the honor of doing this kind of thing for a wedding."

"You're a natural. You've done it before with the Percherons so you should be a cinch to handle the neighboring farmer's horses. They're used to this kind of work. The Belgians from this farm might be smaller, but they're sturdy and up to the task. Bridget really wanted matched light-colored horses which is primarily why we're bringing Adonis and Ajax."

"Anything for the bride, huh?"

"Wedding days are a big deal, especially for the bride. All these tiny details make a memory."

"I'm glad I'm not a groom," Caden said as Kristos pulled slowly out with the trailer so as not to jar the precious cargo.

Kristos grinned. "I get the impression from my brothers that all the hassles of a wedding are worth it in the end. I've seen the expression on their faces when their bride appears and comes down the aisle toward them, and I know I've found the right woman who stirs that kind of feeling in me when my time comes."

"All that gushy stuff. I'm not ready for it," the young man stated.

"When you fall in love, I think you'll find the hassle is worth it."

"You've fallen in love?"

"Oh yeah, I love Eliza."

"I like her. She's a great gal. She's coming to the wedding, right? You can show off your skills to impress her."

"I don't think I need to impress her with this after what we went through in Mexico."

"She's a keeper then, right?"

"I think so." Kristos chuckled. They arrived at the ranch and pulled the Mountain Shadows Stable truck in by the barn. Kristos parked. The men exited the vehicle and went to bring out the horses so they could move around a little before being hooked up to the Cinderella carriage.

"Come on, boys. There you go." Kristos patted Ajax while Caden brought Adonis out. They led the geldings to a corral and released them in there where they both went to drink some water.

Michael strode over to the corral and the men shook hands. "You really brought them. Bridget will be so happy."

"Of course, I brought them. That's what you hired us for. We'll do our best to make this a wonderful day," Kristos said. "You look spiffy. I suppose I need to get my tuxedo on now."

"Sure, it's in the bedroom on the first floor. Take the hallway to the right of the staircase and you'll find it the second door on the right."

"Caden, go check on the carriage and the Belgians. I've met them but you haven't. Ask Steve in the barn and he'll get you acquainted."

"Aye, aye, boss." The young man spun around and headed eagerly to the barn.

Kristos checked out the carriage for delivering guests and it was decked out with white- and coral-colored streamers and flowers. He pointed to it. "Looks wonderful. Not sure coral is my color but for you I'll wear that cummerbund and bow tie."

The men headed toward the house where Kristos' tux and shoes had been put the day before.

"Anything for Bridget. Kristos, I'm almost dizzy at this point. I can hardly wait and yet we still have so much time. I haven't seen Bridget today."

"Steady on, man. Deep breaths. It will be over before you realize it and then you'll settle into everyday life. I'm glad for you. I think Bridget is a great lady."

"You'd better since you're delivering her to the site."

"No worries. My guys are as steady as they come, and the carriage has been looked over carefully and is in top-notch condition."

"I knew you wouldn't fail me. You realize I wanted you to be my best man, but you're so busy with all of this I didn't think it right to saddle you with that as well. Kind of hard to drop off the bride, secure the horses, and rush to the front of the tent before she makes it down the aisle."

"No worries. I'm thrilled to be a part of the day, and I am still in the wedding party. It's all good."

Michael patted him on the back. "Go change and I'll see you later."

"You can count on it." Kristos entered the bedroom and located his tuxedo. He changed his clothing and checked his image in the standing mirror at the corner of the room. He tugged on the bow tie and headed back outside. Thankfully, he wasn't required to wear a top hat. He'd done it before while transporting a bride, but if it grew windy it wasn't a good thing to lose. So far, the day was cool and damp, which lent a chill to the air. Kristos left the house and went to double check the carriage. All was in order. The horses were patiently waiting.

Cars started to arrive, and a young man directed traffic. Caden emerged from the barn on the wagon beautifully cleaned and pulled by sparkling black Belgians. He maneuvered to the area near the house and Kristos strode over to assist the guests into the wagon. Soon it was loaded so Caden took off to deliver them to the location where they would wait for the ceremony to start.

When Caden returned he made a large circle to get the horses in position again.

"How did they handle?" Kristos asked.

"The horses did fine. The wheels slipped a few times, but we managed as long as we took it slow. There are slippery spots on the hills, and the ground is wet and soft in the valley area from yesterday's rain."

Kristos glanced at the carriage. The once red trimmed wheels showed signs of mud. "Take it easy, OK?"

"Aye, aye, boss."

Kristos turned to spy the woman he couldn't seem to stop thinking about.

Eliza and Livie were coming toward the wagon, followed by other wedding guests. Eliza wore a beautiful dress in a soft green color that brought out the green in her eyes, making them sparkle. The movement of the material as she walked gave the impression of elegance. He was proud she was his.

"Good afternoon, Livie, Eliza. I'm glad you could make it." He assisted them into the wagon.

Eliza shivered as she wrapped a green and blue shawl around her. "You're not coming?"

Kristos frowned. "Are you going to miss me? Remember I'm in the wedding party, which is why I suggested you bring Livie. I have other duties and won't be able to be with you very much. You promised me a dance tonight. Don't forget."

She winked at him. "Well, see."

Kristos shook his head and flashed her a smile on his way to assist other guests into the carriage and once again Caden was off. A few more trips and soon the time came for the wedding party to depart. Kristos assisted all the bridesmaids and groomsmen into the wagon along with Michael, and Pastor Blake who was performing the ceremony.

The sky grew dark. Caden left and headed down. Kristos hooked up Adonis and Ajax and brought the Cinderella carriage around to the front door of the house where Bridget awaited. He went to the door and when he entered the foyer he gave a low whistle.

"Wow, Bridget, you're going to knock Michael's socks off. You're beautiful."

She blushed. "Thank you, Kristos. Have we given them enough time?"

"You don't want to give him too much time, plus it will take a little while to get there. I'll take it slow to enhance the drama." He gave her a wink and she giggled. He extended an arm. "Come, my lady. Your carriage awaits."

They exited and he assisted her into the enclosed carriage. It always seemed that what he dubbed "Cinderella's carriage" looked like a white pumpkin. Of course, that was intentional. Most brides wanted the fairy tale.

Kristos got on the seat and frowned at the foreboding sky. The pounding of rain could be heard on the ground and moving closer. He urged the horses to move.

At that moment, the rain began to fall. First in a light sprinkle, slowly growing to sheets of rain pouring down. Kristos struggled to see clearly through the gray atmosphere.

The first part of the journey was slow. Kristos was aware that even with the distance of at least a mile, Michael and the guests could view them approaching. At least everyone else was dry under a tent. The grassy slope down to a short valley was slick, and he urged the horses to go slow and steady. He was already soaked to the skin but at least Bridget was dry, and he had a job to do. When they reached the valley, the rainwater was flowing in a small creek as the deluge continued.

"Steady on, Adonis, Ajax."

The horses slowed. Kristos realized that the carriage wheels weren't turning and the horses were trying to drag it through the mud. He halted them and took a deep breath. He loathed getting off. He tried to get them to move again, but the wheels wouldn't turn. The tiny carriage was stuck.

38

Eliza could barely see the carriage coming as the downpour clouded the scene.

"Oh, no!" Bridget's mother exclaimed. "The carriage is stuck." The woman fanned herself and guests started murmuring about how horrible this was and wondered what would happen next.

Livie pointed. "I can't believe it. Kristos is getting off his perch."

"Oh, my." Eliza shook her head. She watched him try to rock the carriage out. The mud and water now running through that section of land flowed above his ankles. She wouldn't have been able to get a truck out either. "What's he going to do?"

"Guess we'll find out," Livie said.

"I guess so."

One of the groomsmen called out. "Men, the tent roof is filling with water—we need several men to help us gently get it to drain so this thing doesn't collapse!"

Several men jumped to help.

Kristos put the brakes on the carriage and climbed down. He undid the harness for the horses and brought Adonis farther into the water up to the carriage door. He needed to act fast because the entire thing would be floating soon.

He opened the door. Bridget sat with eyes wide open. "Kristos?"

"I'm sorry, Bridget. I'm aware you can ride. I'll help you up and lead you out. You can hold Adonis's mane and I'll take it slow. It's the best I can do."

The bride shook her head and grinned. "This will definitely be a day to remember, that's for sure. Just not for what I had hoped for."

"Hurry, before the carriage starts floating."

Kristos moved the horse closer and assisted the bride to sit on it sideways. He closed the carriage door and made a clicking noise that urged Adonis forward. As they came to Ajax, he grabbed the reins so the horse would walk beside him as well.

"I have ridden horses before, Kristos, but never one this tall or broad and sidesaddle without a saddle."

"You're doing great."

Slowly they trudged up the muddy incline to the tent and when they came closer, Caden rushed out to grab Ajax's reins to lead the horse to a little shelter under some evergreens.

Michael appeared and lifted his arms up to his bride as Kristos held Adonis steady.

"Come on, sweetheart. I'll catch you," the groom said.

Bridget released her tight grip on the horse's mane and slid down into her soon-to-be husband's arms. He pulled her into the tent out of the rain.

Kristos walked over to the other horses and handed Adonis off to Caden.

"Any thoughts on how we'll get out of here?" Caden asked.

Kristos shook his head. "I'm sure we'll figure out something."

Kristos strode back to the tent as the dry guests made their way to their seats. Bridget stood in the back, her flowers had come ahead of her so at least those were fresh and dry. Her mother pushed the hair off her face. Kristos came to her side.

"How fare thee, lovely maiden?" He gave a grin.

She smiled. "You promised to get me here safely. I forgot to ask for dry. I'm grateful I didn't need to walk." She glanced at Kristos' pants and shoes.

He shrugged. "We're here. Go make some more memories."

The ceremony began and a dripping bride was led down the aisle by her dry father. Kristos went to stand at his place behind Jeremiah. Michael didn't spare him a glance. He hoped he hadn't ruined the day, although Kristos wasn't the one who planned an outdoor wedding in fall. He glanced back to the direction they'd come. The carriage was sideways in the stream. Guess it wasn't stuck anymore. Once the ceremony was finished, he'd take the horses down and see if they could pull it out.

Eliza shivered as the damp air grew chilly. She glanced over to Kristos, soaking wet but standing there with regal dignity next to his friends. The bride beamed at her groom as she strode down the aisle. Soaking wet she was still lovely. Maybe that's what love did. It made one shine with beauty from the inside out, regardless of what one wore. If it had happened to Eliza, she'd be crying by now. Or might have refused to leave the carriage.

Would Kristos have forced her? Tossed her up over the back of a gargantuan horse? She huffed at the indignity of the thought.

Pastor Blake started the service. "Life is filled with unexpected events. Circumstances beyond our control. Today you start a new chapter by joining the story of your lives together into one. Now you will no longer travel alone, but as a team. Just as the horses worked as a team to get most of us here," the audience chuckled, including the bride and groom, "Michael and Bridget, you will be a team. You each have your strengths and weaknesses. Michael, you are more serious and like to know the plan. Bridget, you have a more playful spirit that can lighten Michael and together you can pull forward to face the challenges of life.

"God says in His Word that you are never alone. You each have accepted Christ and have learned to lean on Him as your Lord and Savior. Now Jesus has seen fit to bring you two together here today, to mark a point in your relationship where you become united as one, in Him. That will mean negotiation and teamwork. Never forget you are on the same team. You are cheering each other and your marriage to grow stronger every day."

Eliza thought about the way she and Kristos were forced to lean on each other in Mexico.

The pastor continued. "The wind and water, the storms of life—" Bright lightning and an almost instantaneous crash of thunder interrupted the message. "As He so beautifully illustrated, these storms happen but they don't need to defeat you or knock you off your course together. Bridget, I'm sorry this didn't work out as you planned—"

"Kristos got me here safely."

Pastor Blake grinned. Kristos' face grew pink. Or was that the sky growing lighter? The rain stopped and the sun began to peek through.

"Storms will end, but if you can take the trials and move forward in love and loyalty to Jesus and each other, you will weather them well and grow closer to each other."

Eliza wiped away a tear. She longed for that kind of love. Someone unafraid to be there in the storm with her. She already had a hero in Kristos. As much as she struggled to submit to God could she give up her independent streak and rely on Kristos again? This time forever?

He'd been a wonderful teammate in Mexico. She relied on him without hesitation. They'd worked seamlessly as a team.

She relied on her Army buddies.

They relied on her.

She'd let them down.

So maybe she was tearing up not because of the beauty of the moment but because she wasn't worthy of being in that kind of relationship. She couldn't be depended on when things went wrong. When the world blew up around her, she failed.

Unlike Kristos. When the storm raged, he was steady and sacrificed his comfort and clothing to help Bridget and Michael on their wedding day. He'd been steady and faithful in Mexico, even when she fell apart in a hurricane.

She suddenly wondered. How were they going to get back to the house and their vehicles?

The vows were spoken. Eliza swallowed her tears, wanting what she didn't believe she deserved. Kristos would be busy anyway. Maybe they could leave. Watching someone else revel in their happiness in spite of the rain was almost too much to bear.

Pastor Blake spoke. “I now present to you Mr. and Mrs. Thatcher. Michael you may kiss your bride.”

Eliza clapped with everyone else as the bride and groom kissed.

Michael and Bridget strode down the aisle and out into the wet grass and sunshine. Each groomsman and bridesmaid teamed up to follow, Kristos being the final one with one of Bridget’s friends.

He winked at her as he passed by.

She let out a slow exhale. This man was dangerous to her heart. *God what are You up to? Why did I even agree to this?*

The guests were soon all out on the lawn. Kristos wasn’t in the receiving line. He was with Caden discussing options. Soon Kristos was on one of the Percherons and heading slowly in another direction. Nearly a half an hour later, he returned, grabbed the reins of the other Percheron and headed down the hill to the carriage.

“What is he doing?” Eliza asked.

Bridget overheard her. “He’s rescuing the carriage and has possibly found a longer but safer path back to the house.” She shivered.

Eliza pulled her shawl off from around her. “Here. Let this help warm you up. I can’t imagine how you…”

Bridget smiled. “Thank you. That’s sweet of you. As for today, this will be a funny story to tell. Thankfully, photos with my dress and bridesmaids were taken before I headed here. If I hadn’t been so obstinate about getting married here, we could have avoided this drama. It is what it is, and I’m blessed to have a man who was willing to marry me even if I look like a drowned rat.”

“You’re mine and a little rain doesn’t change anything,” Michael stated, putting his arm around her. “Mrs. Thatcher, you’re beautiful to me because that beauty comes from within and out of your love for the Lord.”

The couple moved on to mingle with other guests.

Kristos arrived on the perch of the white carriage now with muddy wheels. The beautiful gray horses sported mud on their legs. Kristos jumped down and opened the door. “It’s a little damp but at this point that's hardly a big issue."

Michael and Bridget laughed as they got into the carriage and the door closed. Kristos hopped back up to the perch and soon the horses and carriage were off, taking a different path. The other driver pulled up and men helped the women up to the wagon. Eliza and Livie were grateful to be some of the first to get back to the barn where the reception would be. Even if the wagon seats were wet.

Once there, Eliza settled into a chair. Her wet behind wasn't comfortable, but since everyone suffered there was no embarrassment. When a waiter passed by with a glass of champagne, she grabbed it. She hoped it would warm her up. She opened her purse to check for her phone, but it wasn't there.

"Livie? Have you seen my phone? I could have sworn I took a photo or two under the tent."

"I don't remember seeing it. Maybe you left it in the car. I'll go check."

Great. All she needed was a lost phone. Her stomach began to ache. Anxiety? Or had that sandwich in the fridge been too old? She shook her head. Too many negative thoughts. Think positive.

No excuses.

But God…

No excuses.

Help me, Lord.

39

Kristos was coming out of the house when he saw Livie heading back into the barn. "Everything OK?"

Livie shrugged. "Eliza lost her phone. You got cleaned up."

"Well, out of the wet tuxedo anyway. Not how I expected to be attending a wedding reception but short of going home it's the best I can do. You said Eliza lost her phone? Where?"

"I'm not sure. She was sure she had it under the tent."

Kristos grimaced. "Let's call it." He dialed it as he walked toward the barn. No one picked up. "Don't tell me. It's on mute?"

"Duh. Of course. We were at a wedding."

Kristos went to the front of the room and found Michael. "Eliza lost her phone. Can we ask if anyone found one?"

"Sure."

Kristos went to the makeshift dance floor and whistled loudly. Everyone grew quiet. "Just wanted to ask if anyone found a cell phone?"

Everyone shook their heads.

"Did anyone see one under the tent?"

More head shaking. Kristos sighed. He walked outside to the wagon used to transport guests and checked all around it. Nothing. He checked around the barn and found some old rubber boots and a flashlight as it was getting darker. He headed out to the path everyone took on their way back from the wedding tent and slowly checked the ground around the ruts of the wagon wheels. Nothing. He got to the tent. Someone had already collected the chairs. He scoured the area without success. He walked the path the original carriages had taken and scanned even farther down where there had been water to see if it had been swept farther along the field.

Nothing.

A blister was starting to form on his foot due to the ill-fitting boots. He trudged up the last incline back toward the house and still found nothing. He returned the boots where he'd found them along with the flashlight and once back in his own work boots, he headed into the reception. He strode over to Eliza, pulled out a chair, and sat down.

"Hey," she said, avoiding his gaze.

"You're phone. Do you have the find my phone application on it?"

"Yeah, but I've only accessed that from my laptop."

"We can try from my phone." He pulled up the application and typed in the number. "Weird. It should make it ring though. I hope whoever has it will hear it?"

"One could hope. You should get back to your table. They are about to serve the food."

"I'll keep trying."

"Thanks, Kristos."

Eliza picked at the food placed before her. She wasn't sure what was in some of it. There was a range of tastes from some steak to something Mexican and something from some other culture. Korean? It was the oddest kind of wedding meal she'd ever tasted. Maybe the bride and groom decided to do a little of each of their favorite foods?

If it were her, she'd likely choose macaroni and cheese. Or mashed potatoes.

"Livie, where's the bathroom?"

"Most barns don't have them. You'll have to head to the house."

"I'll be back."

Upon making her way back to the barn, many of the tables were removed and chairs were set up along the side of the room. The bride had changed back into regular clothing before dinner. The rest of the bridal party followed suit so the bride wouldn't feel so bad about her dress being ruined. The music was in full swing, and a line dance was going on. She located Livie.

"Oh, there you are. I was afraid you'd gotten kidnapped again."

"Just tired. I think we should head home."

"Kristos told me he found your phone but the guy who has it is miles away. It was on a chair, but he didn't notice when he stacked them. It fell out in the truck and thankfully he was unloading when it rang. So, you really can't leave yet."

Kristos strode up to her. "Hey, where were you?"

"I needed the restroom," Eliza said.

"You look pale. Are you feeling OK?"

"Livie said you found my phone?"

"Yeah, the guy should be here in about thirty minutes. Are you up for a dance?"

"I wish I were, thank you. I just want to go home."

He held out his hand. "A slow dance is starting. If you're tired, lean on me. I'll hold you up."

Eliza relented and took his hand. He helped her up and led her to the dance floor. Pulling her close he swayed, slowly moving them around the floor. The lights dimmed and other couples were also in their own little worlds, including the bride and groom.

"You're not a bad dancer," Kristos said as he leaned his forehead against hers.

"You're not bad yourself."

The dance ended and he returned her to Livie who rose. "You still want to go, Eliza?"

Eliza nodded. "I'm just off tonight."

Kristos drew her into a hug and then released her. "I'm glad you could both come. Sorry it ended up being an odd evening. At least the ceremony went off without a problem."

"Yeah, that thunder and lightning was perfectly timed," Livie joked.

"I jumped when that happened," Eliza confessed.

"Understandable. Too bad we don't get that kind of rain when we need it, when the fires start. Drive safely and I'll see you tomorrow at church with your phone."

"Sounds like a plan. Thanks, Kristos."

They strode out to the car in the moonlight.

"Did you know he walked the path to and from the tent and searched for your phone?"

"He did? Why?"

"Because I told him you'd lost it."

"It wasn't his problem to solve."

"What does that matter? He solved it. Why are you so resistant to someone helping you? You need to get over yourself, Eliza."

Maybe I do.

40

liza and Livie were doing physical training at Ivy Gym on Fort Carson but not getting a lot of physical in their PT due to chatting more than exercising.

"How did your recent session of EMDR with Dr. Rodriguez go?" Livie asked.

"Wow. The best word I can use to describe it is intense with a capital *I*."

"Really?"

"Yeah. I've had several sessions and I'm finally able to remember some of the explosion. I'm able to cope with talking about it without wanting to shut down and hide somewhere. I know I've still got more work to do, but EMDR is definitely working for me."

"Did you get a chance to talk to your therapist about your Mexico mayhem?" Livie asked with a smile.

"Yep. We've done two sessions, and I feel like I'm already dealing with it in an extremely healthy, mindful way. I know God wants more for me than avoiding trauma. I feel like I'm alive and able to deal with whatever comes next. Of course, I don't want any more mayhem, as you call it. But I know I'm learning the tools and my faith is going to get me through."

"I'm so impressed with you, girl!" Livie gave Eliza a high five and a huge hug.

Eliza finally got the news. She had her medical retirement date. Thankfully she'd found a ground floor apartment. She hadn't told Kristos yet. She didn't want to say anything until she'd been given a final date. It wasn't that she wouldn't need more therapy, but she was stable enough to make it on her own.

She was ready to start her new life. Kobbe agreed to hire her but was going to let Eliza share the news when she was ready.

She texted her mother the news. Then she called Rachel.

"Hey, girlfriend, what's up?" Rachel asked.

"I'm getting out in a few weeks. I rented an apartment and have a job lined up."

"Cool. You're not moving back to Tennessee?"

"Nope. Kristos is here and I hope my future is with him."

"He'd better be good to you. You still haven't told me all that went on in Mexico."

"He's always been a gentleman. As for Mexico, I may never tell the entire tale. My therapist told me to write it or type it out, so I don't forget anything later. I have no clue why I'd want to remember."

"If you do, send me the document, OK?"

"We'll see. So how are the munchkins doing?"

Rachel spoke about the kids and issues with her husband, her house, and a new job she started along with juggling it all. Eliza grew weary listening to it. Soon, as if on cue, screaming in the background ended the call.

An hour later, Eliza picked up the phone to call Kristos. "Hey, how's your week going?" she asked.

"It's been fine. Got a new horse to board so I'm getting used to taking care of her. Sometimes the rider comes out to exercise the mare."

"That's cool. How do the other horses react?"

"Just another member of the herd."

"I wanted to give you some news."

"I'm all ears."

"I received my retirement date." She gave him the specific date. "I can start moving into my apartment next week. I'll need to get some furniture, especially a bed. Will you be able to help?"

"Be glad to. Do you want to go shopping tonight? I know where the best thrift stores are for furniture, too, although I expect you'll want a new bed."

"Yeah, probably just a twin though."

"Whatever you like. Do you want to meet somewhere since it's a bit of a pain for me to get on post?"

"Sure."

They set up a location and said their goodbyes.

She'd forgotten to tell him about the new job. She'd break the news later.

Kristos was happy to help Eliza. Soon she'd be out of the Army and his hopes of something more permanent seemed possible.

Seeing Eliza back in her cargo pants brought back memories. Her flannel jacket looked good on her. Kristos' denim one was old and worn but suited him. They were quite a pair. They managed to get the furniture selected and the workers were willing to load the bed frame, love seat, recliner, and dresser onto his pickup. He strapped everything in and headed back to the ranch. He pulled the truck into a garage.

"Do we need to unload it?"

"Nah. I shouldn't need the truck before you move and we have another one. I'm fine leaving it here where it will be safe and dry. I think you made some excellent choices. So, when do you want to shop for a mattress and box spring?"

"Does tomorrow night work? They'll deliver."

"Yes. It's a date." Kristos wrapped Eliza in his arms and placed a chaste kiss on the top of her head.

Funny how he had patience in training a horse but lacked it in training himself.

Patience was forced on them in Mexico. Every day he was faced with the frailty of life and fear that it would be their last on earth. He didn't want to waste time but realized Eliza wasn't ready.

He hoped she would be soon.

When he released her, she gave him that smile that sent tingles all over.

"I forgot to tell you I got a job."

"Kobbe hired you, didn't she?"

Eliza playfully slapped his arm. "Way to spoil the moment. Yes. I start after I've moved off post."

"I'll get to see you more often, I expect."

"That could be a benefit or a curse."

Kristos paused. "A benefit because I love being with you and seeing you."

"And a curse because I'll want to be with you, but I need to do my job."

"Not a problem, I love that you'll be close, and I'll see you more after work. I'm looking forward to that."

"Me too."

Kristos pulled her close for one last hug.

Moving day finally arrived and Eliza brought Kristos to post to help her collect her things, including Ramsey. It wasn't as if she owned many possessions, but the bird would not fit in her car. Thankfully, Mrs. Sava offered her delivery van—it was not in use at the moment—to transport Eliza's belongings to her new place. They'd already brought over the other furniture and stuff she'd been collecting for the house at the various thrift shops Kristos had taken her to. Those were fun dates. She enjoyed every moment she was with him.

Kristos entered her barracks and his eyes widened at the size of the bird and cage.

"Ramsey, meet Kristos. Kristos, this is Ramsey, a blue-and-gold macaw."

Ramsey fluffed his feathers and shook his head. "Hello."

"Hello yourself, Ramsey," Kristos said. He turned to Eliza. "I thought you said he didn't talk?"

"What? Are you kidding me? He won't talk to me or to my roommate. That's the first time I've heard any words from him." She put her hands on her hips.

"Ten-hut! Drop and give me twenty," the bird said before breaking into laughter.

"He laughs too?" Kristos asked.

"I never heard that either."

"Well, let's get your belongings. We'll take Ramsey last."

"Pretty bird. Good boy. Hello." The bird followed up with kissing sounds and more laughter.

Eliza was stunned at her bird's behavior. Why would he only talk to a guy? It didn't make sense. Maybe she should give the bird to Kristos.

Once they moved everything into her apartment, Kristos cooked up a simple meal on the stove.

They sat on the two kitchen chairs at a tiny drop leaf table. Kristos grabbed her hand.

"I remember when we had nothing to eat, or very little. You never complained."

"Wouldn't have done any good," Eliza said, relishing the sensation of his hand holding hers.

Kristos bent his head and Elisa did likewise. "Jesus, thank You for bringing Eliza home and giving her a new life and fresh start outside the Army. Thank You for bringing her into my life. I am the richer for it. Bless this food. Amen."

Eliza took a bite and groaned in pleasure. "Macaroni and cheese never tasted so good and you made this from a box mix?"

"With a little extra added in. I'm glad you like it."

Ramsey made kissing sounds and laughed.

"He's entertaining at least," Kristos said.

Eliza shook her head. Annoyed as she was with her bird, she was grateful this man was here, sharing a simple meal, because he treasured her.

What a novel experience. To be treasured. Precious.

He'd treated her that way when they were in Mexico as well. He didn't talk down to her or belittle her or expect her to be weak. He accepted her just the way she was and never tried to change her.

"Deep thoughts?" Kristos asked.

"Yeah. Sometimes my mind wanders back to Mexico. Not the events themselves but memories of us. In spite of all that happened that was bad, my memories of us are sweet and good."

"I've experienced that as well. It's a blessing to have positive memories. I was wondering, I realize you don't work till Monday, but could you come to the barn tomorrow? Maybe we could go for a horse ride," he pleaded.

"I haven't done that before."

Kristos grinned. "Then let me teach you. Mandy would love it. I hear you made a connection with her."

Eliza nodded. "I've had a few more sessions. Kobbe said I can take time out of work for breaks to see Mandy when she is available."

"Best kind of break."

"Fine. I'll be there."

"Ten hut. Drop and give me twenty," Ramsey crowed.

"I think I'll need to teach him some new phrases." Kristos picked up the empty bowls and began washing them and the other dirty dishes.

"You don't need to do that," Eliza protested.

"It doesn't take long. Go finish making your bed. I'll leave soon so you have time to relax and enjoy your new space."

Eliza did as she was prompted.

She gave him an extra kiss on the cheek as he was about to leave.

"What's that for?" he asked.

"Just because you're wonderful."

His face lit up with a smile and he wiggled his eyebrows. "See you tomorrow."

"Bye bye," and more kissing sounds came from the bird.

"See ya." Eliza shut the door and locked it. After years of communal living, she finally had a place of her own.

Squawk! Squawk! Squawk!

"Ramsey. Hush."

She closed the blinds, tossed a blanket over the birdcage to quiet him down, and turned off the lights before heading to bed. It had been a long day but good. She was finally home. Her own home.

Why did it seem empty with Kristos gone?

41

ristos helped Eliza climb onto the saddle. "Relax. Mandy will pick up on any anxiety. Trust her. She's a solid horse and really good. You'll be fine as long as you stay put in the saddle. We won't go far."

Kristos climbed up onto Zena's back and led them through the gate onto a path to the woods. The trees were almost past their full colors and leaves littered the pathway.

When they came to a wider path in the clearing a small waterfall could be seen.

"Oh, it's beautiful."

"It's funny, each of my siblings have a favorite spot on the property. This is mine."

"I can see why. Thank you for sharing it with me."

Kristos turned Zena around and came abreast of Mandy facing the opposite direction.

"How are you and Mandy doing?"

"OK."

Sweat beaded on his brow in spite of the cool fall temperature. Just spit it out.

"Eliza, you captured my heart from the first time we met. After everything we've been through, I cannot imagine spending the rest of my life with anyone else by my side. I love you. Will you do me the honor of marrying me?"

He pulled a ring out of his inner pocket and waited. Eliza's jaw went slack and she stammered to find the words.

"Yes. Yes! Yes!" she said as she held her left hand out to him.

"I have one more question."

Her brow furrowed. "OK?"

"Can we marry on December 31? New Year's Eve?"

"So soon?"

"I don't want to wait to hold you all night long. I want so much more."

She smiled. "So do I. We'll make it work, but as much as your Cinderella carriage is lovely, I don't want to risk getting stuck or freezing to death, so an indoor wedding, please?"

"It's a deal." Kristos' heart soared as they headed back to the ranch.

He got off Zena and helped Eliza off Mandy. He pulled her close and wrapped his arms around her and kissed her on the top of her head. When he let her go, she took a step back.

"I look forward to hugging you forever—and so much more."

Kristos grinned and drew her close, reveling in the fact that she said yes. His deepest desire was coming true.

Eliza could hardly believe it was already New Year's Eve and her wedding day. She wore a white dress with cowboy boots on underneath. Rachel had flown in without her husband and children to be her attendant and was dressed in blue. They had decided to hold the small wedding at the ranch in the corral. Enclosed and heated, it was used for therapy during the week, but now a small bower was erected with flowers and sparkling lights in the center. A few chairs were around in a circle.

Her mother flew in and was wearing an elegant red dress with sequins. Her stepfather was already seated.

"Are you ready, dear?" Joy asked.

"Yes."

"You look beautiful, Eliza," Rachel said. "Let's get this done."

Rachel went down the aisle first and was met by Kristos' brother

Rusty. A string quartet began playing.

"It's time," Eliza said.

"I'm so happy for you, sweetheart," Joy said as she took her daughter's elbow and walked her down the aisle. "Your father would be so proud of the woman you've become. I know I am."

"Oh, Mom." Eliza could barely pay attention as she spied Kristos at the front with his father who would perform the ceremony. Her mother handed Eliza over to Kristos and took her seat next to Nigel.

The ceremony was a surreal dream. In a daze, she could only focus on Kristos until Pastor Sava, now her father-in-law, said, "Kristos, you may kiss your bride."

The kiss took her breath away again. Would she ever be able to breathe normally while married to this man?

Pastor Sava interrupted her thoughts. "Ladies and gentlemen, it is my honor to introduce you to Mr. and Mrs. Kristos Sava." The small crowd clapped as Kristos walked her down the aisle. He pulled her into a side hallway in the barn and put his hands on each side of her face and kissed her again.

About the authors

DEEDEE LAKE

DeeDee Lake is The Connection Expert and lives in Colorado with her amazing hubby of forty years, Seth, and two ridiculous dogs. Her golden-doodle, Bella Rose, can be found busting in when DeeDee is on Zoom with the tiny Shi-Tzu following close behind.

DeeDee is a speaker, author of *Next Step: You've Accepted Jesus, Now What?,* blogger, columnist, relationship coach, part-time adult, potato fan, Navy brat, Army wife, type A, and an extreme extrovert. She's lived in fifty houses and can pack up a house faster than an Olympic skier races down the slope.

DeeDee believes relationships are built one conversation at a time.

She loves Jesus, her man, family, friends, and strangers. She's the owner of Cherish Relations Retreats and Workshops. DeeDee lives out her faith guiding individuals how to experience extraordinary relationships.

If there is laughter and chatting, you can be sure she'll be there! Check out her blog at DeeDeeLake.com or connect with her on Facebook.com/DeeDeeLake.speaker.

SUSAN M BAGANZ

Susan M. Baganz is happily married to Ben and is a native of Wisconsin. She writes adventurous historical and contemporary romances with a biblical worldview.

She speaks, teaches, and encourages others to follow God in being all He has created them to be. With her seminary degree in counseling psychology, a background in the field of mental health, and years serving in church ministry, she understands the complexities and pain of life as well as its craziness.

Her favorite pastimes are lazy…snuggling with her dog while reading a good book or sitting with a friend chatting over a cup of spiced chai latte, or more recently running the skid-loader to help with outdoor projects at home.

You can learn more by following her blog at susanbaganz.com, her Twitter feed @susanbaganz, or her fan page, facebook.com/susanmbaganz.

Acknowledgments

DeeDee Lake would like to thank Susan M. Baganz Lodwick for a friendship that God surely created. Her love, encouragement, acceptance, and willingness to get this manuscript that began thirty years ago to life means so much to me. Meeting at our first CCWC event set the tone for an amazing relationship. To say thank you to my precious husband, Seth, isn't enough. He believed in me when I was ready to stop the presses years ago. His enduring enthusiasm for this project encouraged me more than I can say. Seth continues to bring romance, fun, safety, and love every day of our forty years together. I appreciate all my family and friends who have cheered me on over the years. To my heavenly Father, who loved me before I knew Him, I owe Him my all. Every step of this military life You've gone before me and always had the perfect plan. Thank you, Lord!

Susan M. Baganz would like to thank DeeDee Lake for the love, laughter, and friendship that have brought about this partnership in spite of the miles that exist between Wisconsin and Texas. I'm especially grateful to my hubby, Ben, for his faith and support of my writing career and for showing me what true love and dedication are like. Thanks to my friends: Heidi, Elisabeth, Kaye, Kerry, Beth, and so many more who have supported me on this journey. Thank you especially to God who saved me, redeemed my pain, and has called me to this opportunity to bless others and share the wonder and love of our amazing Lord Jesus. It is an honor and a privilege to be His talmidim. May all honor, glory, and praise be to Him.